THE MAN WHO
CAUGHT THE WEATHER
AND OTHER STORIES

By BESS STREETER ALDRICH

THE MAN WHO
CAUGHT THE WEATHER
AND OTHER STORIES

by

BESS STREETER ALDRICH

D. APPLETON-CENTURY COMPANY
INCORPORATED

NEW YORK   1936   LONDON

CONTENTS

THE MAN WHO CAUGHT THE WEATHER

H E lived next door to us when I was a girl—old
Mr. Parline. To be sure, his wife lived there,
too, but we never saw very much of her. She was one
of the immaculate housewives of that day, whose life
was bounded by the hundred small tasks of a home into
which the modern button-pushing conveniences had not
come. A shy, effacing woman she was—"mousy" de-
scribes her too well to abandon the term for its mere
triteness. Mr. Parline was the one who did the talking,
who neighbored with the rest of us, who came to the
back door bringing us gifts from his garden.

The Parline house sat in the midst of trees and flowers like Ceres among her fruits. We were just then
emerging from the dark age of fences into the enlight-
ened era of open lawns. By your fenced or fenceless condition you were known as old-fashioned or up-to-date.
One by one the picket and the fancy iron and the rough
board fences on our street had gone down before the
god of Fashion. Mr. Parline, alone, retained his—a
neat picket, painted as white as the snowballs that hung
over it, Juliet-like, from their green foliage balconies.

The shrubbery was not so artistically placed as that

I

of to-day. We had not learned to group it against houses and walls, leaving wide stretches of lawn. Single bushes dotted Mr. Parline's lawn, a hydrangea here, a peony there, a tiger lily beyond, in spaded spots of brown, mulchfilled earth, like so many chickens squatting in their round nests.

The Parlines were of English extraction although both had been born in Vermont. There was a faintly whispered tale that they were cousins, but there was no one so intimate as to verify the gossip and no one so prying as to ask.

Mr. Parline was a half head shorter than his tall, slender wife. He was stocky of body, a little ruddy as to complexion, like the color of his apples, a little fuzzy as to face, like the down on his peaches. There was a quiet dignity about him that fell just short of pompousness. "Mr. Parline" his wife called him, in contrast to the "John" and "Silas" and "Fred" with which the other women spoke of their liege lords. Where other women in the block ran into our home with the freedom of close acquaintances, Mrs. Parline alone occa sionally came sedately in at the front gate in a ʳ ₐt brown dress covered with a large snowy apron st⁊ ᵕhed to cardboard stiffness.

It was Mr. Parline who came often. With ₗnat manner which was paradoxically gentle and ₒmpous, he would bring us edibles from his garden all summer long on a home-made flat wooden tray. That garden, as

2

neat as constant care could make it, was the delight and despair of every one who attempted to emulate it. Not a pigweed showed its stubborn head. Not a mullein stalk lifted its thick velvety self. The bricklaid paths, without sign of leaf, might have been swept, even scrubbed. As for the growing contents of the garden, they made a varicolored and delightful picture. In its perfection every cabbage might have been a rose, every beet an exotic tropical plant, the parsley dainty window-box ferns. To Mr. Parline there was no dividing line between the beauty of flowers and the beauty of vegetables. With impartiality he planted marigolds near the carrots and zinnias next to the beans.

"Just a little of the fruits of my labor," was his dignified greeting on those occasions when he tapped at the back door. In the center of the wooden tray might repose a cabbage, the dew still trembling upon the silver sheen of its leaves, around it a lovely mass of the delicate shell-pink of sweet peas. One felt it as much of a sacrilege to plunge the cabbage into hot water as it would have been to cook the sweet peas. Or, he might have several bunches of grapes in merging shades of wine-red and purple, their colors melting into the wine-red and purple colors of shaggy asters. Old Mr. Parline had the heart of a poet and the eye of an interior decorator.

We never saw Mrs. Parline pulling a vegetable or cutting a flower. Occasionally, at evening, she walked in the paths with all the interest and curiosity of a stranger, evidently considering the garden as sacred ground as did the rest of us. Indeed, Mother was at their back door one day when Mr. Parline came up the path with the inevitable wooden tray. There were beets on the tray, their tops cut, their bodies like blood-red hearts, around them white Sweet Williams and crimson phlox. "I was just bringing my wife some of the fruits of my labor," he said in his courteous, half-pompous way.

We laughed about the phrase at home. Ours was a noisy, hilarious, fun-loving family. One member might bring in a mess of dirty potatoes in a battered old pail. "A little of the fruits of my labor," he would imitate Mr. Parline's pompous dignity. Or another, coming in with the first scrawny radishes, might have placed a few limpsy dandelions around them as a floral satire on the contents of Mr. Parline's wooden tray.

If the garden was the old man's hobby, the weather was his very life. It was inconceivable that any one should be so wrapped up in the constant change of the elements. To other busy people the weather was incidental to their labors, the setting in which they performed their tasks. It might be pleasant or inconvenient, but it remained a side issue. To old Mr. Parline it was the important event of the day. He scanned the heavens, read the almanac, watched for signs of changes. Of the last he had a thousand at his command. If the

4

sun went down in clouds on Friday night, if it rained the first Sunday in the month, if a dog ate grass, if the snow stuck to the north sides of the trees—he knew to a nicety what the results would be. To old Mr. Parline the weather was not the background. It was the picture itself. It was not the mere setting for daily living. It was life itself. No government official connected with the Weather Bureau made it more his life's thought. In the kitchen he kept a large calendar upon which he made notations for the day. Every vagrant shifting of the wind, every cloud that raced across the blue was recorded. For what purpose no one knew. *Another slight dash of snow at noon. Temperature 34. Sun came out at 3 P.M.* It seemed so small, so trivial, that a man should give so much time and thought to that which he could not change. He had thermometers by the house, on the north side to show the coldest registration, on the south to get the hottest, in the garden, by the barn. They were like traps everywhere— baited with mercury—little traps to catch the weather.

From Mr. Parline's conversation one gathered that an overseeing Providence had given him exclusive charge of the elements. If his words did not utter it, his manner implied it. "Well, how do you like my June day?" his attitude seemed to be. If the day was bad, he was half apologetic. If it was pleasant, he glowed with satisfaction. The summer afternoon on which we were to have a little social gathering, he

5

came to the back door and with genuine feeling told us how sorry he was that the day was dull and rainy. His manner showed humiliation, as though from the standpoint of neighborliness he had failed us in a crisis. "I am very sorry," he said in his gentle, half-pompous way. "I had thought—had every reason to believe—that it would be sunshiny." We assured him that we bore him no grudge, and he went home relieved, returning with the wooden tray on which lay a heap of ruby cherries, a delicate mass of baby's-breath around them.

Was there a great national event, his talk turned immediately to the weather in which it was consummated. When he read the newspapers he seemed to ignore the main issue of the news. The weather, lurking in the background, was apparently of greater importance to him than the magnitude of the event. On the day of Dewey's triumph, he spoke immediately of the weather, wondering whether it had been dull or sunny in the harbor. At an inauguration there was no comment from him concerning the great issue of the day, the change in the policy of the Administration. He gave forth no acclaim or condemnation of the new head of the Government. His mind dwelt only on the fact that the new President was having to ride up Pennsylvania Avenue in a mist.

Vegetables, flowers, and the weather—they were Mr. Parline's whole existence. Such little things they

6

were, we said. Whether his wife was bored by the triviality of his life, we could not know. She was too reserved for any one to sense her reactions to her husband's small interests. We could see her working about the house all day. Sometimes she brought out quilts and hung them on the line for cleaning. They were of intricate patterns, beautifully pieced and quilted—the Rose of Sharon, the Log Cabin, the Flower Basket, and the Rising Sun. "I'll bet the old man sleeps under the Rising Sun," one of the family remarked and we laughed uproariously at the joke. In the evening Mrs. Parline often came out and strolled through the paths, stepping gingerly about like a stranger, listening to the old man's courteous, half-pompous talk. She was deeply afraid of storms, he had told us years before. And when one saw the first dark clouds looming up from the southwest in summer, or the first gray ones rolling in from the north in winter, one also saw old Mr. Parline hurrying home, his square, heavy body swinging along out of its accustomed slower movements. To get home to Mrs. Parline when there was rain or hail or snow was his first duty. It was the only time when he ever seemed thrown out of his pompous calm. You saw them later through the windows looking out at the storm together.

The Parlines attended a little ivy-grown church where the old gentleman passed the collection box.

The Man Who Caught the Weather

When his own part of the service was over he would take a seat near the door, one eye on the sky. It was as though he must have everything as auspicious as possible when the congregation should return home. One wondered if he heard the sermon at all. A queer old man.

But the queerest thing of all was his strange prophecy that the day would come when the weather could be regulated. We young folks guffawed at that. "He was eccentric before he sprung that one," we said, "but now he's a nut."

In his half-pompous, half-gentle way, he argued it. "In the centuries to come, who knows but that humanity will have progressed to such an extent that men can catch the weather and retain it—hold it for a time to their own choice? You smile at that." He was sensitive to our thoughts. "But strange things have happened. Who would have thought you could catch the human voice in a little box and listen to it through a tube to the ear?" This was all many years ago. "Who would have thought a machine would rise up in the air under its own power? Who would have thought carriages without horses would go about the streets?"

"The whole trouble would be," we joked with him, "you would want rain the day we wanted sunshine, and living next door to us, there would be complications."

"I don't pretend to know how it could be accomplished," he said in his gentle, dignified way. "I merely suggest that in the years to come it may be so."

So the Parlines went on living their quiet lives. Refined, gentle folk, but different—and a little queer.

And then on a spring day, old Mrs. Parline died, as quietly and unostentatiously as she had lived. There was no fuss about it. A hard cold, the doctor coming and going, a neighbor slipping in and out of the back door, a cousin coming out from Chicago to care for her—death. The various members of our family went over to the house. Other neighbors came, as they do in small towns. A man's sorrow is the town's sorrow. In a neighborly community, sympathy takes concrete form. It becomes buns and flowers and apple jelly and sitting up.

Old Mr. Parline greeted us kindly, courteously. Outwardly he showed no manifestations of his grief, except that his face was gray and drawn. He was solicitous of our comfort. He brought in fuel for the kitchen stove and oil for the lamps. He went to the cellar and came back with apples, polishing them scrupulously. He asked us if we were too cool or too hot. He went up and down the tulip beds pulling a few tiny weeds from the soil. Such little things in the face of death! He looked at the thermometer, at the almanac, at the sky, and predicted a pleasant, sunshiny afternoon for the services. A queer old man, we all said. Not even death itself could take his mind away from the habits of a lifetime.

Mrs. Parline was buried in Riverside Cemetery. "It seemed very mild out there this afternoon," he said to us a day or two after the services. "There was a light breeze from the northeast." We knew where "out there" was.

By Memorial Day there was a stone at the grave and a mass of scarlet geraniums which he had transplanted, and some parsley. "How odd," we said, "parsley from the vegetable garden." But he was always odd. We walked around the stone to read the inscription. Propped up against it, in the lush grass, was a thermometer. We laughed a little—but only a little. Some laughter is half tears.

During that summer he seemed lost, a boat without a rudder. It was pathetic the way he went about his housework. He hung the quilts out on the line to clean them—the Flower Basket and the Log Cabin, the Rose of Sharon and the Rising Sun. We would see him, walking about the yard in the evening with a lantern, reading the thermometers.

"Look at that," we young folks said, "he's batty."

"Oh, no," Mother said, "he's lonely."

And then, quite suddenly, we realized that he was going out to the cemetery at the sign of every storm. At the first glimpse of a thunderhead looming up over the trees, we would see him slipping out of the white picket gate and hurrying down the street. In some indefinable way he must have felt that he wanted to carry out that old habit of protecting her.

"It's ridiculous," we said.

"It's beautiful," Mother said.

If we expected his garden to deteriorate, we were mistaken. He took more pains with it than ever. More often he came to the back door with its products for us. Once, some one spoke tactfully about paying him, that he ought to have some compensation for his work. He looked pained. "Oh, no," he said, with gentle dignity. "Please do not speak of it again."

He found out the neighbors' various likes and dislikes. "I put out some turnips for you," he said to Mother. "I do not care for them myself, but I want you to have some." Yes, a kind old man.

And he continued to manage the weather. "I do not want to intrude." He came to the back door. "But I see your family is making preparations to go to a picnic."

"Yes, Mr. Parline. Wouldn't you like to go with us?"

"Oh, no, thank you. You are very kind. But I have work in my garden. I went to a picnic once in my youth. It was a very enjoyable occasion. I wanted to tell you that I think it will rain before night. The wind has switched to the east and the temperature is five degrees higher." The queer old codger.

And then, as the years went by, he began to include

others than the immediate neighborhood in his gifts—
people he had not known before and with whom he
became acquainted in the cemetery.

A cemetery is a friendly place. You talk with people
there whom you have not known in town. "The grass
ought to be mowed," you may say to the wealthy widow
by her husband's mausoleum, or "Do you think the
peonies will be out by Memorial Day?" to the Italian
fruit vender by his baby's grave. So people who talked
to the old man "out there," even though they lived
across town, became the recipients of his garden
products.

For three years he lived his queer, busy life there
alone with his garden and his thermometers.

It was in December of the third winter after his
wife's death that the gray clouds of the big snow
began rolling up from the northwest. Some one saw
him slip out of his gate, lantern in hand, and hurry
down the street.

"You don't suppose that poor old man is going out
there to the cemetery?" Mother was solicitous. She
put a shawl over her head and hurried out a side door.
We could hear her calling, "Oh, Mr. Parline!" When
she came in she had deep sympathy in her eyes. "I
told him I thought he ought not to go out when it
looked so snowy. He said in his dignified old way,
'That's why I want to go. I must get out for a few
minutes before the storm breaks.' I suppose he feels

that he protects her just as he used to. Isn't it pathetic?"

We had supper. Company came. It began to snow —soft, damp, heavy flakes. It was late when it came to us that there was no light in the Parline cottage. Father went over. When he found no one, he went after two other neighbors and together they went "out there." I think from the first they expected to find— what they found. He was huddled up against the stone where he had crumpled while stooping down to look at the thermometer. The doctor said death had been instantaneous, that he had evidently taxed himself hurrying to make the trip before the storm broke.

They brought him home. Neighbors went into the little house, not so immaculate as in the old days, but in order. In the kitchen they talked in low tones about the old man, as though from the front room where he lay he might hear their comments.

A queer old man, they all agreed, but kind, unusually kind. Mother went into the cellar and brought up scarlet-cheeked apples and mellow pears.

"He would have wanted to pass them around," she said, with that understanding of humanity which she always seemed to possess. Scrupulously she polished them before she served them.

The cousin and a young married daughter came. The cousin cried a little, tears that were not especially sad. "I didn't feel that I knew him very well," she

told us. "When I took care of Cousin Sarah he was
always very kind to me. He brought me everything
from the garden and kept me supplied with fuel. But
I never really got acquainted with him. When we did
talk it seemed to be only about the weather. But he
was a good old man."

They took him "out there" where his wife was, and
the dead geraniums under their thick covering of snow,
and the parsley from the vegetable garden, and the
thermometer.

In the evening Mother and I went over and sat
awhile with the cousin and her daughter. They replen-
ished the fire in the kitchen stove with some of the
wood Mr. Parline had brought in. They brought apples and elderberry wine from the cellar. The house
had that lonely feeling which hangs over one from
which a soul has just gone.

Drawn by thoughts of the old man's hobby, Mother
walked over to the huge bank calendar hanging there
on the kitchen wall. The last day of the year it was,
and so the last of the calendar with its one vacant
page. Mother thumbed over the closing pages, each
one filled with the old man's wavering writing. "In-
dications of snow. Wind in the east. Temperature 20
at the north side of the house, 19 at the barn, 18 out
there." Underneath was a home-made set of shelves,
all the old calendars of the bygone years in neat piles,
the dates printed on the backs.

The Man Who Caught the Weather

Through the clean, small-paned window, we could see low clouds breaking and slipping into the east. We were no doubt thinking the same thought—of the old man lying "out there" in the dignity of death, with the scudding clouds and the wind in the west, the old man who had lived close to the wind and the rain, the hail and the snow. Death would not seem so significant to him tonight as the importance of the setting— the rift in the clouds and the end of the storm.

There was the last vacant page on the calendar. He would have wanted it filled. Mother looked at it for a moment, then picked up the short, stubby pencil hanging limply on its long string, and wrote the weather for the day—the gentle old man's long Day: *Shadows gone from the valley—no night—and the need of no candle—sunshine—eternal sunshine—and the Seven Stars.*

THE DAY OF RETALIATION

ANNA BRUNEMEIER dressed a chicken at the sink of the farmhouse kitchen. The strong raw odor of the scalded feathers made her head ache. The unpleasant sight of the entrails sickened her. Her feet pained. She felt unusually tired. But then, she was always tired these days. She arose mornings unrefreshed, dragged through long working hours, and fell into bed heavily soon after supper. She felt burdened, oppressed and clumsy. It is the price of coming motherhood.

It was April, and raining. Not the usual soft, bud-unfolding, misty rain of April, but a fierce, pommeling downpour. Just outside the screened porch door the water rushed out of a tin spout into the rain barrel, filled it, and dropped sloppily over the sides.

Gus, her husband, came to that door now, stepped inside the porch, shook himself like a spaniel and slipped out of his boots. As he came on into the kitchen there was an odor about Gus, too, that sickened Anna —his wet, steaming clothes and the rubber of his yellow slicker.

"Pretty damp," he remarked amiably.

Anna acknowledged it with a dull "Yes."

Gus hunted around on the clock shelf for his jack-knife and, finding it, started back to the porch. As he passed the sink he paused.

"Elsa didn't ever cut the leg off the thigh joint," he volunteered, and pointed a wet, stubby forefinger at the designated piece. "She left the second joint on the leg bone. It made a bigger helping."

He was not cross. He was not dictatorial. His mild voice held no definite disapproval. He had merely given forth a simple statement, casual and informative.

But a hot wave of anger flooded Anna's body, a tingling, uprolling tide of resentment that swept over her and settled in dull red puddles of blood on her cheek bones.

Elsa! Elsa! Always Elsa!

Having deposited his unpremeditated information, Gus got into his muddy boots and went out again into the rain.

Elsa! All the dislike that Anna possessed for the dead Elsa wrapped her now like a garment. All the jealousy that she felt for Gus's first wife concentrated in a dull pain of hatred. If only she could remove the memory of the girl that Gus had loved—still loved—she could be happy. But Elsa was a thorn that could never be plucked from her flesh, an ulcer that grew on the very vitals of her being. If only the dead Elsa would let her alone, allow her to be Gus's wife with no interference. But she seemed to come to Anna—Elsa did—and stand beside her. Soft-eyed and dark-haired and gentle she came. It was as if she said: "Just a year ago these things were mine. At this time last year I went about these rooms. Just so I did my housework. But Gus came and took my hand and spoke tender words. *I* was loved, Anna."

It was an unbearable thought—that Elsa had been the loved one.

The chicken finished, Anna went about other tasks, paring potatoes, chopping cabbage, cooking beans. All the rest of the day at her work she was bothered by the unseen presence of the dead Elsa.

All that day, and the other days of that week, Gus himself brought Elsa many times into the house. Once it was with, "Elsa she culled out her chickens about now and sold the irregulars." Again it was with, "Elsa she baked her bread on Fridays." And one day it was, "Elsa she made *kaffee-kuchen* every little while."

Not cross, not unkind, just casually informative, it wore on Anna's mind like the dripping of water from the eaves. For it rained all week. The creek was high. The world seemed a soggy thing over which there would never again be sunlight.

Anna was never idle. She sewed and baked and swept. She cleaned the cupboards and the downstairs closet, brushing Elsa's coat and sweater which were now rightfully hers, but which nothing could have persuaded her to wear. She hated every one of the gar-

ments. And looking at Gus, sitting smoking by the
stove on the rainy evenings, she half hated him too.

It did not seem possible that one person could be
both so loved and so hated. Every fiber of her being
loved him—his big strength and his good looks—and
yet it seemed, at times, that every fiber of her being
also hated him, loathed him for still loving Elsa. For
she felt it was of Elsa he was thinking, sitting so quietly
by the range on the rainy evenings. She wished that
she could shake him out of his silence, bring him back
to her, have him for her very own.

On Saturday it stopped raining and the sun came
out in a blaze of warmth that fairly pulled the green
from the trees, turning the farmyard into a place of
steaming humidity. Gus came to the door in the late
afternoon and tossed his heavy raincoat into the porch.

"Anna, I got to help Emil Schlappe with a sick
horse," he called. "You feel like you could go after
the cows?"

"I can go." There was something stolid in Anna, a
trace of blood in her that had not changed with two
generations of living in a country where women are
not stolid.

She finished cleaning a window and washed her
hands. Then she took a shawl down from a nail and
drew it around her, not for need of warmth in the
moist spring air, but because there were times when

a woman should wear a wrap. She put on heavy rubbers and started out, picking her way between pools in the lane road. As she walked she was thinking that it was just such a late afternoon and on just such an errand that Elsa had been drowned.

There had been hard rains earlier in the season the year before and the creek had been on this same sort of rampage, rolling sluggishly over the rye land. Elsa had gone for the cows, just as she herself was going now. No one ever knew how the accident happened. There might have been a cow at the edge of the creek and Elsa might have waded into the water to drive her out. She might have tried to get a switch off an overhanging willow tree. Or she might have fainted on the high bank at the far end of the pasture. The whole countryside had discussed the possible cause and had come to no conclusion. The body had been found floating gruesomely against the wire fence down on the Emil Schlappe place. The entire community had sorrowed.

Anna, herself, had been contentedly at home with her parents five miles away when the word came over the phone that Elsa Brunemeier was drowned. It had meant nothing to her then but the excitement of the news, the loss of a none-too-well-known church acquaintance, a general sort of sympathy for Gus.

And then, so strange is fate, last fall she herself had taken Elsa's place.

The Day of Retaliation

She had reached the end of the lane now, and stopped to pick up a cottonwood stick with which to whack old Spotty if she proved lazy. The sun shone warm across the spongy pasture. The ground was sticky, the new wild herbage steaming. The cows were at the far end of the pasture still nibbling the juicy grass. Anna picked her way across to them, her feet denting the soft ground. She could see the high creek now. It flowed darkly through the willows like a pleasant old friend turned sullenly unrecognizable. And Elsa had in some way been a victim of that treachery, a sacrifice to that unfaithfulness.

It made Anna stop and look at the picture, fascinated by the ugly danger concealed there under the willows. She paused to imagine the unpleasant details —finding Elsa, bringing her home, Gus's grief. She, herself, had sat in the Lutheran church through the two long sermons of the service. Brother Roerheimer and Brother Schulte had reviewed the beautiful life of the dead woman. Gus had kept his head bowed in his pew. Had hung over the casket when they were leaving the church. Had called "Elsa, come back," so that every one heard him. Had almost fainted as they finally pulled him away. Even then, she had wondered vaguely how it would seem to be so deeply loved by a nice man like Gus.

And then a few months later, as unbelievable as it seemed, Gus had come over to her father's house in his car to call on her. On his third trip he had asked her to marry him. There was no time to make any special preparation for the marriage. Husking was on and Gus needed her immediately. He had said there was plenty of bedding and linen in the house—all of Elsa's things—no use to wait. So she had come. There had been nothing romantic about it. Just a ceremony at the minister's—and then cooking dinner for corn-huskers.

No, she was not particularly loved. She sensed it. She was a housekeeper, a drudge, a convenient helper. Gus was not unkind. Nor especially kind. Just matter-of-fact and very quiet. And he still loved Elsa. That was what hurt. She would not have minded the work, or the quiet, unsmiling way of the man, or the ill feelings with which her body was now racked. But to live with—and work for—and bear a child for a man who did not love you.... It did not seem right.

She was leaning now against a wet post of the pasture fence whose rotting bark sloughed off on her dress. It was not like Anna to be idle, but her thoughts seemed of more importance to-day than her duties. She clung to the distasteful idea: Bearing Gus a child and he loving Elsa all the time. She wondered if she, too, were to drown in the little stream like Elsa, whether he would care a great deal.

Standing by the fence, idly whacking her cottonwood stick at the bushes, she let her mind dwell on the picture of her own death, imagined the people gathering in the church and sitting solemnly waiting for the mourners to come. She visioned Gus hanging over her dead body—heard him call her as he had called Elsa, "Anna, come back"—saw them pull Gus away from her coffin. It gave her an abnormal desire to hurt him by her own death, to drown herself in the dark waters in order to shake him out of his moody quiet, and make him give his mind wholly to her.

The cows had come slowly and lumberingly across the pasture now, snatching greedily at a few last choice morsels of lush grass. Reminded of duty, Anna relinquished her dark thoughts of drowning, turned and plodded behind the cattle.

Gus was not at home when she arrived at the house. She put potatoes in the oven, sliced ham in readiness for frying, and set the table for supper. Then she climbed the narrow stairs to her bedroom.

As one throwing fuel on the fire of her jealousy, she opened the top drawer of the shining pine dresser where Elsa's things still lay. In orderly precision they stared back at her—the collars and cuffs and the folded aprons. They affected her strangely, these intimate things of the woman she hated. For half a year she had seen them there in the drawer just as Elsa had left them, and not once had she ever touched them. All her own things were across the room in a highboy she had brought with her from home.

Now she reached forth a cautious hand and picked

up a lace collar. The thought of Elsa's white neck rising from it maddened her even as it fascinated her. She laid the collar down and picked up other things one by one. She wanted to crush them, to tear them, in a symbolic crushing and tearing of the love Gus held for their owner. One fragile undergarment she wrung between her strong hands until it lay crumpled and torn in her lap. The act gave her an unholy pleasure. Replacing the rumpled garment, she reached for a green plush handkerchief box at the back of the drawer and drew it out. The lid lifted to her trembling, jealous fingers and disclosed a tumbled array of handkerchiefs.

Vaguely she wondered then at the confusion of the contents, in marked contrast to the neatness of the rest of the drawer.

With an inborn sense of orderliness she began straightening the squares of cotton and linen. Her hand, slipping under them, touched paper.

For only a moment Anna hesitated, and then she drew the paper out. The two folded sides of a thin sheet separated themselves in her hand almost without her volition.

"April nineteenth. My dearest Fred," said the letter.

Anna stared. *My dearest Fred!* Some intuitive thing deep within her consciousness knew the contents even then. Fred was the name of the young fellow with whom Elsa had kept company before marrying Gus. Her heart stopped with chilliness for a moment, and then raced hotly on. One long ink-stained blur across the page blotted out the words so that part of the closely written letter was illegible. A corresponding long ink stain ran across the soft whiteness of a handkerchief.

April nineteenth! The date on which Elsa had met her tragic death in the high waters of the treacherous creek. Wide-eyed, Anna was taking in the words that remained unblotted, the broken sentences left to carry their startling revelation.

"——can't go on longer with Gus . . . loving you all the time . . . living a lie . . . stand it longer . . . when we were students in the Lutheran college . . . awful mistake . . . always wanted to marry you . . . crazy this way . . . about out of my head . . . since you were here . . . couldn't sleep . . . come to my decision . . . write you definite plans . . . must burn this . . . no one ever find it . . . always your own Elsa."

Anna stood and stared wildly at the blurred streak, sweeping across the page like the hand of God blotting out part of the confession—stared at the ugly black ink stain on the soft whiteness of the handkerchief like the ugly black sin on the soul of Elsa.

Again and again she read the shocking message beginning with "My dearest Fred," and ending with "must burn this . . . no one ever find it. . . ."

The Day of Retaliation

And no one *had* found it—not then. And no one at all but the very one who most needed to find it. As though the sky had opened and dropped its message of peace to Anna! As though Fate had taken care of the secret for a year, saving it in the cheap plush handkerchief box until Anna should come for it!

More calmly now she tried to think out everything. More carefully she set together the little bits of evidence. The burning love-letter had been written before Elsa went for the cows on that fatal day. And what of the ink blur besmirching the page? And of the corresponding blot on the handkerchief? Might not the writer have been frightened at some one coming unexpectedly into the house? Did Elsa in her fear of detection snatch up the letter, hurriedly run to the handkerchief box and cram its inky paper into the hidden pocket? Did Death, then, lurking in the dark waters of the old creek immediately afterward take its toll of the wife who was not true?

Anna lifted her eyes from the amazing thing in her hand and looked out of the window toward the sullen creek. Elsa, the good, had sinned. Elsa, the worshiped, had deceived. Elsa, the loved, had not loved. Why, she, Anna, was the good one of the two. *She* was the true one. *She* would be the loved one when Gus found this out. *When Gus found this out.* The words poured into her heart like a softly flowing ointment, miraculously soothing and healing the raw, smarting wound that had hurt her so long.

She heard a sound downstairs—the closing of a screen door—so that she hastily shut the drawer and placed the paper in the bosom of her dress. She walked hurriedly down the narrow stairs, her hand at her breast where the letter lay like a weapon ready for use.

Gus was coming in the door with a little pail of cookies from Mrs. Schlappe. With a soothing calm flooding her whole body, Anna greeted him cheerfully. Instinct told her that the time for the amazing revelation was not ripe. After supper, when Gus would sit smoking and silent, thinking of Elsa, she would tell.

In that new tranquil manner she prepared supper. After the meal she washed the dishes, set her bread, and took up some sewing by the kitchen table. With the rise and fall of her breathing, the letter against her breast rose and fell too. She felt a security in its faintly crackling presence, a sense of holding the upper hand over Gus. For a long time they sat so—Anna, sewing, feeling the fluttering nearness of her child and the fluttering nearness of the letter; Gus, idly smoking, staring at the shining blackness of the range.

After a time Gus rose to wind the clock and lock the doors. And Anna had not told. When she went up the narrow, built-in stairway to bed she hurriedly took out the amazing letter, opened the green plush handkerchief box and slipped the paper into it. Then she locked it and placed the tiny key in another drawer. Tomorrow, if even once he mentioned the name of Elsa, she would turn on him and tell.

It was toward noon the next day that Gus, coming up to the house, said to her: "Elsa she used a different broom for the porches." It was not cross, not dictatorial, just casually informative. And surprisingly, it did not seem to hurt Anna to-day. She smiled to herself as he said it. Yesterday at this time it would have been almost unbearable. To-day it had lost its sting. Yesterday she would have known nothing to reply to him. To-day she might have answered if she had chosen. But she did not choose. She would wait until he said something more biting, something that she could not stand, something that cried out for an answer. And the answer would be waiting upstairs in the green plush handkerchief box.

A week slipped away. Several times Gus brought unknowingly the presence of Elsa, the loved, into the house with him. Once it was with "Elsa she churned oftener," so that Anna, tired from much pushing up and down of the old-fashioned dasher, almost turned on him with the weapon of her news. But she held herself, and waited for something more crucial.

The week slipped into a month and the month into August. And Anna had not yet told. Always she was waiting for that more bitter thing—that critical thing which she could not endure.

The Day of Retaliation

Heat descended on the community now, the torrid, corn-growing heat of the midwest. Anna, in her clumsiness, picked up apples and dried them.

"Elsa she sometimes made fresh apple-cake," Gus volunteered, not cross, not dictatorial, merely informative.

But the time had not yet come. Some day he would say a more biting thing and she would turn on him. It was as though she waited for all the references to Elsa to accumulate at some special time—as though she wanted the dramatic touch to come as a great crisis to the humiliation of her love for Gus.

When Gus was out working, Anna sometimes took the letter out of the box and gloated over the blotted, revealing lines, the written evidence which would smite his love for Elsa. She held imaginary conversation with him. The day when she would be goaded into telling, Gus would look at her in amazement, breaking his stony silence with: "I don't believe it."

"Oh, you don't?" she would retort with scorn. "Wait, and I'll show you."

By September, with the corn safely maturing, there was no rain. So dry was the grass that it made a rustling, crackling sound when the chickens walked in it. Anna canned grapes. The heat from the sun and the heat from the range seemed to burn her like fire from two giant caldrons. Gus, coming into the kitchen, passed the range. Then he paused and turned back. "Elsa she dipped out some of the juice first and made jelly of it before she canned the rest," he volunteered.

A fly buzzed aggravatingly around Anna's perspiring forehead. A bit of hot juice splashed across her hand. Suddenly the thread in her brain snapped—the slender, cautious thread that held her secret. At last Gus had cut the fragile thing with the knife of his criticism.

Anna whirled to him, her face livid with the heat and something else. Her gray eyes flashed wild. She flung out her hand.

"Oh, Elsa! Elsa! Elsa!" Her voice rose in a crescendo of madness. All day it had been coming and now it had come. "Elsa!" she shrieked. "Always Elsa. Some day I'll tell you. . . ." She threw back her head and laughed, high, mirthless laughter. "When I tell you . . . one of these days about Elsa. . . ."

She looked at Gus, standing there speechless, his mouth dropped open in amazement. She wanted to hurt him, shame him out of his calm, compel him to love her. "I'll tell you *now*," she shrilled suddenly. Anger and jealousy were boiling up in her like the thick, purple sauce in the kettle. "Right *now*. I'll go get it . . ." She dropped the long-handled dipper on the table, and the sweet grape juice dripped stickily onto the floor.

She ran clumsily from the room to the foot of the built-in stairway. She, who for weeks had walked ploddingly at her tasks, now ran frantically, her foot hitting and overturning a chair. Gus followed her stupidly.

The Day of Retaliation

The color had slipped away from under his summer-burned skin so that it gave him a peculiar mask-like expression of fright. "Now ... right now," she called back, her voice high, strident. "Then you'll talk some more again of your nice Elsa!"

Up the stairs she ran, lifting the cumbersome weight of herself violently. At the head of the stairs she flung herself across the hall into her bedroom and ran to the dresser. With hands fumbling madly for the key to the handkerchief box, she suddenly sank to the floor.

"Gus!" she called. "Send for help, quick!"

In a daze she could hear disconnected sentences from Gus at the phone: "No ... don't wait ... right away. Get off the line, you curious coyotes!" He was calling the Schlappes. "Tell Emil to bring your mother, quick!" Gus's voice was no longer mild.

People came. They moved about Anna strangely—sometimes dimly and far away, sometimes coming close like huge, distorted giants with false faces. She was conscious that she was saying foolish, meaningless things, but they were quite beyond her volition. Gus's face came and went with the others, white and staring. Once she made an effort to speak to him: "The grapes, Gus! I got to get up and finish the grapes. Elsa she always finished...." But she was swept away on a black wave which her struggling senses thought was the swollen water of a sullen creek.

The Day of Retaliation

A long time later—whether a day or a year or an eternity she did not know—she floated back to rest on the shore. Her first sensation was the lightness of her body that for weary weeks had been so cumbersome. Through the window she could see starlight shining. Queer, but it made her think of the rays of some star of which she had heard—a star that stopped once —somewhere.

Vaguely she sensed a rustling, pecking noise over in the basket near her bed. And quite suddenly her mind cleared and she knew. It was her baby, A deep feeling of peace enveloped her.

And then she saw that it was not starlight at all, but the first faint rays of the sun shining slantwise through her bedroom window.

Out in the hall on the couch she could see old Mrs. Schlappe nodding sleepily. Anna called her weakly. Mrs. Schlappe jumped and sat up straight.

"My baby—which is it?"

"Oh, ya. . . ." The old woman got up laboriously and hobbled over to the bed. "A fine girl."

"Where's Gus?"

"Gus?" The old woman could scarcely get herself awake. "Gus . . . oh, him? Vy, Gus has vent up to Omaha to get a nurse . . . a *trained* nurse. Between you 'n me 'n de gate post, you don't need a *trained* nurse any more'n I do. I've took care of t'irty-t'ree voman. I been countin' 'em up. Like as not I've missed some, too. It's t'irty-t'ree anyway, and out o' all dat number only four of 'em died and seven or eight babies. But you couldn't stop Gus, I tell you."

The old woman's voice went querulously on: "I say to him, 'All right, if you vant to pay forty-two dollar a veek ... it's all right mit *me*.' 'N' he say ... de softy ... 'I'll pay forty-two dollar a *day* if it'll save my Anna.' So doc televoned. He say a goot one is shust registered. Ain't dat folderol? Like a hotel. So Gus has vent. It's a vonder he t'ought I was goot enough to lay here by you. He acted *gans närrisch* over you. Valked de floor 'n talked about you till doc make him go outdoor. ... I guess you got him scare talkin' about a note you hide."

Anna was fully roused now, all her faculties clear.

"What did I say?" She raised her body weakly on an elbow. "Tell me quick. What did I say?"

The old woman pushed her back. "Here, none o' dat. You lay down. I'll bring you de baby. Don't you vant to see your baby?"

Anna's voice was authoritative. "Tell me what I said."

"You say foolishness a-plenty all right, about a note dat you hid avay and locked under de water of de creek bed already yet. You say Gus couldn't find it for de key is in de kettle of grape sauce. But most of 'em do like dat. I know a voman vonce who say ven she get up she is goin' to poison de neighbor takin' care of her ... and dem goot friends."

The old woman brought the sleeping baby and placed it in the crook of Anna's arm. Fascinated, Anna watched it stretch its arms in little sleepy, objectless motions and then open its eyes. Gus's eyes—large and blue. Gus's hair—dark and wavy. Gus's mouth—full-lipped and generous. For a long time Anna lay without taking her rapt eyes from the face of the child.

Subdued noises downstairs roused her from her long reverie and then, clumsily tiptoeing, his hat in his hand, Gus came into the room and up to the bed.

Anna looked up to the man hanging wonderingly over her. "Gus, you're disappointed?"

"Not on your life. I'm glad it's a girl."

"Ain't she nice ... her round little head and her funny little hands?"

Anna's plain face was glorified. Gus laid his big hand gently on her hair as though a clumsy touch might brush aside some magic light he was seeing there.

"Gus. . . ." Anna looked up at the man bent protectingly over the bed. "I been thinking ... poor Elsa ... she never knew what I know now ... the feel of a baby in the crook of your arm. It made me sorry for her ... and I been thinking it would be kind of nice ... if we call the baby Elsa."

Gus's face turned red, a brick red that ran below the tan of his skin. "I got no wish to quarrel with you,

Anna." He twisted his hat on nervous fingers. "But I told quite a few folks already yet about the baby . . . and when I was drivin' past the newspaper office . . . the editor was standin' out in front . . . 'n I guess I felt kind of important about it. . . . Anyway, I drove up by the curb and told him, too, and the paper was just goin' to press. Maybe you'll give me Hail Columbia for this . . . but already yet I told the editor to put in the paper that her name was little *Anna*.

"Gee, Anna——" He broke off suddenly and dropped on his knees by the side of the bed. "I'm glad I got you safe. You had me crazy. I thought I was goin' to lose you. Anna, if I'd lost you I'd a-gone too. You was out o' your head from the start, I guess. Anna, do you remember runnin' up the stairs talkin' about Elsa, how you had something you was goin' to tell me about her? You must have been out o' your head, wasn't you?"

Anna nodded. She slipped cool fingers through Gus's hair. "Sure I was, Gus. Don't pay any attention to it. I must have been plumb daffy!"

And then Gus rose hastily, edging away with a lingering look at Anna, because the new nurse was coming in. The nurse was tall, cool-looking, calm-eyed. She came over to the bed and took Anna's hand in her own capable one. Anna clutched at the hand in her eagerness.

"Listen," she said quickly, very low. "Before any more time goes by I want you to do something for me."

The Day of Retaliation

Her voice shook in the intensity of her earnestness. "There's a blurred-looking letter in a—in my handkerchief box, over there in the right drawer of the dresser. The box is locked and the key is in the left drawer behind some aprons. I want you to get the letter out and take it downstairs to the cook stove. Don't let Gus—my husband—see what you're doing, and don't let that old Mrs. Schlappe even catch a glimpse of what you've got. You burn it in the range. Stay there right by it till there ain't a scrap left. Promise me that, and then I'll rest or do anything you say."

"You're not asking me to do something you'll be sorry for when you get up?"

"No—oh, no! I'll never be sorry. I can't rest with it there!"

With hawk's eyes Anna watched the nurse take out the letter. With straining ears she listened to the departing tap of her slippers on the wooden stairs. With taut nerves she waited until the white-uniformed woman came back. Then she raised herself a little so that her hot, searching eyes could read the calm ones of the other. "Did you burn it?"

"Yes."

"All to ashes?"

The nurse nodded and smiled. *"All to ashes!"*

Anna Brunemeier dropped contentedly back on her pillow, and lifted the baby's little pink, clutching hands to her cheek.

ALMA, MEANING "TO CHERISH"

ALMA was nine years old when she came to live with Grandpa and Grandma Drew—a nondescript little person with freckles like so many pale raisins across a tip-tilted nose, big blue eyes that made her thin face look top-heavy, and ashy-light hair tied tightly back in horsetail formation.

Because Alma's dead father had been an only child, Grandma Drew had never sewed for a little girl; so she made the child's dresses rather like her own of the early eighties, with very full skirts gathered on to deep yokes. Alma knew they were not right, but she didn't know just what she could do about it. Once when she had ventured to suggest something ready-made, Grandma explained patiently, tearfully, that they couldn't afford it, that there was some money in the bank for Alma, but that it must never, never be touched until after high school, for if they were economical and did not use a dollar of it, Alma could go away to college some day. If the little girl vaguely sensed that an occasional dress in hand would have been worth two in a bush on some potential campus, she would not hurt Grandma's feelings by saying so. And after all, it gave

one a feeling of importance to realize that one had
money in a big gray stone bank.

The big stone bank belonged to Mr. Withers—and
Grandpa Drew (who was really old Peter Drew) took
care of Mr. Withers's yard. The Drew house, a small
one-story frame, stood on Eleventh Street next to the
alley and at right angles to the garage end of the
Withers home, which fronted on Sherman Avenue.

To the diminutive Alma the Withers place constituted the last word in grandeur. Paradise itself probably could contain nothing more lovely than that which
lay beyond the privet hedge. The house was of dark-
brown brick with gay striped awnings and a stretch of
sparkling glass windows clear across one side. In spring
the yard was a riot of snowy bridal wreath and blood-
red tulips and blue irises. There were white garden
seats, a winding brick path, and a pool where a green
iron frog spouted water impudently at an iron bird
that was either a heron or a stork.

Grandpa had other yards, too, which he sometimes
scrupulously groomed, but for the most part he was
busy at the big Withers place where the bridal wreath
and the crimson tulips and the blue irises took his
attention until the roses came on.

When Grandpa mowed, Alma would sit on the steps
and pretend she lived there at the great house with the
sun parlor and the gay awnings. She would lose herself

38

so deeply in the pretense that she fancied she could hear people driving past say enviously,

"Wouldn't it be grand to live there like that lovely little girl?"

It is quite possible, however, that she caused very little envy in the hearts of her observers, for there was no one in the whole community who did not know that S. T. Withers lived there, and that he and his wife had one son, Rexford, and not even a lovely little girl, to say nothing of one with freckles across a tip-tilted nose, a horsetail of ashy-light hair, and dresses with yokes.

To Alma, the three Witherses were all that storybook people could possibly be. Mr. Withers was tall and slender, with an iron-gray mustache, and he walked springily, not like Grandpa, who plodded heavily. Mrs. Withers was slight and dark and sparkling. Her dark eyes laughed, and when she talked, her voice laughed, and when she served tea out on the brick terrace, her hands moved over the cups like white birds fluttering. Rexford was fifteen, and he had everything a prince could want, including a watch and a kodak and a bicycle. Alma did not know him. She merely knew all this by the simple process of peeking. Only once, just before he went away to a boys' school, did she come face to face with him near the pool where the green frog sat spouting all day.

He said, "Hey there . . . kid . . . how are you?"

And Alma said "All right," and began humming with

assumed nonchalance and hippity-hopped back home through the hedge.

He did not even know her name. But Alma was glad of that, for she had no deep admiration for it. It was too short and sounded too babyish. Just Alma. It had no meaning. If she could have renamed herself the way the teacher said the Chinese did, she would have been Rosamond Dorothy Drew. Always when she sat on the Withers steps waiting for Grandpa, she thought of herself as Rosamond Dorothy instead of the babyish Alma that had no meaning.

And then one day at school when she was browsing about idly in the back of the big dictionary, she found some pages titled "Common English Christian Names. I. Masculine. II. Feminine." Quite suddenly her research work in department two became feverishly intensive. It was scarcely possible, of course, that it would be there. *Abigail . . . Ada . . . Alice . . .* It was there . . . *Alma. Alma,* meaning *to cherish.* As she was quite in the dark about what it meant to cherish, she laboriously looked that up, too. It seemed that it was *to hold dear, to treat or keep with tenderness or affection, to nurture with care, to protect and aid, to harbor in the mind, cling to.*

Just what it was that she was to hold dear, to harbor in the mind, cling to, she had not the remotest idea. In fact, she was fifteen before she knew.

But one does not jump from nine to fifteen as nimbly

as it is written. One lives through long painful years if one doesn't like funny-looking dresses but loves the maker of them—if one is obliged to hear one's grandfather called "Old Peter" by other children when one knows what a nice old man he is. But to offset the distressing experiences, Alma's freckles at fifteen were gradually and mysteriously disappearing into the soft pinkness of a lovely skin, her ashy-light roll of hair looked neat against the white column of her neck, and she was beginning to make her own clothes. Anent this last, she had figured out that if the material must always be cheap, dresses must be made cleverly, so she wore slim, plain brown ones with sheer white collars and cuffs, or blue batiste that matched exactly the shade of her eyes.

Not once did Grandpa or Grandma touch the money for any of these modest expenditures. It was safely there in Mr. Withers' gray stone bank gathering interest like some golden-fingered magician and waiting until the time when Alma would be ready for college.

No longer did she go over to the big yard with Grandpa. A sophomore in high school, she was too old now to hang about childishly. But she was still not above peeking through the hedge at times to watch the gay life over there. Rex was in Yale, but he always came back for the Christmas holdidays and for a few weeks each summer before he and his mother went north to their lake cottage. For those few weeks of each year there were exciting doings beyond the hedge.

"Mr. Rexford Withers gave a dancing party . . ." or "Mr. Rexford Withers was host at a dinner . . ." would head the *Courier's* society column. These parties were always exclusively for The Crowd.

The Crowd was a group as inextricably set apart from the rest of the young people of the town as is the Supreme Court from its associates, as definitely limited by boundary lines as the Withers yard by its hedge. For the most part the members were from the homes that faced the park or those farther up on Sherman Avenue—Irene Bentley, who was Rex's girl, and the Barlow twins, Sallie and Nancy, and Ted and Marian VanScoy, and Bob Robertson, and a few others.

They fascinated Alma, peeking surreptitiously through the hedge to see them drive in, gay and noisy. She used to imagine how they would look later coming down the winding mahogany stairway that she had glimpsed through the door—the girls in their modish gowns and the young men in their evening clothes. It was ideal—the way life ought to be lived. The background against which they moved was a standard of perfection—not one of golden-oak furniture and geraniums in paper-covered tomato cans, and Grandpa's pipes and papers lying about.

The Christmas vacation that Alma was fifteen was the gayest holiday time over at the Witherses' she had ever known. Lights blazed from the basement to the third floor. Rex was home from Yale, Bob Robertson from Amherst, Ted and Marian VanScoy from the State University. The Crowd went in and out constantly. The paper announced Irene Bentley's and Rex's engagement. When the lights ceased to burn and the gay affairs were all over, Alma felt that nothing would be worth while until the coming of the summer when she could again be an onlooker at a life that was ideal.

But when spring came on, with the tulips nosing up through the moist turf, events happened that changed everything. The Witherses' Christine told Grandma through the hedge that Mrs. Withers hadn't been well since Christmas, that they had taken her to the hospital now, and no one could tell how it was going to turn out. Then even before the outcome was certain, the astounding news came that Mr. Withers's bank had not opened that morning.

When Grandpa and Grandma heard it, they went white and stared at each other as though bereft of their reason. "The money," they said in unison. "The money for Alma's college education."

Alma had forgotten all about that phase of the catastrophe in thinking with horror that the Witherses could never live that lovely way any more, that all the gayety of The Crowd was a thing of the past, that life could never again go on over there as it had done. She wouldn't for the world have wanted Grandpa and

43

Grandma to know, but she was more sorry about that than on account of her own loss.

The town was wild about the closing of the bank. Threatening talk flew about because Mr. Withers had lost people's money, but Grandpa said he could not associate the things they were saying with the kindness of the man for whom he worked, that there must have been great forces behind it for which Mr. Withers was not to blame.

Mrs. Withers did not get well. Christine, with red eyes, told Grandma across the hedge that she guessed the news had killed her, but Grandma said that if bad news alone could kill, lots of folks who were living would be dead.

Rex was home from Yale, but no longer was The Crowd over there. Just Rex and his father. Alma could see them walking up and down the brick walk where the bridal wreath was bursting into white froth. Sometimes she would hear Rex trying to coax his father to go into the house, but he would only walk up and down —up and down. Alma on her side of the high hedge ached with responsive anguish for the anguish of Rex and his father. Up and down—up and down—

It was one evening when Rex was in the house that Alma heard the weird staccato sound in the garden like something cracking and saw Grandpa rush faster through the hedge than she thought he could move. Alma, too, was rushing after him when Grandma called her sharply to come back and wouldn't let her go at all. It was true—Mr. Withers had killed himself on the seat by the pool where the green frog sat. All those things had happened to the Withers family between the gayety of the holidays and the blossoming of the bridal wreath. It seemed unbelievable that all this made no difference to the garden—that the crimson tulips bloomed as lovely as ever, and the blue irises.

A few days later when Grandpa came home, he said he had a good piece of news to tell. Mr. Withers' insurance money which would have gone to Rex was to be turned over to the depositors. Grandpa said that he heard the place had been in Mrs. Withers' name, and Rex was going to keep it, that except for enough money to get to New York, he was turning over the insurance, and that Alma was to get seventy cents on the dollar now instead of the fifty or sixty she might have had. Alma knew she should have been pleased about it, but somehow she couldn't be.

Christine, who was moving her things away, told Grandma through the hedge that Irene Bentley wasn't going to marry Rex after all, and that, to Alma, seemed the hardest of all to understand. If Irene had loved Rex at holiday time, why did she not love him when the irises bloomed?

The next night just before time for the flyer, Rex and his dog came through the hedge. Rex had on a dark suit and a turned-down hat pulled over his eyes,

45

and he gave Grandpa a key to the house and said to keep the yard up a little and he would send money. He had not paid any attention to Alma standing near until he was turning to leave, when he said,

"Hey ... kid ... would you mind feeding Jack for me?"

Alma took an impulsive step forward. "Oh, I'll do ... *anything*." It was a cry of human sympathy from the depths of a grieving fifteen-year-old heart.

Rex said, "Thanks," and started back through the hedge with Jack trying to follow him so that he had to stamp his foot and tell him sharply to go back. Then suddenly he called Jack and put his arms around him and buried his face in the dog's shaggy coat.

And Alma ran into the house and cried for Rex and for all the lost loveliness of life. And from that day on she knew what it was that she was to cherish.

For the next day or two Alma could not bear to look over toward the big house, so forlorn now that it seemed a human being from which the living soul had fled. But Grandpa went over several times. He set out the gladioli bulbs as though nothing had happened, and trimmed the terrace.

On the third day he said to Grandma:

"I think you better unlock the door and go in. I can see through the window, and, boylike, he's left food on the kitchen table, and there are ivy plants in the sun parlor."

46

Alma, Meaning "to Cherish"

So Grandma, walking slowly with rheumatism in her bad leg, and Alma went through the hedge and over to the big house, carrying the key to Paradise. When Grandma was unlocking the big hall door, Alma knew that never again in life would she experience that same, queer, suffocating feeling of expectancy. The house where she had glimpsed such lovely things was to be entered. And with no prying eyes to see. Just she and Grandma going in as though they owned it.

They opened the big door and stepped in. The great mahogany stairway curved down into the hallway— darkly gleaming against the white of the woodwork. The sun came through a window on the landing and caught and held all the soft lights of the rug. Alma stood and visualized The Crowd coming down the stairs, heard them laugh as they descended—Rex and Irene Bentley and the Barlow twins and Bob Robertson and the others. And they would never come laughing down the stairway again. She felt a sadness that was overwhelming in its intensity.

For a little while she and Grandma walked about, tiptoeing, peering into the various rooms, shy as trespassers. The drawing-room was in dull green with mahogany furniture, and the walls were satin. The dining-room was dark and paneled, and Grandma thought it was kind of gloomy, but Alma knew it was just right. There were fireplaces and books, rugs as thick as Grandpa's blue-grass lawn, and a grand piano

from which a single silver-framed picture of Rex
watched them with his dark smoldering eyes. It gave
Alma an uncanny feeling of guilt.

They went upstairs, Grandma pulling herself up by
the mahogany railing. One bedroom was all in rose
color with stiff taffeta curtains tied back over china
knobs. One looked as though the blue irises and the
tulips from the garden had been scattered over all
the fat chairs and the bedspreads. And then there was
Rex's room. They could tell by the college pennants
and the pictures of The Crowd. The bed was tumbled
and unmade. So Grandma took off the pillowcases and
the sheets and tied them in a bundle to take home to
wash. If Grandma hadn't been there, Alma knew she
would have cried. But she didn't want even Grandma
to know how she cherished the memory of Rex.

There was a stairway to the third floor, and Grandma
told Alma she'd better run up and see if everything was
all right there. She was gone so long that Grandma
called to know what was the matter. There was nothing
at all the matter except that Alma, in the great stillness,
had fallen to dreaming of the young people who had
come there to dance on the shining floor and who would
never come again.

They took the perishable food home. Grandma wrote
it down on a little pad in her kitchen: "Seven eggs, a
loaf of bread, three strips of bacon, and a quarter pound

of butter." She would keep it so she could pay Rex back if he came home that fall.

But Rex did not come home. Grandpa took up the bulbs and nailed boards across the basement windows. Leaves blew into the pool and covered the green frog and the iron legs of the heron-or-stork.

Then spring again. And Grandma and Alma went over to the big house because Grandma thought they ought to take out the quilts and look them over for moths. This time she took home the canned fruit in the basement and used it. But each summer thereafter she would can the exact number: eight quarts of cherries—ten quarts of strawberries—five quarts of peaches—to have them ready for Rex.

It came to be as the years went by that Alma had cleaned everything. She had even taken all the lovely dresses out of the closet, brushing them tenderly as though attending to some religious rite—the black lace over silk and the dark wine-colored velvet and the black velvet evening coat with the white satin lining. Sometimes Grandma said Alma was foolish to put all that work on it when she wasn't getting any pay, but Alma would never answer her.

For no one was getting any pay, not even Grandpa any more. The money had come from Rex for a while and then it ceased. But each year Grandpa trimmed the honeysuckles and the bridal wreath and the roses—cut back the blue irises and set out the gladioli bulbs.

Alma, Meaning "to Cherish"

He never told any one that he was no longer the gardener.

"You'll get old Peter Drew after you," people would say to any one attempting to trespass. And every one thought he was the hired caretaker.

Alma went away to college and very soon she was twenty-one.

But one does not jump from fifteen to twenty-one as nimbly as it is written. One lives through happy, important years. And if one has not had many dollars in the first place and must, perforce, get along with only seventy cents for each one of these, one must be very careful to dress cleverly, to see that one's good looks become genuinely lovely and one's happy disposition makes countless friends. If one can do this, the other thirty cents do not matter so much.

It was June with the crimson ramblers queening it over the old garden—and Alma, graduated from college the week before, was now making her first summer pilgrimage to the Mecca of her childish dreams. The place looked run down, she was thinking. Grandpa was getting older and slower, and six years is a long time for a home to be without a tenant. Grass was matted between the bricks of the path, the green frog had lost one of his bulging eyes, and the heron that might have been a stork was tipping a little giddily on his thin iron legs.

Alma, Meaning "to Cherish"

She was thinking that Grandpa had told her Rex's taxes were delinquent for the last legal time, and the place would be sold if he didn't come home and see about it. The news saddened her, but she quickly put it from her mind for a happier thought—that three of her sorority sisters were driving through town that afternoon on their way to Yellowstone and would stop for an hour or so. She was wishing that Grandma wasn't bedfast and nervously fussy just now about callers, and that the golden-oak furniture by some wave of a magic wand could be . . .

That was as far as she went in her wishing, for inspirationally she knew she was entertaining the girls in the Withers home. Why not? Hadn't she and Grandma cleaned in every corner of it? Didn't she feel quite at home there now? Wasn't it a happy solution? Temptation, unlike vice, is not necessarily a creature of frightful mien.

With gay energy she set about making preparations. She aired the stuffy house and went over it with her dust cloth and floor mop. She set bowls of crimson ramblers about, and with only a slight stab of conscience took down some Spode tea things. She would bring over an alcohol burner for the tea, for, of course, there was no electric current now.

After all these energetic preparations, two o'clock found her sitting on the steps of the Withers porch watching for the car. The girls would be looking for

the Eleventh Street address, and so she must not let
them drive by.

It gave her a queer feeling to be sitting there on the
steps just as she used to do when she was little. For
her own amusement she repeated her childish formula,
"I'm the lovely little girl who lives here." Which was
50 per cent more true than in the old days, for had
she but known it, two women driving by at that moment
and seeing her there were saying,

"Didn't Alma Drew turn out to be the prettiest
thing!"

She recalled her old feeling of awe for The Crowd.
How queer the way life had treated some of them.
Irene Bentley was assisting in her husband's store.
The Barlows had been having a hard time. Marian
VanScoy was working in a tea room. Rex's taxes were
unpaid. The Crowd now represented a whole economic
upheaval. It would have taken a treatise on world
conditions to have written about them as they had been
and as they were now.

There they came—the girls—driving slowly and
looking for the house. Because the Witherses' number
was hidden by ivy vines, they would not notice the
discrepancy in the address. She waved at them, and
the car slipped up the drive and came to a stop near
her. There were gay greetings and noisy laughter, so
that instinctively Alma gave a swift thought to the
fact that they must have looked and acted quite as

Alma, Meaning "to Cherish"

The Crowd had in years gone by. Jack lumbered around the corner of the house and wagged a friendly tail with feeble dignity.

The four went into the house, and the college reunion against the background of the mellow old furnishings became a very pleasant thing for Alma. She felt neither uncomfortable nor strange. If she had made any plan to explain to them that she was borrowing the house because of Grandma's illness, she did not do so at once, and when the first opportunity had gone by, she found she could not tell at all. She evaded false statements adroitly and made gay inconsequential answers to pertinent questions. As, who was the good-looking man in the silver frame on the concert grand? "Just a neighbor boy," she said—and *that* was over.

No one knows why these uncannily strange things happen—why, for instance, out of all the days of all the years that had gone by, this was the day on which Rex Withers came home.

Alma had been saying, "When I started to read it, I found it so interest . . ."

The words snapped off on a broken syllable. For a key was turning in the lock of the side door that had been closed for six years, and Rex Withers was opening it—was standing on the threshold of the room. His face was grave. Unsmiling he stood, looking with somber eyes at the group, apparently showing neither surprise nor annoyance, merely suspended thought concerning the situation.

Alma's mind seemed blank, her body paralyzed, as though neither mentally nor physically were her faculties or members able to function. Rex had come, and she was entertaining guests in his home. Obviously something must be done about it. For that long vibrant moment she stared across at him, and then quite suddenly her brain sprang into action like a soldier called to duty.

Immediately she became Alma Jekyll and Alma Hyde. Nerves taut to the finger tips, Alma, the college graduate, who in four years of training had learned to carry herself graciously through various social crises, was walking up to Rex with extended hand, was saying:

"Why, Rex, I didn't know you were in town. How are you?"

And Rex was saying gravely: "Very well. And how are you?"

"These are sorority sisters of mine who are on their way to Yellowstone and whom I want you to meet. Let me present Mr. Rex Withers, Adele—Miss Langdon."

"Ah, the neighbor boy," Adele said with bright pertness.

"Yes, the neighbor boy . . ." the girls took it up in jesting tone, so that the blue eyes of the other personality, the Alma Drew who was only the gardener's little granddaughter, darkened with embarrassment and fright, met the questioning eyes of Rex Withers, and said with all the force of her mentality:

"Don't give it away. Please play up to me."

And he did. If he was mystified, he did not show it, for in the next half hour he assisted materially in keeping the conversation on the general and remarkably safe topics of Yellowstone Park, the new books, aëronautics, modernistic paintings, daylight hold-ups, and the habits of owls. And when Alma went to the kitchen to get the tea things with a gay, "I'm both hostess and maid," Rex asked if he could help. Alma said no, that each one was to carry out her own things.

When they had gone out to the terrace in laughing single file, Jack came lumbering up, gave his bleary old-man look at Rex, and began pumping his tail wildly, so that Adele Langdon said pertly,

"Aha . . . I have it . . . you're the favorite caller."

For the next hour Alma Drew, with the one endeavor in life to keep the situation in hand, quite possibly proved she had missed her calling, for no actress ever put on a better performance. And all the time over her head the sword of Damocles was swinging . . . and swinging. . . .

But all groups of sixty minutes do eventually pass, and Adele was saying:

"Time's up, girls. Signing off. We promised an aunt of mine we'd honor her with our presence this evening.

Three down and one hundred miles to go. I wish you could go with us, Alma."

So did Alma. If only she could have put on her hat and crawled into that back seat, never to look behind, never to come back—merely to have thrown herself comfortably and peacefully into Old Faithful geyser!

And now one of the girls was saying, "Alma, this is just the way I would have imagined you—all cool and unperturbed like this, with an old garden behind you." And to Rex Withers, "She fits in the picture, doesn't she?"

Rex Withers looked for a moment into the depths of his mother's old Spode tea-cup. "Perfectly," he said.

There were farewell quips and laughter. Rex moved his own car so that the girls could get out. They backed, turned by the garage, waved gaily, were gone. And Alma Drew and Rex Withers stood alone on the brick terrace.

Alma did not let a moment pass. "I know what you're thinking," she said courageously, "and the worst isn't terrible enough. I don't know why I did it." The relief of getting the horrible thing off her mind was immeasurable. "I want you to know I have never done it before. Grandma and I came in every year and cleaned . . . and kept things in good condition . . . you'll find them so, I am sure. But not until to-day did I ever take advantage of having the key. To ask the girls here. . . ." She spared herself not all all. "It was cheap . . .

chiseling. . . ." She talked on and on with self-flagellation. Silence might have been golden, but Alma was off the gold standard.

Rex was looking at her with the somber, smoldering eyes she remembered so well.

"Wait . . . do I understand you're apologizing for . . ." he motioned toward the old house there behind them in the mellow June sunlight, "for being here?"

"If it could be called by so mild a thing."

"Let's walk," he said suddenly, picked up one of Alma's hands and tucked it under his arm. Down the brick walk straight to the pool he went . . . by the white seat where . . . it had happened.

It did not seem strange to Alma to be walking down that brick path with Rex. It seemed very natural, as though she were living over something that had happened many times before in another world. Perhaps that was because it had happened more than once in the world of dreams.

Still with Alma's hand tucked under his arm he was saying:

"It's my turn to talk now. To make it clear what I want to say to you, you must know that the first year away was—well, not so good. The world pretty well collapsed for me that spring here at home. When I went east, I tried to get into something . . . but couldn't seem to get going. I had always expected in a careless fashion to go in with Father here in the bank . . . so when I was thrown out on my own . . . Well, you know these little robins that can't seem to get to picking up their own worms? I couldn't even find any worms. It appeared that there was no place for a bright young college man whose ideas of work had been mostly those revolving about his fraternity's social affairs. Once I got so low that I almost thought I, too . . ." He made a passing gesture toward the white seat, so that Alma said with a little cry,

"Oh, no."

He grinned and patted her hand. "Oh, I'm all right now. The world's a pretty decent old place. Banking being in the blood, I suppose, I finally landed a job in a bank; and two promotions in five years aren't so bad. I'm no moneyed plutocrat, but things are jogging along very well." He dropped his lighter tone and said gravely: "All those years I hung on to the place here like grim death. It seemed dumb not to sell . . . but I couldn't quite bring myself to it . . . with their things all here. Fate must have had a little something to do with it, though, for Robertson of Dad's old bank, reorganized, ran on to me when he was east a while ago, and finding that I wasn't doing so badly, offered me the assistant cashiership here."

"Here?" said Alma, and caught back the excitement in her tone with, "That's very nice for you."

"The offer was tempting," he went on, "but whenever I thought of coming back, it seemed too dreadful to contemplate . . . unbearable. I decided to come and prove to myself that it couldn't be done . . . to live here. Perhaps you can sense how I had to steel myself to do it? I've lived this home-coming over a hundred times . . . and the experience was terrible. And now, after all that . . . when I get here . . . to find you. I don't understand. It isn't awesome nor unbearable . . . and I think I am staying. It isn't . . . not even very sad. It's merely peaceful and homelike . . . as though I'd found . . ."

Suddenly as though he realized he was rushing things a bit, he broke off and bent to look into Alma's lovely face.

"And so you're the little kid next door? Old Pete . . . Mr. Drew's granddaughter. And you've been away to college? Say, you're not engaged or anything, are you?" he asked in sudden alarm.

"Yes," she said blithely, "for a year—to the school board."

And they both laughed the gay untroubled laughter of youth.

"And your name is Alma," Rex went on. "I guess I never even knew your name. It's funny . . . I've known a lot of girls, but somehow I never happened to know one by the name of Alma. I'm glad I never have . . . for now it's just you."

Alma turned blue eyes to him—eyes that contained mirth and something infinitely more tender.

"It means," she said—not shyly nor sentimentally

59

as femininity might once have done, but humorously and daringly, quite in the modern way—"it means *to cherish, to hold dear, to treat or keep with tenderness and affection, to harbor in the mind, cling to.*"

And the green fog leered impudently with his one good eye at the heron that probably *was* a stork.

BID THE TAPERS TWINKLE

THE Atkin house sat well back in a tree-filled yard on a busy corner of town, its wide frame porch running around two sides, thirty feet of it facing Churchhill Avenue, thirty feet facing Seventh Street, its long brick walk sloping across the lot to an iron gateway in the exact corner, as though with impartial deference to both streets.

The arrangement might have been almost symbolic of the character of old Mrs. Atkin, who had lived there for many years, so impartially gracious to her well-to-do Churchill Avenue callers and her hired help from Seventh Street.

Old Sara Atkin had known the town longer than any one now living in it. Indeed, she had arrived as a bride only a few weeks after the first timbers were laid for the sawmill which became the nucleus of a village. She had seen a store go up near the sawmill, a single pine room with a porch across the front, onto which a man threw a sack of mail from the back of a pony twice a week. She had seen the first house built—a queer little box of a cottonwood house; had seen another follow, and others; then a one-roomed school-house and a stout frame church with a thick spire like a work-

61

worn hand pointing a clumsy finger to the blue sky. She had seen whips of cottonwood trees set out at the edge of the grassy streets, had watched them grow to giants, live out their lives and fall to the ground under the axes of the third generation. She had seen a shining roadway of steel laid through the village and the first iron horse snort its way into the sunset. All these things and many others had old Sara Atkin seen.

John Atkin had gone back to Ohio for her and brought her by wagon and ferry to his bachelor sod house on land he had purchased from the railroad company for two dollars an acre. She had been nineteen then, her cheeks as pink as the wild roses that sprang up in the prairie grass, her eyes as blue as the wild gentians that grew near them.

A few years later they had moved into a new three-room house with a lean-to and turned the soddie over to the stock. John Atkin had possessed the knack of making money where some of his neighbors had not. He had started a general store and a sorghum mill, had shipped in coal and lumber, had prospered to such an extent in a short time, that they were able to build the present residence, a castle of a house for the raw prairie town—so unusual, with its parlor and back parlor and its two fireplaces, that people had driven for miles in their top buggies or buckboards to see its capacious framework and the mottled marble of its mantels.

When it was completed, new furniture had come for

it too—walnut bedsteads and center tables and a tall hall rack with a beveled-glass mirror. But the house which had once been such a source of pride to the whole community was merely a fussy and rather shabby old place now, with its furniture outmoded. John Atkin had been dead for many years, and Sara, whose cheeks had once been like wild roses, was a great-grandmother.

In the passing years the town had taken on an unbelievable size, and even a bit of sophistication, with its fine homes and university, its business blocks and country clubs. It had grown noisily around Sara Atkin; the tide of traffic now banged and clanged on the paved corner that had once been rutty and grass-grown.

But even though a filling station had gone up across the alley on the Seventh Street side and rather high-priced apartments on the Churchill Avenue side, old Sara would not leave, but stayed on in the fussy house with the walnut hall rack and the marble mantels.

She lived there all alone, too, except for the daily presence of one Jennie Williams, who came ploddingly down Seventh Street each day to work. Once, in Jennie's high-school days, Sara had taken her on temporarily until she could find some one else to help. But Jennie had grown fat and forty waiting for Mrs. Atkin to find another girl.

This morning she came puffingly through the kitchen door in time to see Sara Atkin turning the page of the drug-store calendar on the kitchen wall and pinning back the flapping leaf so that the word "December" stood out boldly.

Old Sara greeted Jennie with a subtle, "Do you know what date this is, Jennie?"

She asked the same darkly mysterious question every year, and, as always, Jennie feigned surprise: "Don't tell me it's December a'ready, Mis' Atkin?"

Yes, it was December; old Sara Atkin's own special month—the one for which she lived, the one toward which all the other months led like steps to some shining Taj Mahal. It was the month in which all the children came home.

"It's true, Jennie. Time again to bid the tapers twinkle fair. Did I ever tell you how our family came to use that expression, Jennie?"

Jennie had heard the explanation every year for a quarter of a century, but she obligingly assumed ignorance.

"How's that, Mis' Atkin?" As a stooge Jennie Williams could not have been surpassed.

Sara Atkin's white old face took on a glow. "Well, it was years ago. My goodness, I don't know how many —maybe forty-one or two; I could figure it out if I took time. But our Dickie was just a little chap—that's Mr. Richard Atkin, you know, my lawyer son—and he was going to speak his first piece in the new schoolhouse on Christmas Eve. The piece he was to give began:

Bid the Tapers Twinkle

"We hang up garlands everywhere
And bid the tapers twinkle fair.

"When you stop to think about it, Jennie, that's a hard line for anybody to say, let alone a little codger with his first piece. I can just see him—he had on a little brown suit I'd made him and was so round and roly-poly, and he stood up so bravely in front of all of those folks and began so cute:

" 'We hang up garlands everywhere
And bid the twapers tinkle tair.'

"He knew something was wrong—every one was grinning—and he stopped and tried again, but this time he got it:

" 'And bid the taters pinkle tair.'

"Every one laughed out loud and he said, 'I mean:

" 'And tid the bapers finkle fair.' "

Sara Atkins laughed at the little memory so dear to her old heart, and Jennie politely followed suit with as extensive a show of hilarity as one could muster after hearing the anecdote for twenty-five years.

"Richard never heard the last of it. And after that whenever Christmas was coming we'd always say it was time to bid the tapers twinkle fair. I guess all big families have jokes that way, Jennie."

"I guess yours more than most folks, Mis' Atkin. My, I never knew anybody to make such a hullabaloo over Christmas as you Atkinses do."

It was just faintly possible that a bit of acidity had crept into Jennie's voice. The coming month was not going to be exactly a period of inertia for fat, slow Jennie. But to old Sara it was merely an invitation to indulge in a line of reminiscences, so that it was almost a half hour before Jennie needed to start working.

Jennie Williams was right. The Atkins made much of Christmas festivities.

There are those to whom Christmas means little or nothing; those whose liking for it is more or less superficial; those who worship it with a love that cannot be told. Sara Atkin had always been one of these last. Christmas to her meant the climax of the year, the day for which one lived. It meant vast preparation, the coming together of the clan. She had never been able to understand women to whom it was merely half interesting, sometimes even a cause for complaint. From the first Christmas in the sod house with a makeshift tree for the baby to the previous year with twenty-one coming, she had sunk herself in loving preparation for the day. No matter what experiences had preceded it— drought, blizzards, crop failures, financial losses, illness —she had approached The Day with a warmth of gladness, an uplift of the spirit which no other season could bring forth.

Bid the Tapers Twinkle

In those old pioneer days she had neighbors who possessed no initiative by which to make Christmas gifts out of their meager supplies. She herself had known that it took only love and energy to make them.

There had been two sons and two daughters born to her. They were middle-aged now, but by some strange magic she had transmitted to them this vital love for the Christmastime, so that they, too, held the same intense ardor for the day. In the years that were gone sons and grandsons had wrangled with wives that they must go to Grandma Atkin's for Christmas. As for the daughters and granddaughters, they had made it clear from the times of their engagements that it was not even a subject for debate whether they should attend the family reunion. To the Atkin descendants at large old Sara Atkin *was* Christmas.

So now the annual preparations began. Life took on a rose-colored hue for old Sara and a dark blue one for Jennie. Rugs came out to be beaten and curtains down to be washed. Permanent beds were made immaculate and temporary ones installed. A dozen cook-books were consulted and the tree ordered. Jennie in her obesity and obstinacy was urged gently to try to make more effective motions. Once in her happiness old Sara said chucklingly:

"Jennie, Doctor Pitkin was wrong. Life begins at eighty."

Bid the Tapers Twinkle

To which Jennie made acrid reply, "Good land, don't tell me you've took up with a new doctor at your age, Mis' Atkin."

Eva, dropping in from a bridge afternoon, found her mother on the couch at the close of a day's preparations, a pan of strung pop corn at her side. The daughter was perturbed, scolded a little.

"Mother, what is there about you that makes you attack Christmas this hard way? You'll make yourself sick. Why don't we all go to the University Club? We can get a private room if we get in our bid right away."

"What—a club? On Christmas? Not while I have a roof over my head."

"But you do so many unnecessary things. No one strings pop corn any more for a tree. That was in the days when there weren't so many decorations."

"There's no law against it," said old Sara. "Or is there," she twinkled, "since the government has so much to say?"

In a few days Eva dropped in again. She had something on her mind, was hesitant in getting it out, averted her eyes a bit when she told it. "Mother, I hope I'm not going to disappoint you too much, but Fred and I think our family will have to go to Josephine's for Christmas. She's the farthest away . . . and can't come . . . and would like to have us . . . and . . ." Her voice trailed off apologetically.

Old Sara was sorry. But, "You do what's best," she said cheerily. She must not be selfish. It was not always possible for all of them to be with her, so she would not let it disturb her.

She told Jennie about it next morning. "There will be five less than we thought, Jennie. My daughter, Mrs. Fleming, and Professor Fleming and their daughter's family won't be here."

Jennie was not thrown into a state which one might term brokenhearted, interpreting the guests' attendance as she did in terms of food and dishes.

The next evening Sara Atkin had a long-distance call from Arnold. He visited with his mother with alarming lack of toll economy—in fact, it was some little time before he led up to the news that they were not coming. He and Mame and the boys were going to Marian's. Marian's baby was only nine months old and Marian thought it better for them all to come there.

When she assured him it was all right old Sara tried her best to keep a quaver out of her voice. In her disappointment she did not sleep well. In the morning she broke the news to Jennie with some slight manipulating of the truth, inasmuch as she told her there was a faint possibility that not all of Arnold's family might get there.

When the letter from Helen arrived next day she had almost a premonition, so that her eyes went immediately down the page to the distressing statement. They were not coming. They couldn't afford it this year, Helen said—not after the drought. It hurt Sara worse than the others. It wasn't a reason. It was an excuse. That

wasn't true about not affording it. It had been a bad
year of drought, but Carl had his corn loan. If she had
died they could have afforded to come to the funeral.
And she could not bring herself to tell Jennie they, too,
were not coming. She had too much pride to let Jennie
know that Helen and Carl, who had no children to
provide for or educate, thought they were too poor to
come home for Christmas.

She had scarcely laid the letter and her glasses aside
when the phone rang. It was Mr. Schloss telling her
that the turkeys were in. "I'll save you two as always,
Mis' Atkin?"

"Yes," said old Sara. Two turkeys for no one but
herself and Richard and Clarice and their son Jimmie,
who was sixteen. But she would not admit that the Atkin
reunion was to be composed of only four people.

Before breakfast the next morning the night letter
came in:

SORRY CAN'T COME MOTHER STOP JIMMIE HAS HARD
COLD CAUGHT IT PLAYING BASKETBALL STOP HOPE
MESSAGE DOESN'T FRIGHTEN YOU STOP THOUGHT LET
YOU KNOW RIGHT AWAY STOP SENDING PACKAGES STOP
WILL BE THINKING OF YOU ALL DAY CHRISTMAS

RICHARD

Old Sara got up and shut the door between herself
and the kitchen, for fear that Jennie would come in
and see her before she had gained control of herself.

Twenty-one of them. *And not one was coming.* It was unbelievable. She sat stunned, the telegram still in her hand. She tried to reason with herself, but she seemed to have no reasoning powers; tried to comfort herself, but the heart had gone out of her. All her life she had held to a philosophy of helpfulness, but she knew now she was seeing herself as she really was. A great many people who had no relatives for Christmas gatherings made it a point to invite those who were lonely. They went out into the highways and hedges and brought them in. The Bible said to do so. Old Sara didn't want to. Tears filled her old eyes. She didn't want lonely people from the highways and hedges. She wanted her own folks. *She wanted all the Atkins.*

Jennie was at work in the kitchen now. She seemed slower than ever this morning, trudging about heavily in her flat-heeled slippers. Sara did not care, did not hurry her, gave her no extra duties.

The morning half over, the phone rang, and it was Mr. Schloss again. "Ve got de trees dis mornin', Mis' Atkin. Fine nice vons. I tell you first so you can get your choice same as always. Can you come over?"

Jennie was listening, craning her head to hear. Something made old Sara do it. "Yes, I'll come over."

Mr. Schloss led her mysteriously through the store to the back. "I like you to get the pick. Folks all comin', I suppose? I never saw such relations as you got to have dose goot Christmases. Like when I'm a boy in

Germany. Most folks now, it ain't so much to dem any more."

He sent the tree right over by a boy. Sara and Jenny had the big pail ready with the wet gravel in it. The boy told them Mr. Schloss said he was to stay and put it up. They placed it in the front parlor by the mottled marble fireplace, its slender green tip reaching nearly to the ceiling. Jennie got down the boxes of ornaments and tinsels and placed them invitingly on the mantel. Old Sara started to decorate. She draped and festooned and stood back mechanically to get the effect, her old eyes not seeing anything but her children, her ears not hearing anything but silence louder than ever noise had been.

For the next two days she went on mechanically with preparations. Before Christmas Eve she would rouse herself and ask in some people—the food and decorations must not be wasted. She would probably have Grandma Bremmer and her old-maid daughters. They would be glad to get the home cooking, but Christmas had never meant very much to them. It was just another day at the hotel. Not a vital thing. Not a warm, living experience. Not a fundamental necessity, as it was to the Atkins.

In the meantime her pride would not allow her to tell Jennie or the merchants or the occasional caller who dropped in. "Our family reunion is to be cut down quite a bit this year," she would say casually. "Some of them aren't coming."

Some? Not one was coming.

In the late afternoon before Christmas Eve snow-flakes began falling, as lazily as though fat Jennie were scattering them. The house was immaculate, everything prepared.

"Shall I put all the table leaves in, Mis' Atkin?" Jennie was asking.

"No," said old Sara. "You needn't stay to set the table at all. The—the ones that get here will be in time to help."

"I've got a package I'm bringing you in the morning," Jennie informed her.

"So have I one for you, Jennie. Come early . . . we . . . we'll open them by the tree."

"Well, good night then, Mis' Atkin, and Merry Christmas."

"Good night, Jennie—and Merry Christmas."

Jennie was gone and the house was quiet. The snow-flakes were falling faster. The house was shining from front to back. Beds were ready. The tree was sparkling with colored lights, packages from all the children under its tinseled branches. The cupboards were filled with good food. So far as preparations were concerned, everything was ready for the family reunion. And no one but herself knew that there was to be no reunion.

Later in the evening she would call up the Bremmers. But in the meantime she would lie down in the back parlor and rest. Strange how very tired she felt, when there had been so little confusion. She pulled a shawl about her and lay down on the old leather couch.

Through the archway she could see the tree, shining in all its bravery, as though trying to be gay and gallant. Then she nodded and it looked far away and small. She dozed, awakened, dozed again. The tiny tree out there now had tufts of cotton from a quilt on it, bits of tinfoil from a package of tea, homemade candles of mutton tallow. It was a queer little cottonwood tree trying to look like an evergreen—a tree such as she had in the pioneer days.

She could not have told the exact moment in which she began to hear them, could not have named the precise time in which she first saw them vaguely through the shadows. But somewhere on the borderland of her consciousness she suddenly realized they were out there under the crude little tree. Arnold was examining a homemade sled, his face alight with boyish eagerness. Eva and Helen were excitedly taking the brown paper wrappings from rag dolls. Dickie was on the floor spinning a top made from empty spools. Every little face was clear, every little figure plain. For a long time she watched them playing under the makeshift tree, a warm glow of happiness suffusing her whole being. Some vague previous hurt she had experienced was healed. Everything was all right. The children were here.

Then she roused, swept her hand over her eyes in the perplexity of her bewilderment, felt herself grow cold and numb with the disappointment of it. The children were not here. When you grew old you must face the fact that you could have them only in dreams.

It was almost dusk outside now, with the falling of the early December twilight. Christmas Eve was descending—the magic hour before the coming of the Child. It was the enchanted time in which all children should seek their homes—the family time. So under the spell of the magic moment was she that when the bell rang and she realized it was not the children, she thought at first that she would not pay any attention to the noisy summons. It would be some kind friend or neighbor whose very kindness would unnerve her. But the habit of years was strong. When one's bell rang, one went to the door.

So she rose, brushed back a straying lock, pulled her wool shawl about her shoulders and went into the hallway, holding her head gallantly.

"Merry Christmas, mother. . . . Merry Christmas, grandma." It came from countless throats, lustily, joyfully.

"Bid the tapers twinkle fair, mother."

"He means bid the taters finkle tair, grandma." Laughter rose noisily.

She could not believe it. Her brain was addled. The vision of the children under the tree had been bright, also. This was another illusion.

But if the figures on the porch were wraiths from

some hinterland they were very substantial ones. If they were apparitions they were then phantoms which wore fur coats and tweeds and knitted sport suits, shadows whose frosty breath came forth in a most unghostly fashion in the cold air of the December twilight.

They were bursting through the doorway now, bringing mingled odors of frost, holly, faint perfumes, food, mistletoe, evergreens; stamping snow from shoes, carrying packages to the chins—Eva and Fred, Arnold and Mame, Dick and Clarice, Helen and Carl, Josephine and her family, Marian with her husband and baby, Richard's Jimmie, and Arnold's boys. They noisily filled the old hall, oozed out into the dining-room, backed up the stairway, fell over the tall old walnut hatrack. They did not once cease their loud and merry talking.

"Aren't we the rabble?"

"Did you ever know there were so many Atkins?"

"We look like a Cecil B. DeMille mob scene."

"Mussolini should be here to give us a silver loving cup or something."

They surged around old Sara Atkin, who had her hand on her throat to stop the tumultuous beating of its pulse.

"But I don't understand. Why did—why did you say you weren't coming?" she was asking feebly of those nearest to her.

Several feminine voices answered simultaneously—

Eva and Helen and Dick's wife. "To save you working your fingers to the bone, mother. The way you always slave—it's just ridiculous."

"We decided that the only way to keep you from it was just to say we weren't any of us coming, and then walk in the last minute and bring all the things."

"Carl and I couldn't think of an excuse." It was Helen. "So we laid it to the poor old drought. And we'd a perfectly dreadful time—writing and phoning around to get it planned, what every one should do. I brought the turkey all ready for the oven. . . . Carl, where's the turkey? Get it from the car."

"Fred and I have the tree outside and——" Eva broke off to say, "Why, mother, *you've* a tree?"

Clarice said, "Oh, look, folks, her packages are under it. And she thought she was going to open them all by herself. Why that makes me feel teary."

Old Sara Atkin sat down heavily in a hall chair. There were twenty-one of them—some of them flesh of her flesh. They had done this for her own good, they thought. Twenty-one of them—and not one had understood how much less painful it is to be tired in your body than to be weary in your mind—how much less distressing it is to have an ache in your bones than to have a hurt in your heart.

There was the oyster supper, gay and noisy. There were stockings hung up and additional Christmas wreaths. There was Christmas music from a radio and from a phonograph and from the more-or-less unmusical throats of a dozen Atkins. There were Christmas stories and Christmas jokes. There were wide-eyed children put to bed and a session of grown people around the tree. There were early lights on Christmas morning and a great crowd of Atkins piling out in the cold of their bedrooms and calling raucous Merry Christmases to one another. There was a hasty unwanted breakfast with many pert remarks about hurrying up. There was the great family circle about the fireplace and the tree with Arnold Atkin, Jr., calling out the names on the gifts, accompanied by a run of funny flippancies. There were snow banks of tissue paper and entanglements of string. There was the turkey dinner. And through it all, after the manner of the Atkin clan, there was constant talk and laughter.

The noise beat against the contented mind of Sara Atkin all day, like the wash of breakers against the sturdy shore.

All of this transpired until the late Christmas afternoon, when the entire crowd went up to Eva's new home near the campus.

"Don't you feel like coming, too, mother?"

"No, I'm a little tired and I'll just rest awhile before you come back."

They were gone. The house was appallingly quiet after the din of the passing day. There was no sound but the pad-padding of Jennie Williams in the kitchen.

Bid the Tapers Twinkle

Old Sara lay down on the couch in the back parlor. Through the archway she could see a portion of the disheveled front room, over which a cyclone apparently had swept. The tree with its lights still shining gaily stood in the midst of the débris.

In her bodily weariness she nodded, dozed, awakened, dozed. Suddenly the tree blurred, then grew enormous; the green of its branches became other trees, a vast number of them springing from the shadows. They massed together in a huge cedar forest, some candle laden and some electric lighted, but all gallant with Christmas cheer. Under the branches were countless children and grown people. And then suddenly she almost laughed aloud, to see that they were all her own. There were a dozen Arnolds, a dozen Helens—all her boys and girls at all their ages playing under all the trees which had ever been trimmed for them. It was as though in one short moment she had seen together the entire Christmases of the sixty years.

She roused and smiled at the memory of having seen such a wondrous sight. "Well, I suppose there'll not be many more for me," she thought, "but I've passed on the tapers. They all love it as I do. They won't forget to light the tapers after—after I'm gone."

Then she sat up and threw off her shawl with vehement gesture. "Fiddlesticks! Imagine me talking that way about dying—as if I were an old woman. I'm only eighty-one. I'm good for a dozen more Christmases. My

79

body isn't feeble—at least—only at times. As for my mind—my mind's just as clear as a bell."

She rose and went out to the dining-room. Jennie Williams was trudging about putting away the last of the best dishes. Some of the women had helped her, but there were a dozen things she had been obliged to finish herself. She was tired and cross with the unnecessary work and the undue commotion. Her feet hurt her. She liked the peaceful, slow days better.

"Well, Jennie, it's all over," old Sara said happily. "We had a good time, same as always. We've had a grand day to bid the tapers twinkle fair. Jennie, did I ever tell you how we Atkins happened to start using that expression?"

Jennie jerked her heavy body about and opened her mouth to answer determinedly, for she felt her provocation was great. But she stopped suddenly at the sight of old Sara Atkin standing in the doorway. For old Sara's sweet white face glowed with an inner light, and the illumination from the tree behind her gave the appearance of a halo around her head. Suddenly Jennie Williams had a strange thought about old Sara. It was that Mary the Mother might have looked that way when she was old.

"No," said Jennie kindly. "I don't believe you ever have told me, Mis' Atkins. How *did* you?"

TRUST THE IRISH FOR THAT

OLD MAGGIE O'RILEY sat in a wheel chair by her kitchen window. She stared out at the garden, the cow shed and the chicken house, desolate-looking in the clearing against the great wall of dark pines. It was late September in the north country, and there was nothing left in the garden but a few frostbitten tomatoes. For the rest there were dead beet tops, dried bean vines and weeds.

It ought to be cleared off and spaded for spring, old Maggie was thinking. Last year at this time she had spaded it and worked the dirt over until it looked as square and flat as a huge stove top. And she would never do it again.

The cow shed out there by the pines was apparently no different from usual, but old Maggie knew that Daisy was not inside it. They had taken Daisy away and sold her because an old woman in a wheel chair cannot take care of a cow. The chicken house, too, was empty. The neighbor boys had loaded the boxes of Plymouth Rocks on their trucks and taken them to the dealer over at the Corners because she could never again go out to feed them.

Never! It is the most cruel word in any tongue.

Trust the Irish for That

The chair in which old Maggie O'Riley sat was new, of shining oak and rubber-tired. "A lovely chair," Mrs. Schulter, her nearest neighbor, had said when she helped unpack it. The big chair had come all the way up from Minneapolis by train and truck after Mrs. Schulter had written the letter and sent the money from the sale of Daisy.

Yes, it was a nice chair, Maggie had agreed grimly. But it held you with iron hands. Its wood drew you and absorbed you into itself. Its rubber-tired wheels sucked at your heavy old limbs and clutched them tightly in their grasp.

Maggie looked down now at those two limbs that a few weeks ago had so unexpectedly failed her, had so suddenly turned traitor to her. They had taken her back and forth between the house and the garden, the chicken yard and the cow shed, the woods and the lake shore—back and forth tirelessly for years. They had made her no trouble, given her no complaint. They were part of her. They were herself.

And then, as though they had been concealing something from her, concocting a joke behind her back, they had suddenly failed her. It had proved a cruel, malignant joke. For now they were no longer a part of her, no longer her own self. They were alien things, heavy, cumbersome, like knotted white-birch logs. Dead timber!

Maggie looked sullenly down at their outlines under

the gray calico dress. Dead timber! Useless! Maggie had always made use of everything around the little house in the woods where she lived alone. With a neatness that was proverbial with the few neighbors, she had kept up the place in the clearing. And if there was no use for a thing she either buried it or burned it. But this time it was different. There was no use in the world for two dead legs, and yet she could neither bury them nor burn them.

For all the rest of the afternoon Maggie sat looking out toward the cow shed, the chicken house and the garden with the dark wall of pines in the distance. She might have sewed. She might have read. But old Maggie O'Riley's hands, gnarled and rough from much spading and cow-tending, were clumsy with the needle. And as for reading—that was a secret of Maggie's.

Even the Schulters, who had lived close to her for two years now, were unaware of it. A few times when she had been cornered she had slipped out of it cunningly, had laid it to her glasses that were broken or mislaid. And even the Schulters had not guessed that old Maggie O'Riley could not read.

This afternoon, Maggie was more grieved than ever about her condition. There were people in the world, she was thinking, who did not like to work, lazy folks who shirked the burden of labor. And all she would ask of life would be to go about and work hard again. *How* she would work! Up and down the little place she would go tirelessly. Never would she stop except for sleep, if they would only come to life again—those dead legs.

Suddenly a wave of rebellion swept her. It seemed that it must not be true that she was this way. It could not be. She told herself that she would rise above it. She would not let it be so. She would get out of the hated chair and step on the floor.

With magnificent strength of will she threw herself forward. But only the trunk of her body moved. The dead, immovable weight held her fast. *Och! Mother of Christ!* It was true. Old Maggie broke into sobs, great wrenching noises that came from the depths of a racked soul.

The dusk deepened. The old woman saw the Schulters' light appear like a star against the black pines. But she did not move. She knew it was time for her supper, that it was ready for her in the lower part of the cupboard within easy reaching distance, but she made no move to wheel herself over to it. Instead, she gave herself up to thinking of the thing that had come into her mind a week ago.

At that time she had put it aside as wicked, but from much brooding over it during the monotonous days, she had begun to ask herself why it was so bad. She went over it again in her mind, while the dusk settled thickly over the unspaded garden, the empty chicken yard and the cow shed where no living thing stayed.

Trust the Irish for That

This was it: Up on the highest kitchen shelf was a little box of white powder. If she should put a little of that powder into her coffee some morning, and drink the coffee as though nothing were different, she would go to sleep in her chair. Very soon she would rise up and slip away from her body—leave her body sitting there in the hated new rubber-tired chair. She imagined herself looking down on it, looking back at old Maggie O'Riley sitting there asleep.

She believed it would make her laugh to look down and see old Maggie sitting there so helpless in the chair, while the soul of her swept up and away from Maggie—away from those dead old legs. Her imagination stopped at that picture. She could not quite conceive what incidents would follow. She only knew that it would be worth the doing—to have that fine exhilarating feeling, that buoyant sensation of getting away. Maggie could not put it into words. She only fondled the sensation and it was all of those things: buoyancy, exhilaration, freedom.

For a long time she toyed with the subject. The church forbade it, but it did not seem wrong. It was not really like killing one's self, she argued. People killed themselves with guns and ropes and in other terrible ways. But this—this was just a little white powder. All there was to it was to drink her coffee with a little cream and a little sugar—and a little white powder. She herself would not be harmed. She would go away free. Only those old dead legs would be left behind.

The church ought not to mind that. It seemed so fraught with ease, so filled with relief for such small effort. A little white powder! And then for reward—that great moment, that laughter-provoking moment of looking back and crowing over old Maggie O'Riley's dead legs.

Even the Schulters would never suspect. To find an old woman dead in her chair sometimes happened. They had found old Mrs. Mendenhall that way over at the Corners four or five years ago. If she sat close to the stove and threw the little box into the fire just as soon as she drank the coffee....

She mulled over the details in her mind. She would have everything ready. There was no one to care a great deal. Mrs. Schulter would probably throw her apron over her head and cry a little, for they had been close friends for these two years. But after all, she would be relieved. She would not have to come over any more and get old Maggie into the chair or help her back to bed. Ernie and Emil Schulter would not have to take their time to do her chores.

She ate no supper at all. When Mrs. Schulter came over to help her to bed she was still planning craftily. For a long time she lay thinking of the various catastrophes that might overtake her in her present wretched state. She might get so much worse that she would be bedridden. The Schulters might move away. Mrs. Schulter might get sick. Some other unforeseen thing might happen. Yes, it was best. She was quite calm about her decision.

The next morning when Mrs. Schulter came over, Maggie was ready for her. She assumed a forced cheerfulness as Mrs. Schulter helped her dress and get into the chair. At first, weeks before, when the thing had happened, Mrs. Schulter had brought over all of Maggie's meals and cared for the little three-roomed house. But with the arrival of the chair Maggie had insisted that such work cease. "No," she had said, "if it's got to be, it's got to be—and it's me that's goin' to do my own work."

They had all been good to her. Schulter had come in with his plane and hammer and chisel, and had pried off the old-fashioned threshold boards between the rooms and planed them smooth, so that the chair would slip easily from kitchen to sitting-room to bedroom. Emil and Ernie took turns filling the wood box and bringing the water. "Anything else, Maggie?" they would call loudly, thinking that because she was old and helpless she was also deaf.

Emil had sawed off a broom handle for her and she had learned to sweep from her chair. It took her a long time, but Time was something Maggie did not begrudge. Time was something of which she possessed a great deal. And her shoulders were still strong and active. It was only those old leaden limbs that would not let her go. So this morning when Mrs. Schulter said, "Anything else, Maggie?" Maggie was ready for her.

"Yes," she said, " 'tis the medicines on the top shelf I'm wantin' down lower. There's a toothache one and the peppermint I might be needin'. Would ye be kind enough to clean off the top shelf and get 'em close to me?"

So Mrs. Schulter, thinking, perhaps, of the canned blueberry pies that she must make, swept everything into a lower shelf.

Maggie eyed her as she handled the boxes and bottles. But Mrs. Schulter paid no attention to the labels. Maggie watched surreptitiously—peppermint and castor-oil, the toothache medicine, liniment, sassafras, the little white powder. . . .

All morning, at her slow, laborious tasks conducted from the chair, like a silver thread through her thoughts ran the idea of the release after sleeping. It was something to look forward to, like a meeting with a friend or a tryst with a lover. She would think it over a long time to be sure of her decision, but always it would lie there before her—the way of escape.

In the afternoon it rained, a slow, cold fall drizzle, with the pines dripping clammily. Maggie wheeled herself to the kitchen door and called to Collie to come into the sitting-room. Collie, in his simple dog fashion, was thoroughly amazed. Such a thing had never happened in all his days.

"Come on, Collie," old Maggie called. "You might's well come on in here with me now."

But Collie whined and thumped his tail on the kitchen floor and would not come in. A long time Maggie coaxed, but Collie was bashful, as though pleased at the invitation but too wary to commit himself, so that she gave up trying to get him in.

For the two or three days following, old Maggie existed in an apathetic way as though the intense agonizing rebellion had died down like the forest fires of the north country when the lake shores are reached. And then the unforeseen thing, that she had half predicted, happened. Trouble came to the Schulters.

It was an early October day with pine needles ankle-deep in the woods, bare branches on the pin cherries and birches, mallards at the lake edge, the sun pale in the clearing—and old Maggie tied to a chair. Just before noontime it was that she saw the men go past her house and made out from her window that they were carrying Emil Schulter into his house. Emil, who had been on a vacation from his work as a forest ranger, swinging along that very morning with his young, powerful strides, had been brought home injured.

Maggie at the window an hour later saw the doctor come from his long drive through the woods. He was in the house for several hours.

Trust the Irish for That

It was late evening before Mrs. Schulter could get in to Maggie. Mrs. Schulter told her more about it. Emil had been over to the Corners in the truck. Something had gone wrong with the steering gear and he had run into a tree.

"It'll be weeks before he's out again, months maybe," his mother said. She threw her apron over her head and broke out crying. "To see him there helpless, wantin' me right by him all the time . . . always so big and strong and full of life." Then she thought of Maggie and added apologetically: " 'Tain't so hard for you, Maggie. You're old and you're a woman. 'Tain't half so hard for you."

Maggie said nothing. Yes, she was old and she was a woman. But it was hard. She looked at Mrs. Schulter sitting there swaying back and forth in her misery and crying about her boy. Even before this happened, Mrs. Schulter had worked all day long, and now with this added burden of taking care of Emil. . . .

"You can't come over to take care of me any more. 'Tis too much to ask. I ain't worth it. It's me that ought to 'a' died insteada hangin' on good for nothin'."

Mrs. Schulter wiped her eyes. "Don't you say that again, Maggie. I'll manage. I'm strong yet. The Lord don't give us more than we can stand."

When Maggie was in bed she told herself that the little white powder was the answer to the problem. But she would not take it just yet. It would only add more

to Mrs. Schulter's burdens. It ought rather to be when
Emil was over the first danger. And it would be so
simple—just her usual coffee with a little cream and a
little sugar and a little white powder.... Then sleep,
and that wonderful moment of rising up and floating
away from the cumbersome body, shuffling it off like a
locust; that great moment of looking back and laughing
to see old Maggie O'Riley sitting heavily there in the
chair.

In a few days they lifted Emil, too, into a big chair
by the window. From across the clearing he waved his
hand to Maggie. It seemed queer to look out and see
the bulky outline of Emil Schulter sitting idly there.
Even at that distance Maggie could sense his restless-
ness, the constant turning of his head from side to side.

Late in the afternoon of the second day that Emil
sat by the window, Maggie saw all the other Schulters
come out of the house together: Schulter and Mrs.
Schulter and Ernie, who worked in the garage at the
Corners. Ernie and Schulter fixed a wire up on their
chimney. Then they got down off the house and ran it
across to a pine tree. A clothesline! *The hat of St.
Peter!* Why were they putting it up that high for? The
Schulters were daffy. Maybe they could raise and lower
it some way for more sunshine. But that wasn't
sensible. The sunshine flooded the clearing for several
hours each day when there was sunshine at all.

Emil directed the work from the window, leaning on

the sill. There was a great deal of talk. Maggie slipped her window up carefully that she might hear, so hungry was she for the talk. Schulter had his pipe in his mouth. Sometimes he took it out and called back to Emil, arguing about the wire. *Och,* if she could only walk, she would go over and ask them what in time they were doing.

Mrs. Schulter did not come over until the hour to put Maggie to bed. Then she was excited and in a great hurry. "It's the radio they've been puttin' up for Emil," she told Maggie. "It's goin' to be wonderful. We can get to hear the music from Minneapolis." She was anxious to get back.

It made Maggie feel sensitive. She thought it over in bed. There was some quirk to it. The Schulters were not so bright. It wasn't sensible. She thought of the wire out there in the dark stretched from the chimney to the tree. No, it wasn't sensible that any one down in Minneapolis could sing a song that the Schulters would hear up in the pine country—a song that could run along on a wire down the Schulters' chimney. Somebody was just making them think so.

Most of the next afternoon through her window Maggie could see Emil sitting quietly enough. In the evening she could make out that the whole family was there together in the main room.

When Mrs. Schulter came over at bedtime she began at once: "We got the singin' from Minneapolis all right. It was grand. You'd 'a' thought they was in the same room."

Old Maggie listened incredulously. It wasn't sensible —such talk.

The next few days Mrs. Schulter did not come over except in the early mornings and to put Maggie to bed. Maggie sat idly at the window after the necessary tasks were finished. And she knew she would sit there all fall and all winter and all spring. The gray fall and the white winter she might be able to stand. But the green spring! Spring again with the partridges drumming and the hens wanting to set and the warm sandy loam crumbling through other people's fingers. *Och . . . Mother of Christ!* Every morning Mrs. Schulter asked cheerfully and hurriedly if there was anything more she wanted. But Maggie could see how anxious she was to get back to her injured boy.

"There's nothing more, thank ye," Maggie would say humbly.

Mrs. Schulter would put a final stick of wood in the stove. "Be careful, Maggie, when you do it yourself. I always think of you alone with the fire and wonder if you're careful."

"I'm careful."

All day now she could see Emil near the window working on something. He picked up some object and put it down again, over and over. His mother waited on him constantly. Of course she would wait on her boy and get things to amuse him. Maggie told herself that it was foolish to care, to think they had forgotten her. But she could not help but recall the days when Mrs. Schulter had brought little things over to her: a dish of custard, a glass of chokecherry jam, a bit of news from the Corners.

She brought nothing these days, told her no gossip. She was always hurried, breathless, almost impatient. Maggie brooded over it in her helplessness, nursed her sorrow. Once she wheeled herself to the cupboard and took out the little white box. So small it was, so harmless-looking and so powerful. She told herself she was cowardly. Why did she put it off? If she had any backbone she would set the very morning.

And then came the next Monday when Mrs. Schulter, with her washing and her waiting on Emil, did not get over until hours later than usual. All morning Maggie lay helpless. It was after ten when Mrs. Schulter came, tired and hot and apologetic.

"Everythin' was at once, Maggie. The dishes and the washin' with the clothes boilin' over and me havin' to stop in the very midst of it and get somethin' for Emil. I never saw a mornin' so rushed."

It hurt Maggie anew. She was put off until after ten. She quivered with the pain of it. Well, to-morrow it would not matter. Mrs. Schulter could come over at seven or eleven or not at all. When she came over in the evening, she would find Maggie asleep in her chair by the stove. Never to bother her again!

All day from her chair Maggie cleaned the house. She put everything in shape. Tuesday morning it was to happen. Coffee with a little cream and a little sugar, and a little white powder—and then that high buoyant sensation of getting away from her loathsome self, away from those dead limbs; that great moment of gay wonderful laughter—of high-winged release.

All afternoon she sat by the window. The slanting rays of the pale October sun hung over the lonely little house.

Suddenly something was happening over at the Schulters'. They were coming out of the house and over this way—all of them—Schulter and Ernie and Mrs. Schulter. Emil, too, sat leaning out of the opened window, watching. The men-folks were carrying a lot of contraptions: a black box and wire—a great coil of wire. Mrs. Schulter was laughing. The men-folks were grinning. *The hat of St. Peter,* what was ailing them?

They came in the back door. They filled the tiny kitchen. Maggie, frightened, wheeled her chair out toward them.

"Maggie, it's for you!" Mrs. Schulter's voice was high and excited. "Emil made you one, too, from a secondhand one with some parts missin'. The week and more he's put every minute on it. 'Twas for this I had to quit my washin'. 'Maggie must have one, too,' he tells us the minute we had his put up. 'Settin' there like she is all day. ''Twill put new life into her,' he says. And Ernie bringin' him the parts from another old one a summer tourist left at the Corners. And me bringin' the tack hammer and the bit and brace every minute of my time, till I thought I'd never get a thing done, let alone takin' care of you.

"I felt terrible neglectful, but Emil, he's that set on finishin' it quick. It made me torn betwixt the thought of my neglectin' and the anxiousness of you havin' the singin' and the speakin' too. It seemed for all the world like I was harmin' my own mother, Maggie, leavin' you go that way—me losin' her when I was little makes you seem like my own."

The men-folks were setting the contraptions together. They bored a little hole at the edge of the window and pulled a wire through. Schulter's pipe smelled all through the house. They strung a long wire from Maggie's chimney to the old cow shed. Collie ran excitedly before them.

"Jenkins said the old automobile battery was wore out," Ernie was telling his father; "told me to help myself to it, but it'll hold juice for Maggie for a spell yet."

Maggie could scarcely adjust herself to all this commotion after the quiet of the past days. And she worried about the wire running through that little hole at the side of the window, having a distrust of wires in general.

Trust the Irish for That

All at once they had finished. And Mrs. Schulter had thought of the bread in her oven, and was running back home. Schulter took his tools and went away. Ernie stood in front of the black box and the horn that craned its neck like a goose, and turned the little wheels. A band began playing on the inside of the box. It did not seem sensible. But with her own ears Maggie O'Riley heard the fife and the drums.

"Here, Maggie, I've only a minute to stay." Ernie shut off the music. "Listen, while I explain. You'll have to do the best you can with it by yourself till Ma gets back over. See here! You'll get on to it pretty soon. You get your long wave lengths here and your short ones here."

Ernie might as well have been repeating the *Iliad* in the original.

"There ain't much I can tell you about it now for to-night, except just to turn the dials and get what you can. You turn *this* and when you get your station, to tune in better you turn *this*."

"What if I'd turn wrong, Ernie? What would happen?" Maggie was fearful.

Ernie laughed. "Oh, 'tain't goin' to blow you up. You just wouldn't get anything. And before you go to bed you turn this around. There ain't a chance in a dozen there'll be lightnin' this late, nor a chance in a million it would strike if there was, but if it did, it would run down into the ground."

Trust the Irish for That

Maggie did not like anything running around loose in her house, mice or lightning. And she did not want Ernie to leave her alone with the machine.

"You're all right. You'll get onto it," he assured her. "Remember, first you turn *this* and then *this* and then *this.*"

And then Ernie went away. And Maggie sat in front of the little black box with the striped wheels. She would not have felt more helpless in front of the steering apparatus of an ocean liner.

"*This* and then *this* and then *this,*" Maggie said over her lesson. And then she took the plunge. She turned *this*. There was a long whistle-like sound. She was agitated, but she kept her head. And then she turned *this*. There were a few faint notes of singing. Then they died away. Almost immediately a man was saying something about signing off.

Maggie sat in front of the mysterious black box and waited. Nothing happened. The man had said he was signing something and she figured that he would come back after he had signed it. But there was nothing but a sound of squeaks and rushing air.

After a time Maggie decided upon another Columbus-like venture. Cautiously she turned the little black wheels. And right in the room a man started to sing:

> "Oh, the days of the Kerry dancing!
>   Oh, the ring of the piper's tune!
>   Oh, for one of those hours of gladness . . ."

Trust the Irish for That

Old Maggie had not had one hour of gladness for months, but suddenly her heart was leaping to the piper's tune.

> "When the boys began to gather
> In the glen of a summer night ..."

Old Maggie could see them as plain as day—Michael and Patrick and Terry. Ah, well! It was because there had been only one Terry in the world that Maggie had never married.

> "And the Kerry piper's tuning
> Made us long with wild delight."

It was all there before her. The work was done. The peat was gathered. The moon was shining through the trees. All the young folks had come into the glen. She could see the dear faces ... Kate's and Teresa's and Eily's. And Terry was coming toward her.

> " 'Lads and lasses, to your places,
> Up the middle and down again.' "

Terry touched her hands. She slipped her own into them. And then a strange thing happened. Old Maggie O'Riley seemed to leave her body. She rose out of it and joined the throng of young people dancing on the green. She was red-cheeked and lithe and spry. With Terry she was dancing. All the magic of youth she had in her feet. And she looked back at old Maggie O'Riley sitting there so helpless with the immovable limbs. Threw back her head, she did, and laughed at old Maggie, so old, so helpless, with two dead logs for legs. She made sport of her—old Maggie, tied to a chair. "Is it grindstones ye're havin' for feet?" she mocked. "Watch me!" she called and danced the faster.

> "Ah! the merry-hearted laughter
> Ringing through the happy glen!"

Faster and faster she danced. "Look at me," young Maggie O'Riley called to old Maggie O'Riley, "you wid yer dead legs! Is it the wings like the lark I have? Or maybe 'tis the thistledown I am!"

> "Loving voices of old companions
> Stealing out of the past once more..."

They had whirled to the trees at the edge of the glen. Terry held her close and kissed her, so that she half swooned at the sweetness of it.

> "And the sound of the dear old music,
> Soft and sweet as in days of yore."

The song died away on its last lovely melting note. A man's voice was saying briskly that this was Minneapolis.

Old Maggie sat back heavily. *Saint John the Kind!* It was so. From away down in Minneapolis a man had sung to her up in the pine country—sung the gayest and dearest old tune of them all.

Trust the Irish for That

And now Ernie Schulter was hurrying over again. All dressed up he was, to go after his girl at the Corners.

"How you comin', Maggie?" he called. "Did you like it?"

"'Twas heaven itself," said Maggie. And then she was wanting to know: "Who did it, Ernie? Who got it up—was smart enough to know how to fix the little black boxes to catch the music?"

Ernie laughed. "You mean, discovered that sound could be transmitted? Oh, I guess you'll have to give a man by the name of Marconi the credit for that, Maggie."

Maggie repeated the name after him reverently.

And then Ernie was gone and Mrs. Schulter was back with a fresh loaf of bread. And together they listened to a sermon and dance music and a talk on tree culture. Praying and prancing and pruning—it was all the same to Maggie, so eagerly did she drink it in.

After it was over, she could not get to sleep for excitement. She was not forgotten. The Schulters had not neglected her. Emil had made her the magic box. Ernie and Schulter had put it up. Mrs. Schulter had said she was like a mother to her. All evening she had forgotten herself, forgotten the old legs that were like dead birch logs.

Now she would always know how to forget them. With a few turns of the little black wheels she knew how to rise up and away from old Maggie O'Riley sitting there so heavily in the chair.

On Tuesday morning she poured her coffee. She put in a little cream and a little sugar. And that was all. When she had finished her breakfast she wheeled over to the cupboard. From it she took a little white box. Then she wheeled herself over to the stove and put it in the fire.

All the morning she worked at her accustomed small tasks. She would not permit herself even to glance toward the enchanted black box. It was after eleven when she finished. She wheeled herself to the lighting switch and turned it cautiously. With fine bravado she turned the wheels of the box. A man's voice was droning monotonously: "This completes the market quotations for the day. Signing off at eleven-twenty-nine, Central Standard time."

Signing off! You couldn't fool old Maggie a second time. Signing off meant *quitting*. She chuckled at her own smartness. Then she turned the wheels and heard a violin playing. But at that moment she saw Ernie Schulter drive into the clearing. She wheeled herself hurriedly to the window and raised it.

"Ernie," she shrilled, "sure, and I feel grateful to that Mar O'Connor you told me about. You could tell he was Irish, pulling music out of the air that way. Trust the Irish for that!"

Then she closed the window, wheeled herself over to

the stove and took up her dinner. It was early for it she knew, but she wanted to get it over so that she need not miss a single thing that might come running over the wire from the cow shed.

HOW FAR IS IT TO HOLLYWOOD?

GRETA GARBO and Mae West sat on the back fence and swung their legs over the tops of the milkweeds and the boxes of empty tin cans.

Greta was small and dark, with black hair cut like a boy's, and restless, jack-in-the-box movements. Mae was fair and pleasantly plump with a wide-eyed and innocent complacency that, if one were very critical, could justifiably be termed stodginess.

Miss Garbo lived at the Brysons'. In fact, she was known to Mr. and Mrs. Bryson, her sister Louise, the neighbors, teachers, and most of her playmates as Angie Bryson. Miss West lived at the Thomases'. In fact, she was known to Mr. and Mrs. Thomas, her brother Bob, the neighbors, teachers, and most of her playmates as Emma-Jo Thomas. To carry the statement still further, even to a truthful conclusion, it was *only* to Emma-Jo that Angie was Greta Garbo; and inversely and frankly, it was *only* to Angie that Emma-Jo was Mae West.

A talented and wordy gentleman who once said "The play's the thing" might almost have foreseen the coming of Emma-Jo Thomas and Angie Bryson. The play was indeed the thing in life just now. The masquerading, personifying, emulating—whatever the game was, it had been going on now for three weeks, and so completely had the two sunk their little-girl personalities into character that once Angie, forgetting she was in school and so forced temporarily to abandon the pretending, had called Emma-Jo by her name of "Mae," to the mystification of her classmates and the red-faced mortification of Misses Garbo and West.

In truth, the aforementioned school had become a decided nuisance of late, interfering as it did constantly with the making of Greta's elaborate costumes and Mae's jewelry. All day they toiled at the disagreeable tasks inflicted with humiliating regularity upon them by the exigencies of a public-school system, until that magnificent release at four o'clock when they could throw off the debasing shackles that bound them to a world of which they were no longer an integral or interested part.

At that magic hour they simply ceased to be such mundane creatures. Chrysalis-like, from the drab cocoon of school life they would emerge and become the great Garbo and the popular Mae West—their minds, their hearts, their very souls sunk into character. And only those who understand a certain phase of imaginative childhood can comprehend how possible was this merging.

So on this Thursday afternoon the two actresses sat above the milkweeds and tomato cans and swung their legs.

How Far Is It to Hollywood?

Although it was only Thursday afternoon, quite surprisingly three whole days of freedom loomed before them. Almost unbelievably, there was to be no school the next day, for the pupils from near-by country schools were coming in to town to take the county examinations, and the room constantly if unwillingly occupied by the Misses Garbo and West was the one happily chosen for the giving of the tests.

Thursday afternoon, Friday, Saturday, Sunday— world without end! The lovely and strange interlude trailed on into infinity in the immensity of its length.

Gratefulness for this unexpected intermission on the part of her who was known as Mae West was pathetically immeasurable. And all on account of problems. Now it must be known that Mae was the craven possessor of that complex known as "dumbness in arithmetic." It was terrible. It was like unto a disease. The mere sight of a problem confused her. Anything beginning "If a man..." had the immediate effect of sending her into a mental lethargy.

Reading she loved; geography was interesting; language not so bad. But problems! "Find the area of a farm..." the teacher was forever writing on the board. It was so silly and so unnecessary to actual living. Men always knew the areas of their farms. Uncle Jasper had a farm and he knew it was one hundred and sixty acres without any figuring. Cousin Mel's was eighty acres. He could tell you the minute you asked him.

How Far Is It to Hollywood?

"If a train goes so-many miles an hour—how many miles is it to Denver?" Angie's father was a conductor and he could tell distances everywhere. You could hardly catch him on anything. When Emma-Jo asked him that time how far it was to Denver and put down his answer by the problem, the teacher had said it wasn't right. It had shaken Emma-Jo's faith in the teacher.

After reading a problem through two or three times, Emma-Jo's mind seemed to lapse into a form of coma. This was because she never had the slightest idea what to do first. Occasionally when some one started her off on one, told her the initial step to take, she had sudden and unexplainable inspirations by which she was able to continue to the bitter end. It was due to these lucid, if infrequent, moments that she received any grade whatsoever.

This time, the problems for Monday had been on the board. There were two of those impossible ones beginning, "If a man . . ."; one almost equally bad, "If a train leaves at . . ."; and the inevitable and silly "If a farm. . . ." But the worst of all was the last. "If there are telegraph poles one hundred feet apart from here to Hollywood, and there are sixty-eight thousand, seven hundred and forty-two of them, in terms of miles how far is it to Hollywood?"

That one was perfectly dreadful. The teacher must have made them up, too, for she had held no book in her hand when she wrote. How *could* she have thought up that last horrible one? Emma-Jo could not know that the problem might have sprung from the same fountain as her own suppressed desires, for the teacher was very pretty and very young. All she knew was that if you lived almost in the middle of the United States and the teacher made up a problem like that Hollywood one, the answer was sure to be composed of four or five figures.

Emma-Jo had brought the problems home. She always did. Even if the teacher said no one was to take them, Emma-Jo managed to smuggle them home with all the slyness and finesse given to transporting anything of contraband nature. It is safe to say Emma-Jo Thomas had bootlegged more problems than all the rest of the pupils put together.

Sometimes her father helped her, sometimes her mother; Bob, once in a great while when he was home. Strangely enough, Bob, of the same flesh and blood, was working with figures for his living, as he was a bookkeeper in the State Bank at Hawksbury. But whoever "helped," it always resulted in that person becoming almost wholly the author and finisher of results.

But now she put away the thought of the problems as the Maid of Orleans might have thrust aside the thought of her doom. For was there not before her all of Thursday afternoon, Friday, Saturday, Sunday? It seemed so very long until Monday morning; until one must know with awful finality in terms of miles how far it was to Hollywood.

"Well, let's get started." The restless and wholly imaginative Angie was desisting from her leg-swinging activities.

"All right, let's." The complacent and stodgy Emma-Jo was assenting.

They slipped across the tin-filled boxes and into the welcome vacancy of an unused yard. And it was as though they left their Thomas and Bryson skins hanging on the fence like two dull locusts—for suddenly they were the glamorous Garbo and the sumptuous West.

The people who had moved away from this particular neighboring house three weeks before were really responsible for the present state of affairs in the lives of the two little girls. For since they had been donated a vacant house and yard, it followed that something must be done about it.

Angie, with her natural Robinson-Crusoe mind, followed by her Friday in the pudgy form of Emma-Jo, had been exploring the premises by the time the departing moving van had turned the corner. Everything had been securely locked excepting the screen door to the back porch. In that haven, an almost unbelievable wealth had been found lying there before the naked eye and immediately available for use. *Just dozens of movie magazines!*

Because Emma-Jo's mother held a peculiar notion

about supervising her offspring's reading, Emma-Jo had
never seen enough of them in her life. Angie, whose
mother had no foolish scruples about overseeing her
daughter in much of anything, was familiar with every
phase of the industry, including the plots of the plays
marked "for adults only."

Until dusk descended and penetrating voices from the
less interesting world of reality called shrilly through
the gloom, Angie and Emma-Jo had pored over the
fascinating contents. They had scarcely been able to
wait until school was over the next day before getting
back to the happy hunting ground.

In the week that followed, the mental and emotional
processes by which the little girls became metamor-
phosed into two actresses of the screen were so intricate as to be beyond the understanding of the adult
mind. From choosing the actresses they were to im-
personate, on through constant conversation in the
actual rôles, and with the setting of the play in the
silence of the vacant yard where no prying grown person
came, it had become very easy to change their personalities. The thing is quite possible to that portion of
humans unhampered as yet by such phases of life as
jobs, taxes, politics and monthly bills.

"Hops on being Greta Garbo," Angie had taken her
choice with superb nonchalance.

"Who had I better be?" the less grasping Emma-Jo
had asked.

How Far Is It to Hollywood?

"Let's see." Angie had run the studio favorites over in her mind. "Mae West," she had suddenly dictated, "with just *loads* of jewelry."

It had appealed to Emma-Jo—especially the jewelry, which was so miraculously easy to obtain here in the vacant yard. There were white-clover diamonds, syringa pearls, nasturtium-leaf emeralds, violet amethysts, and large rubies from a vine whose name she did not know.

The new Mae had set so diligently to work making bracelets, necklaces and earrings that Greta, who had to supply much of the imagination for both, finally insisted there was more to the play than the mere manufacturing of jewelry.

But this afternoon the buxom Mae began her usual task of making fresh jewelry, her adornments being of such delicate nature that a daily renewal was necessary. Angie, however, was not so materialistic. She had a far-away expression in her eyes that would have done credit to the one for whom she had named herself. She seemed lost in contemplation of something far from mortal ken. Almost would one have said she was seeing visions and dreaming dreams. Perhaps it was the languid spring-like atmosphere that put the call of the road into her mind. Perhaps it was the intoxication of the free days before her. Mayhap she was descended from one of the Maidens of Odin and was only now sensing that she could conduct the worthy to Valhalla.

Whatever the motive, suddenly she pulled her pudgy

fellow thespian into the cool cavern of the back porch and said in the low, intense tones of one laboring under great stress: "Mae, listen. Why don't we go to the *real* Hollywood?"

The eyes of Mae the Second widened in darkened alarm. "Oh, we couldn't—not really. We're too—too young." Emma-Jo's life was circumscribed by old-fashioned family law.

But to Angie, whose family life included the new freedom, the idea held possibilities. She even brought forth arguments to that effect. "Lot's of 'em went when they were young. Jackie Cooper did. Look . . ." she threw out her hands in conclusive proof—"look at Shirley Temple."

Emma-Jo looked. She had only to gaze at one of the fifty-seven varieties of pictures pinned to the inside of the porch to see the young lady who was definitely younger than herself. She began slipping—did Emma-Jo.

"But how?" Indeed, how? Aye, Angie, there's the rub.

But Angie was made of initiative as well as imagination. Together the two are invincible. "We'll earn our way as we go. We'll start to-morrow. We'll take things to sell at each town; with some of the money we make, we'll buy more things to sell. Out there we'll get into the pictures. Then we'll write back—and send money to our folks. Emma-Jo, wouldn't you like to send money to your folks? Remember"—her voice dropped to dramatic pitch—*"your father is going to lose his job."*

Emma-Jo wilted under the accusation. Didn't she know it? Why, for months, now, Father had been talking anxiously to Mother about what they were to do. To be able to send money home to him—it gave her a warm little feeling of gratitude toward Angie and a ready acquiescence to the plan.

There were other recent troubles in the clans of Bryson and Thomas. Emma-Jo's brother Bob was engaged to Angie's sister Louise, or rather he had been, but something had happened—the girls did not know what. All they knew was that there had been many tears on the part of Louise and much solemnity on the part of Bob. But neither the lachrymal condition of the one nor the melancholy state of the other could make any difference in the friendship of two small girls with parts to play daily in the privacy of a vacant yard.

So it came about, after some conversation concerning the troubles of the families, both financial and romantic, that the acquiring of picture jobs seemed a natural procedure on the part of the two most talented members of the same.

Angie, who decided there should be an oath between them about going, was all for pricking their fingers and bringing forth real blood to make it binding, but Emma-Jo, turning a little pale, insisted that she did not care to get her finger confected, so they merely shook hands which was virtually as substantial and far less gory.

That evening, when Emma-Jo's mother kissed her good night just as a faint silvery new moon was caught in the top of the maple tree, nothing but altruistic thoughts of helping her father kept the counterfeit Mae West from breaking out into loud lamentations and thereby spilling both tears and the beans.

Came the dawn, and much secret preparation, including fresh jewelry for Miss West—a white-clover diamond necklace, a half-dozen syringa-pearl bracelets, a crescent ruby brooch effected by means of a pasteboard background, and lastly, the invention supreme, huge hoop-shaped earrings, looking faintly like fruit-jar rubbers in those spots where the diamonds were thin.

This Friday was Club Day for the feminine heads of the families of Bryson and Thomas. Mrs. Thomas, however, was not going. She said she had plenty to do at home and she thought a mother's place was right there, where she could oversee her child on a day when there was no school. But Mrs. Bryson was going. She had worked long on her paper, "Modern Child Training *versus* Old-Fashioned Methods," and no upsetting rearrangement of school hours would keep her from reading it.

It was easy for the two potential travelers to have picnic lunches put up, for both families knew what long hours the girls spent in the vacant yard. It was not so easy, however, to get things to sell en route.

How Far Is It to Hollywood?

When they met and took an inventory of resources, Miss West had accumulated a small glass of jelly, some caps for toy guns and a package of radish seeds. Miss Garbo's plunder consisted of a pair of Louise's silk hose, a card of buttons and the current number of her father's railroad magazine. Each apologized faintly for the humble characteristics of the contributed merchandise, but hope springs eternal, and one can never tell just what a fickle public craves.

From the alley back of the vacant yard, each carrying a basket, their faces turned toward the klieg lights, the two set out. Ah, well, older and wiser moths than Angie and Emma-Jo have fluttered their feeble wings in the direction of that fascinating radiation.

When they left the last of the scattering cottages behind and were really out on the paved highway, Emma-Jo had a sudden and illuminating inspiration. *She could count the miles to Hollywood.* Then, as quickly, the idea died with the remembrance that she was leaving school and would not have to answer the problem at all.

Cars passed them. After some time, one drew up and a hearty voice called, "Want a lift, kids?" It was a man from back home. They felt a mild surprise to see him here, as though in leaving their town behind they had severed connections forever with its inhabitants. He wanted to know right away whither they were bound.

How Far Is It to Hollywood?

"Center Schoolhouse," the clever Angie informed him, while the less adroit Emma-Jo opened her eyes and mouth at the astounding statement.

They got out at the country schoolhouse, and when their temporary but inquisitive benefactor was out of sight, began trudging on toward the West.

Their second invitation to ride was from a man and woman who had been visiting in town, and now their luggage strapped on the back of the car gave mute evidence that they were shaking the dust of the village from them. The little girls accepted the lift but at Robbinsdale they got out and prepared to do business. The little town lay basking in the sleepy noon sunshine, apparently in a deep somnolence until it should be awakened to the privilege of buying buttons, jelly, hose, railroad magazines, gun caps and radish seeds.

Miss Garbo immediately chose the south side of the street as looking more prosperous; Miss West, perforce, took the north. But neither patricians nor proletarians were visibly affected by the bargains offered at their front doors.

To Miss West, especially, were the constant rebuffs trying, for she was made of more sensitive, less audacious stuff than Miss Garbo. It was very warm. Her jewelry was shriveling. A toe on her left foot hurt. Up and down the front walks to various houses she pursued her way without apparent results.

In front of an unpainted cottage an old man sat

tipped back in a chair against a tree. He was deaf, and Emma-Jo had to shout about her wares. It embarrassed her exceedingly to be yelling about radish seeds, jelly and gun caps.

"Guns," he said; "wall, now, I ain't shot a gun sence the war." He dropped his chair down on its front legs, pointed a shaking old finger at her and shouted: "What year was the Civil War? Quick, now."

It was worse than problems. She said faintly: "I guess I'll be going now, thank you," and fled precipitately.

At the next house a woman with a long face like a horse's came to the door.

"Would you"—Emma-Jo gulped at her Dobbin-like appearance—"would you like to buy gun caps, jelly or radish seeds?"

The woman glared. "Have you got a license?"

Emma-Jo was frightened. Bob and Louise had been going to get a license before they quarreled. "I wasn't going to get married," she said faintly.

"Well, I should hope not. Have you got a license to sell things in this town?"

"No," said Emma-Jo faintly.

"Then you ought to be reported to the town council."

Emma-Jo almost ran. She had to wink fast to keep the tears from falling. Her heart was beating violently. She looked behind her, half expecting to see the town council in a body coming down the street. But there was no one but Angie, who was motioning to meet her over in the park.

It was a crushed little Emma-Jo who sought a shady seat to ease her hurting foot. Not so, Angie. Angie was mad through and through. She took it out on the town. She thought of a great many violent things to say about it and the inhabitants thereof. She said she would like to put the buttons in their food, plant radish seeds in their old park so radishes would grow up all over their old town and smother their flowers and grass. She was all for going right on out of the place as soon as they had eaten lunch. "I wouldn't—I wouldn't *lower* myself to sell them anything," she stated to her peddler partner.

They ate their lunch and were well on their way to Hawksbury by two o'clock. Hawksbury was larger; people would have more sense there, Angie said. But they must plan not to pass the bank where Bob worked. It was just possible Bob might not see eye to eye with them about this western trip.

It was getting warmer. Their baskets were bunglesome. Cars passed. They began to look wistfully after them. Some men in a big shining car must have noticed their longing looks, for the car slowed. There were two men in the front seat and one in the back.

"Want a lift, girls?" they called. Strangely enough, it was Angie who hung back, Emma-Jo who was ready to meet unknown people. It was such a nice-looking car, she thought, and the men were so well-dressed. She even climbed in ahead of Angie. Her feet hurt, and it seemed providential to have the problem of transportation settled.

There appeared to be some difference of opinion among the three whether or not it was a good idea to take them in; one man evidently did not like the plan. The one in the back seat was talkative. "Where you bound for, girls?"

It was Emma-Jo who volunteered: "Hollywood."

"That's just where we are, too." He liked his own joke, it seemed.

"All the way?" asked Emma-Jo.

"Sure. We've just signed for the pictures. We're to play Uncle Tom, Topsy and little Eva." And he laughed again.

One of the three was surly. He swore at the talkative one—words that no Bryson or Thomas ever used. Angie with her quick wits was worried. But Emma-Jo would have risked a great deal to ease her aching feet.

They were getting into Hawksbury now, and even the talkative one was sitting silent and tense. "Please don't drive past the bank," Emma-Jo said politely. "My brother works there—and he doesn't know I'm going away."

One of the men glared at her.

Angie said quickly: "We'll get out here, thanks."

How Far Is It to Hollywood?

"Oh, no, you won't."

The one in the back seat had changed, too. He wasn't laughing any more. He said in a low voice, "Yes, we're going by the bank. We're going *into* the bank." He uncovered a queer-looking gun and turned it toward them. "You're to do just as I say, sisters. When we come out, you're to be standing on the running board. Whichever one stirs off the running board, this guy at the wheel he'll blow out her brains. Get me?"

Angie, having attended more than one gangster picture, had "got" him long before his speech was ended. Emma-Jo had, too, now. She had found fault with her brains at problem time, but such as they were, she wished mightily to retain them.

The car stopped in front of the State Bank of Hawksbury, facing the long slope that led to the highway. The little girls stood on the running board, frightened and obedient, waiting for the thing to happen: the thing that Angie had long since sensed, that Emma-Jo had never dreamed.

The two men went into the bank, while the third kept the engine running, swearing under his breath. Soon they came tearing out, with their guns up, and threw some bags into the car. It started almost before they were in, down the hill toward the highway.

The two little girls, one on each side, hung on tightly. The highway stretched straight before them. A mile beyond, to the left and right, several roads turned into the thick woods along the river bank. The men were arguing excitedly about which turn was to be made on a woods road.

Emma-Jo thought she was in a nightmare. She would wake up soon and see the silver moon caught in the top of a maple. But no, she was on the running board of a car tearing madly down the highway. They would soon make a turn, too, and Bob and the Hawksbury men would not know which way to come to find them. In "hare and hounds" they dropped little pieces of paper to leave a trail. Although in the grim reality of what was happening to her she was no longer Mae West, she remembered the former actress' jewels and dropped one of the wilted bracelets in the highway—then another—and another.

When they were gone, she surreptitiously yanked at the pasteboard crescent brooch. In a few minutes now they would turn into one of four roads. Her sharp little teeth bit through her white-clover-diamond necklace, and when the turn was being made almost on two wheels, she dropped that, too, where it lay like a long accusing finger, pointing out the way they had gone.

It was just at that moment that Mrs. Bryson, reading her club paper, was saying, "Children without complete freedom have no chance to develop their initiative," wishing her neighbor were there to hear.

The girls could see a car standing down the woods road, now. The driver of their own car suddenly turned into the edge of the woods, bumping along until he stopped back of a clump of trees. The men were out, tearing over to the car waiting at the side of the road.

The talkative one said: "So long, kids. Give my love to Janet Gaynor."

They were gone. The girls climbed down slowly from the running boards, looked at each other a moment with no words, peered out through the underbrush, and tiptoed out to the road. But soon other men were coming in cars, evidently after the bank robbers. So the two waited until all had gone by; then they started back toward Hawksbury. For reasons best known to themselves, neither mentioned going on to the Coast.

When they trudged into Hawksbury, a great many people were in the bank. They went in, too, with their market baskets, and pushed through the crowd.

Bob was in a back room with a bandage tied around his head and, strangely enough, Louise was there, holding his hand right in front of every one. When Bob and Louise saw Miss Garbo and Miss West, their eyes stared as though they would pop out of their heads. But because Miss Garbo was hot and tired, or, mayhap, because Miss West had no jewels, Bob and Louise thought they were merely their two little sisters.

The bank robbery was over. Club was over. The trip to Hollywood was over. The crime, intellectual, and romantic waves had all receded into the sea of an exciting past.

Twilight was soon to settle down in the small midwestern town which numbered the Thomases and the Brysons among its citizenry. Many words had been spoken into the atmosphere anent the various activities of an unusually active day.

Mrs. Bryson had said that it had all come out right— that the whole thing proved that if children were left to their own resources, were thrown on their own, so to speak, they could take care of themselves in any crisis; also, that the only punishment a child should ever have was the self-knowledge that it had bungled matters—and Angie now knew she had bungled. Mrs. Thomas said it proved that when a mother took her eyes off her brood, any thing was liable to happen; also, that getting Emma-Jo safely back home did not minimize the fact that she had done wrong, that inasmuch as the punishment should fit the crime and the crime had been running away, Emma-Jo was to stay in her room all day Saturday, getting her schoolwork in the meantime.

So it came about that Emma-Jo sat now by her open window with the problems in her lap. The sweet spring evening smelled like syringa pearls and a faint silvery moon rode in the sky like a crescent-shaped brooch.

Some one was hoo-hooing in the yard below. It was

Angie. The statement is significant. It was not Greta
Garbo—merely Angie. All the illusion was gone. Angie
did not look like Garbo at all; she looked just like a
little dark-haired girl of Emma-Jo's own age. All the
glamour was gone, the romance dead.

Perhaps Angie felt the same way, for she was
calling the old name: "Emma-Jo."

Emma-Jo called, "Here I am, up here."

Angie had a plan, it seemed. She was saying: "Come
on down. Dad gave me money to go to the show. Can
you get your folks to let you go, too?"

To Emma-Jo the possibility of getting her folks to
let her go to a show was as remote as the silvery moon.
There was no use struggling against Fate.

"No," she said, "I can't. I've got to stay in my
room all day to-morrow for—for doing what we did."
The sight of Angie, free as the wind, money on her
palm, no punishment fitting the crime, brought a sudden gush of tears to Emma-Jo. It was then that all
unconsciously she fell back into character. "Angie,"
she said, between gulps, "come up and see me sometime."

Angie left on the wings of freedom, and Emma-Jo
picked up her problems. Life can be very hard, for if
Sunday comes, Monday is not far behind.

She tried the two problems beginning "If a man . . .";
then moved patiently on to "If a train . . ." Very soon,
realizing there was no use in further endeavor, she

124

tackled "If a farm..." She gave that up almost immediately and came then to the last. "If there are telegraph poles one hundred feet apart from here to Hollywood, and there are sixty-eight thousand seven hundred and forty-two of them, in terms of miles how far is it to Hollywood?"

She read it through three times, looking at it with a dulling lackluster eye. Miles—telegraph poles—feet. If some one would only tell her which one of them to start with. She experimented impartially with addition, subtraction, multiplication and division, and when not one seemed to give satisfactory results, she succumbed to the mental lethargy which was stealing upon her.

And under any circumstances, she comforted herself, the problem was not sensible. If you were going to Hollywood by train or aëroplane, the conductor or pilot could easily tell you how far it was. If you drove your own car, your speedometer would register it. And if you were not going at all, you didn't need to know. *And she was not going.*

LOW LIES HIS BED

THE west-bound flyer was pulling into Parker City three days before—

Still, if one had been there it would not have been necessary to specify the time of year. Too many conspicuous characteristics of the period would have been about one; too many pointed allusions to it made by the passengers. Bunches of holly on the furs of four gay college girls, their eyes as bright and shining as the berries. The occasional swift rush of hard snowflakes against the car's double windows. All the racks overhead containing packages of grotesque shapes. The high strident voice of a child in the rear of the pullman: "But Mother, he couldn't get down *Elsie's* chimbly, *could* he, Mother?" The traveling man across the way: "Christmas trade picked up any, Bill?"

To old Mrs. David Daniel Parker, sitting stiffly on the plush seat, the sounds and sights of the holiday time came indistinctly, like little waves washing against a stone statue at the water's edge. Indifferent alike to the exuberant laughter of the young girls and the child's excited questioning and the results of any one's selling ability, she stared straight ahead, her eyes fixed rigidly on the blue velvet hat of the woman ahead of her, using the shininess of its cut-steel buckle as a sort of tangible object to which she might tie her rousing emotions.

They had been subdued of late years—those culprit feelings; had become far more obedient to her than the limbs of her frail old body. Joy. Sorrow. Love. Fear. Regret. She had known them intimately in her long years of life and been violently swayed by them all. But they had been held in check so long by an inflexible will that they were subdued now, too cowed to bother her often with their insistent tuggings—in the last years had become but memories.

And now that they were awakening and creeping stealthily through the chambers of her heart, she tried to tie them to the glimmer of a steel buckle in the seat ahead. A poor hitching post for winged Memory!

Old Mrs. Parker was thin, slender of shoulder, her faded old eyes palely brown behind her gold glasses. The snow-whiteness of her hair under her soft black hat made a scarcely perceptible line against the waxen hue of her face. Her coat was of finest seal and only a close observer would have noticed that the sleeves were short from having been turned in and the elbows showed long elliptical patches of skin.

She sat firmly erect, her black-gloved hands folded on an ebony cane. At her side were two worn bags embossed in scarred gold with D. D. P., their once-expensive leather covered with a dozen faded foreign labels. Another bag hanging limply from one of the crossed wrists was lettered in matching gold. Mrs. Parker knew that in the bag were a change of glasses, two neatly folded handkerchiefs, a purse containing four dollars and a rather important paper.

Although it was thirty-five years since she had been here, she knew by the swaying of the coach that they were passing around the bend now. That would be by the old picnic grounds, she thought, but she did not look out to verify her intuition—merely gazed stonily ahead, centering her attention on the shining buckle, as though she watched defiantly to see that Memory did not escape to annoy her.

Then suddenly, the train was stopping, and the buckle was leaving, and she became panicky, looking about her rather wildly. The porter came immediately, assisting her to her feet and taking the bags—the two worn bags of fine leather. But old Mrs. Parker kept the other in her hand—the one with the glasses and the handkerchiefs and the last four dollars of a half-million—and the rather important paper which was to admit her to the Old Ladies' Home.

It took her some time to get down the steps, the black gold-handled cane making the descent with tapping assistance. A man and a woman with beaming fat faces came to her through the crowd.

"I'm Mrs. McIntosh," the stout woman said—"the matron, you know. My husband—*Mr.* McIntosh, Mrs.

Parker. And we're so *glad* to have you—and just at Christmas, too."

The stout man repeated the idea, echo-like, "Yes. Yes. And we're glad, indeed, to have you come at Christmas time."

Old Mrs. Parker had a brief moment in which she thought how very much alike the two looked. Their round fat faces slightly red-veined, their double chins, their prominent blue eyes, the very shape of their glasses were similar, as though they might have changed clothes and no one been the wiser.

They took her arms, one on each side like symmetrical pillars of support, and began to assist her to a waiting car.

"I can walk alone, thank you," said old Mrs. Parker, tall and slim and erect. And tapped out her own support across the station platform.

In the car they heaped attentions upon her, raised a shade, tucked the robe about her, pressed a cushion upon her, with their warm hospitable parrot-like ways.

"You'll want the shade raised, won't you?"

"Yes, raise the shade for her."

It took both of them to complete every move and statement.

"Let's put the cushion at your back."

"Yes, the cushion!"

It irritated old Mrs. Parker, tall and slim and erect. They drove through the business streets bustling with pre-Christmas activity, gay with their greens and their fat little trees, across a park and a residence district. The matron called her attention to the new court-house and the new post-office and a widened boulevard.

"And here's our lovely Home." The woman pointed ahead.

"Yes, that's the Home." The man nodded.

In one fleeting glance Mrs. Parker saw the long two-storied building back of clumps of big trees, bare now in the pale wintry weather—and shivered slightly. Immediately she was calm, telling herself not to let it happen again.

They were almost into the driveway when the matron exclaimed, "Oh, Edward, how careless! Whatever was the matter with us? Why didn't we think to drive up Jefferson Avenue past Mrs. Parker's *own* old home where she used to live so long ago?"

"Well, I declare! That *was* careless—the big old house where she used to live." He brought the car to a standstill on the curve of the drive.

"No. Go on. We'll go another day. Mrs. Parker will want to have tea now and rest."

"Yes, tea and rest."

They were out now and in the warm lobby. Christmas was in here, too—long drapings of evergreen from wall brackets and bright red wreaths in the doorways and poinsettia plants on stands. Across the far end of the hall sauntered an old lady with flashing knitting needles and gay-colored wools tucked under her arm. Two others peeped surreptitiously from a near-by doorway. Old Mrs. Parker winced and closed her eyes briefly.

Then the matron had taken her up to the second floor in a smoothly running elevator, had escorted her to Room Twenty, had shown her the bath and the ample closet, asked if she could help about the settling, explained the dinner hour, bustled about hospitably, rearranged a drape—was gone.

Old Mrs. David Daniel Parker stood leaning on her cane, unmoving, in the center of the room. And so life had come to this. She was an old woman, worn out physically, burned out emotionally.

The door to the hall was still open, and through it came the sounds of soft footfalls, low voices, a bit of music. She did not want to see any of the other—other old ladies! She did not want to see any one. Now or ever. If she could just stay here alone in this room— until the end. . . .

She walked over to the door to close it, noticing for the first time the printed slip fastened on its polished surface. With peering eyes she stepped closer to read it: "This room has been furnished through the courtesy of the Parker City Thursday Club."

Her own old club, the one she had helped organize, whose social meetings had usually been held in the ample rooms of her lovely home, in the city that had been named for her husband's people.

For a time she stood, unseeing, then closed the door, tapped back to the soft depths of a large chair and sat down heavily. She could faintly hear music again in the building, the muffled sound of the elevator stopping, old laughter down the hall. Hard snowflakes tapped sharply against the pane like so many grains of white sand. The branches of an elm outside the window rubbed together in crisp rhythm. The shadows of the December afternoon lengthened, while old Mrs. David Daniel Parker with staring eyes sat stoically in the big chair donated through the courtesy of the Parker City Thursday Club.

An insistent rapping on the door roused her, brought her back from that long bitter trip into the realm of Memory. With labored movement she pulled herself to her feet and went again to the door.

A short old woman stood in the hallway, smiling up at her with toothless greeting. "Velcome home, Mis' Parker."

"Thank you," said old Mrs. Parker stiffly.

"I guess you don't know me." The old woman's short fat body shook with silent merriment as she wagged her head in mirthful glee. Her face was as seamed as a relief map with its rivers. Her coarse gray hair was screwed into a doorknob twist and across her ample bosom a safety pin was nobly endeavoring to assist a row of buttons in their effort to hold the two sides of her blue print dress together.

"No, I do not know you." Old Mrs. Parker stood, tall and aloof and unsmiling.

"I'm Anna. Anna Kleinschmidt who used to vash for you." And she held out the hard old hand that had rubbed ten thousand shirts. "I thought I'd come and velcome you."

The soft blue-veined hand of Mrs. Parker took the red one. "Oh! I remember. How are you, Anna?" It was not unkind in tone, nor kind. Just a statement without emotion. A question with no interest.

"I'm goot, I t'ank you. So goot that I ain't got a vorry in the vorld. And who could be better dan dat?" She smiled her cavernous smile.

"You work here?"

"Oh, no!" Old Anna Kleinschmidt bridled a little. "I *live* here—all de time. Room Fourteen, and my own bat'tub." It was not necessary for Mrs. Parker to know that, largely, she kept her overshoes and umbrella in that useful adjunct.

"Oh, yes. I see." For her part, old Mrs. Parker was through with the interview. She did not feel arrogant toward old Anna, was in no way too haughty to hold conversation with her; but she did not want to talk to any one, queen or washwoman. She wanted only to be left alone. Peace—it was all she asked.

But old Anna did not consider that the volunteer

welcoming committee of one had ceased to function. "I earn all my money by myself to come here. All but one hundred dollars. And den my arm gif out. And who do you suppose hear of it and say I shall come at vonce viddout vaiting and gif the rest of the money himself?" She paused for dramatic effect. "Mr. T'eadore Harms!"

Yes. Theodore Harms would do that.

Mrs. Parker knew him well. He had been her Harry's chum, had spent many a long-gone night under her roof, had worked in her husband's bank, had gone away and made a fortune. And so he had paid part of old Anna's way at the Home? How could she tell old Anna that if Theodore Harms had not paid *all* of her own expenses she, Mrs. David Daniel Parker, must needs have gone to the poor farm instead?

But old Anna had more to ask: "And Mr. Parker died, didn't he? Tsk! Tsk!"

"Yes." Anna need not know that it was by his own hand.

"My man died, too. My Emil. You remember? So goot, so kind to me. Alvays collect my vash money. Sometime even carry home the clothes himself. Alvays say, 'Mamma, don't pump all dat vater now; vait till it stop storming.'" And still old Anna was not through: "And your son, you lost him, too—your Harry?"

"In the war."

"And your daughter, too?"

134

Low Lies His Bed

"Yes."

"Tsk. Tsk. Poor dear! Poor dear!"

But Mrs. Parker was turning away now. She could not stand more.

"Vell," old Anna had a parting word, "a merry Christmas to you. Ve vill velcome you gladly."

A merry Christmas indeed! When there was nothing more in life. Nothing but bitterness and blackness and emptiness.

In the two days that followed, old Mrs. Parker lived in the midst of Christmas commotion and planning, but the activity of it washed like waves unnoticed against the stone statue that was herself. Once from a north window she had caught a glimpse of the cupola of her own old home through the winter trees, and had pulled down the shade.

But in the late gray afternoon of Christmas Eve she had raised the shade, almost against her own volition. Irresistibly some unseen force had seemed to draw her to the window again. An early light turning on from a near-by building threw the cupola into relief, its outline as distinct as a child's paper-doll house. At that moment a light flashed on in the tower room, two of the windows just discernible through the trees.

Suddenly old Mrs. Parker had a great desire to go down there. For the first time since coming she wanted to look upon it, desired deeply to see it lighted this

135

Christmas Eve, to torture her sick mind further with the sight. With self-inflicted bruises she wanted to add to the anguish of her heart.

She began planning, craftily, as only those who are mentally ill can scheme. She knew they would be assembling for the tree soon after dinner in the big reception room. It would be necessary for her to be at the dinner table, so that no one would suspect her unusual plan. If her wraps could be handy she might be able to get out in the confusion that would follow the dinner.

With painstaking deliberation she wrapped her soft black hat and a scarf inside her coat, turning the fur side inward so that the worn lining only was visible. Her galoshes she would wear to dinner. No one would notice them under the long black skirt and she could not risk taking the time to put them on at the last moment. She went down early in that zero half-hour just preceding the meal when all were tidying themselves for dinner, and deposited her bundle in a small coat closet near the side entrance. The excitement of what she was doing gave her the first real interest in life since she had come.

When the bell rang, the old ladies came from their rooms, some spryly, some feebly, but all childishly eager.

The dinner tables were sparkling and gay with greens. Poinsettias paraded proudly down the center of each, and there were cards of crusted snow-covered bells at the plates.

There were several tables in the large room. Old Mrs. David Daniel Parker, who had eaten at the tables of governors and senators, ship captains and millionaires, sat at the same one with old Anna Kleinschmidt, who in her darkest days sometimes had not eaten at all. There were three others at that particular table besides the matron—an old Mrs. Tuttle, as little and brown and twittery as a partridge; an old Mrs. Murphy, large and solid and immobile, as though, having found a resting place after many weary years, she wanted only to experience the luxury of fixity; and an old Mrs. Sargent with magenta cheeks, flamboyant earrings, unbelievably ink-black hair and a distinct line of demarcation between the gay youthfulness of her face and the wrinkled column of her neck, like a gay Marie Antoinette head on the shoulders of Whistler's Mother.

Mrs. McIntosh pinned a sprig of holly on each old lady, on the flat old silken chest of Mrs. David Daniel Parker and on the mountainous gingham one of old Anna Kleinschmidt, and on all the others.

Old Anna sat next to Mrs. Parker and was excited to the point of hilarity. She drank her tea with gusto, smacked her lips over the soup, was exuberant as a child that there was to be chicken. It was as though she were having all the good things of life at once, as though she were experiencing enough food, warmth and light for the first time in her life.

"Oh, if Emil could see me now," she whispered to Mrs. Parker. "My Gott. Eatin' oyster soup until I could bust."

It would have been exceedingly distasteful to Mrs. Parker in other days, but now she did not care one way or the other. She looked upon her neither with dislike nor liking; was merely callous to those about her.

The dinner was over. All the old ladies were moving toward the parlors, some with excited exclamations in anticipation of the pleasant evening to come. Mrs. Parker with her cane stood by the coat-closet door waiting until the last one should go in. It was old Mrs. Sargent, preening before a glass, giving her too-inky hair a pat into place, her too-showy earrings a loving touch.

The hall was empty now. Old Mrs. Parker slipped into her ancient seal coat and her soft black hat and stepped out upon the side porch. It was colder than she had thought when in the shelter of the warm house, so she buttoned the coat tightly, turning up the collar, and tied the scarf over her hat. Then she started slowly down the drive, tapping her way along with careful steps.

Now that she had left the drive of the Home and was out on the street, she realized there was greater familiarity about the little city than she had sensed in her ride up from the station. There was the old Rhodes place looking fairly natural behind the street lights, and the Kennards's house, though changed into a duplex, was still recognizable. They brought back vivid memories of social events in a day when society was composed of a definite membership.

Old Mrs. Parker, tall and erect, tapped as rapidly forward as her bad limb would allow. Two blocks down this way and one over to the east. She had lost sight of the cupola of her old home, which up to this moment had guided her like a beacon.

Suddenly at the end of the second block her knee buckled, and she stumbled and would have fallen if she had not been close to a low brick wall. She clung to the iron railing above the bricks for a time until she felt that she could go on. But the damage was done; the knee had been twisted and pained with every step. It was snowing and colder.

She was frightened now, and thought with longing of the restful security of Room Twenty. She must get back somehow. That block around the corner to her old home seemed suddenly too long a journey to be attempted. She wanted to cry with disappointment as though she were missing a definite engagement there, as though in reality the family expected her.

But some one was coming down the street, some one short and squat with duck-like waddling, a shawl over her head.

Low Lies His Bed

Old Mrs. Parker had never been so glad to see any one. She grasped the outstretched hand of old Anna as though it were a life belt.

Old Anna was merry with chuckles at the smartness of her own mind. "I miss you and I look in your room, and vhen I find your coat gone, I know shust vhere to go. I say, 'Anna, vhere in de whole vorld vould you like most to go on dis Christmas Eve?' 'Back home,' I say to myself. 'Vell, dat's vhere Mis' Parker go, too.' " She chuckled. "Come, now. I help you."

With her cane on one side and old Anna on the other, Mrs. Parker went on.

There it was—the wide porch and the white pillars familiar against the dark bricks. Lights shone in every room, and each pane held its Christmas wreath. Beyond the French windows a tree stood tall and proud and erect. Like old Mrs. David Daniel Parker. Several children were dancing about near the shining thing, and occasionally the form of an older person came into sight.

And then a strange thing happened. To the woman standing there on the walk, clutching her cane and old Anna, the scene was so familiar that she herself became an integral part of it. Although her frail old body stood, tall and erect, in the snow and the cold, her spirit seemed to merge into the family group there in the high-ceilinged room. The sensation was sharply poignant, infinitely precious.

Low Lies His Bed

Suddenly something broke—ice that had long covered her heart—sweeping out on a wave of Memory. Instead of a bitterness, she felt only tenderness at the familiar sight. In place of coldness, warmth.

"Ain't it nice," old Anna was saying, "dat it shust go on and on—Christmas lights and Christmas trees and Christmas spirit? All over town, no matter who lives in 'em, de nice Christmas candles burn on. In yours; in mine. My old house across de tracks—I go over to see it dis afternoon. De folks got nine kids, and dey vas all hollerin' about Christmas and tyin' holly on de dog—same as mine used to do." Old Anna shook her fat sides. "Come, shall ve go home now?"

"Yes. I'm ready to go—home."

There was the slow snowy walk back to the Home, where for a moment they saw the matron open the door at the side porch, heard her say something about "letting in a bit of fresh air" and a familiar echo from farther in the hall. "Yes, a little fresh air."

They waited under the trees until the door closed and the bulky shadow was gone, then they mounted the wide steps and went into the cheery warmth of the building.

A great circle of chairs was being made about the tree and all the old ladies were seating themselves with girlish commotion. It seemed they were going to sing. The carolers had been there and sung and the radio had given forth much melody, but now the old ladies were going to make Christmas music of their own. To create! Ah, that was the thing that could stimulate.

"Here, Mrs. Parker." "Sit here, Mrs. Parker." She was still new enough to be given a preferential politeness.

So old Mrs. Parker, as tall and erect and proud as the Christmas tree, seated herself between the matron and old Mrs. Tuttle, who was as little and brown and fluttery as a partridge.

They took hold of hands to form a huge circle of arms around the tree.

"My, how cold your hand is," the matron said solicitously, "almost as though you'd been outdoors."

Old Anna Kleinschmidt leaned across old Mrs. Murphy. "It's the excitement and nervousness," she said to the matron, and as though she had just made a discovery: "My Gott! Mine is, too. See?" And she put her hard old hand against the matron's cheek to prove her point, and then shook with noiseless laughter.

So with their hands—wrinkled old hands that had trimmed a thousand trees—they formed a circle around the tree with its shining star at the top.

Old Mrs. Sargent, who had been a music teacher, gave the pitch, and the others joined in, their voices not quite in key, a bit cracked and hoarse, entirely aged— but energetic.

Low Lies His Bed

"Brightest and best of the sons of the morning!
  Shine on the darkness and lend us Thine aid:
  Star of the East, the horizon adorning..."

Surprisingly, old Mrs. Parker felt a lessening of bitterness, a lifting of shadows. Nothing was different. She was still here on the charity of Theodore Harms— not nearly so independent as old Anna, who had earned all but a hundred dollars; still sleeping on a bed furnished through the courtesy of the Thursday Club. But after all, she had lived a full life; with all these other old women had kindled Christmas fires on the hearthstone of a home.

"Cold on His cradle the dewdrops are shining,
  Low lies His bed with the beasts of the stall."

Yes, another had known anguish and sorrow and a lowly bed.

Old Mrs. Parker merely hummed the tune under her breath, but old Anna Kleinschmidt shouted it lustily:

"Angels adore Him in slumber reclining,
  Maker and Monarch who cares for us all!"

WILL THE ROMANCE BE THE SAME?

O N AN afternoon in the merry month of May, Mrs.
Mary Wakely, forty-seven, clothed in a kitchen
dress with a towel bound round her graying hair, sat
on the floor of the attic in her home, sorting pieces of
cloth from an old scrap-bag, and was not so merry.

There are those who will scent at once the battle of
spring house-cleaning in the air.

Mary Wakely was the capable wife of Sam Wakely,
the active mother of six hilarious Wakelys, the energetic
overseer of a big house, and consequently the holder
of that undistinguished position which the world at
large in jocular vein lists as "no occupation."

The Wakely house sat in the middle of a grassy yard
in the middle of a small town in the middle of one of the
middle western states. And as the United States is the
most important nation in the world (save in the preju-
diced eyes of the inhabitants of a few other countries) it
follows without controversy that the Wakely home was
quite the center of the universe. And so it was, just
as all the homes of the Browns and the Smiths and the
Joneses are the center of the universe, to the Browns
and the Smiths and the Joneses.

The whole place had a lived-in look, which is a polite

way of saying that it was not quite as neat as it ought to be. Because the Wakely family was large, and expenditures waxed equally large in that bold proportion which bills bear to the size of families, not everything was in repair at one and the same time. When the lattice under the porch was in perfect condition, the screens would begin to have a faded, peeled look. When the screens were finally repainted, the porch boards would show signs of warping.

Every spring the dandelions slipped up brazenly in the clover and bluegrass. And every spring, with exasperated repetition, Mary Wakely made a noble gesture toward eradicating the pests, but with indifferent success. Always in the middle of the task, neighbor boys came for Tod or Ken or Bo to go fishing, and neighbor girls dropped in to hold giggling converse with Gwen or Louise. When Mary Wakely saw her family melt away, one by one, she invariably remarked apologetically to the butcher knives and bushel-baskets: "Oh, well, let them go. It's the very happiest time of their lives." Which was quite the key to Mary Wakely's character, a little too lenient maybe, a bit too sentimental perhaps.

To give the roster of the Wakely family sounds like calling the roll in a classroom. Mary Wakely (née Bohanan) had been the town belle twenty-five years before when she married Sam Wakely. Sam was a bookkeeper then in the Oakville State Bank, but a kindly providence removing one man above him, and a wrathy board of directors removing another, he had been cashier now for many years. The husky and noisy results of the Wakely-Bohanan nuptials were: Hal Wakely, aged twenty-four, Louise, aged twenty-one, Gwen and Ken, who arrived together seventeen years before, Thaddeus, who had almost forgotten that dignified appellation in the "Tod" under which he had moved and had his very lively being for fifteen years, and Paul Bohanan Wakely, called "Bo" by Oakville friends and enemies, who trailed along seven years behind Tod.

It seems almost a matter for abject apology that, added to this number, there were also Aunt Dell Wakely and Hettie Hess, both of whom the family had inherited along with the old Wakely estate. Aunt Dell was Sam's aunt, a fleshy, florid, fatuous woman who believed that she had been marked for apoplexy for years. But the stubbornness with which she met all minor issues bidding fair to thwart her, had so far refused to yield to the various "rushes of blood" so frequently and eloquently described in detail to the family. Hettie Hess, of problematical age, who often remarked acridly that she wished to the land she had some meat on her bones, might have passed in more sophisticated circles for a maid, but not in Oakville. To be sure she worked for her bed, board, and a stipend; but on days when her "rheumatiz" sent her to lie on a bony, twinging shoulder, or days when she felt an additional grievance to-

ward life in general and the Wakely youngsters in
particular, she simply sent word that she was not coming downstairs. No, one could scarcely insist that Hettie
Hess was the typical modern maid.

On this specific day in merry spring, Mary Wakely
and Hettie Hess were cleaning house. And Mary
Wakely in a kitchen dress with a towel bound round
her graying hair, sat on the attic floor sorting an old
scrap-bag's contents, and was not so merry. For there
were so many things stored away on the third floor that
the task looked stupendous. All of the old Wakely
things left from another generation were there, and
some of the Bohanan ones which Mary had brought
over home when her mother died, old Wakely and Bohanan dresses, bonnets, cushions, pictures, curtains,
quilt scraps, patterns. Every year Mary Wakely put
forth strenuous, if subtle, efforts to get rid of them, but
Aunt Dell would puffingly climb the narrow built-in
attic stairs, settle herself in an old arm chair, and watch
the sorting process with an ancient but alert eye.

Surreptitiously, Mary would attempt to throw out
some of the flotsam left upon the shore of time, impersonated by the floor of the attic, but the covert act
could never be consummated without Aunt Dell seeing
it. A few moments before this, Mary had attempted to
rid the figurative beach of some of its wreckage in the
form of an old bird-cage, to be met with Aunt Dell's,
"Dear, dear, that's Dicky's little house. I can remember

so well how he always chirped when we put seeds in this very same little dish. I couldn't bear to see that thrown out, Mary. I believe I'd hear his little chirp in my sleep." So Mary, with superb resignation, had replaced the battered home of the departed Dicky, lest such dire consequences as a phantom cheep cross Aunt Dell's heavy slumber.

And now, as Aunt Dell appeared to be engrossed in an old photograph album, Mary slipped away from the piece-bag and casually edged a wire dress-form toward the top of the stairs. But Aunt Dell was on the job instantly.

"You ar'n't intending to throw *that* away, are you, Mary?" Her voice held volumes of reproach.

"Why, yes, I was, Aunt Dell. What good will it ever be to us?"

"Oh, I wouldn't think of it, Mary. Why, you might want to fit something on it some day for one of the girls when they are away to school."

To be sure the form was as foreign to present-day maidenly figures as though it were of some prehistoric female. Wide-shouldered, padded, wasp-waisted, it looked like a wire skeleton of Queen Elizabeth. But back to the cluttered shore of time Mary Wakely rolled it, with a fleeting wicked thought of the language the fastidious Louise and the artistic-minded Gwen would use when she told them.

Hettie Hess was dusting a pile of old things in another corner. "A mess, I call it," she was grumbling. But that was scarcely an innovation. She always grumbled. The family thought no more of Hettie's constant mumbling than of a continuously leaky faucet. It might be annoying if one stopped to think about it, but if it could not be repaired, why stop to think about it? She mumbled and grumbled her way through the day's work, her mind a little at loose ends, going off on tangents; her sentences never finished, trailing off into nothing.

Just now she brought a pile of dog-eared books and dumped them aggrievedly down by Mary Wakely. "Them old scrap-books . . . that there corner . . . I declare, Mis' Wakely . . . leaves tore out . . . I suz . . . every year . . . pick up 'n pick up. . . ."

Mary Wakely opened the top scrap-book. Originally it had been a book of her father's, recording the uprisings and the downsittings of the members of a lodge known as "The Knights and Ladies of King Arthur's Round Table," although just how the ladies happened to be sitting in at that particular round table she had never known.

Over the erstwhile memoranda of the lodge knights and their ladies, verses were pasted. Mary herself had pasted them in when all the world was young and joyous and romantic, when Sam Wakely and Matt Dorring and George Hines had all wanted to go with her. How had she ever found time to paste poems in the old secretary book? Her days were so rushed, now, so filled with countless necessary activities, that it did not seem possible she had ever had leisure to cut out poetry, to say nothing of pasting it back in a book. She turned the pages of the long-forgotten record of flamboyant ceremonies. There was Kipling's *Vampire,* Riley's *Old Sweetheart Of Mine,* a bit of *Khayyam.* There were verses from Meredith's *Lucille.* Several pages ran to Ella Wheeler Wilcox—*Love's Window, Love's Task, Love's Rainbow.*

Aunt Dell sat heavily in the rocker and sorted pieces of calicos, returning them all jealously to their boxes. Hettie's voice grumbled its far-away accompaniment: "I declare ... same old things ... dust 'em 'n dust 'em ... I suz ... every year ... such a mess ..."

Where had they gone, those old thrills, that old romantic feeling she and Sam had felt for each other? How golden and dream-filled and illusioned life had been! Mary Wakely, forty-seven, maturely heavy, in a kitchen dress, with a towel bound round her graying hair, sat and turned Time's pages.

> Was his love then, the love of the river? And she—
> Had she taken that love for the love of the sea?

She could hear Sam's deep mellow voice as he read the smooth, singing verses aloud. She could see him, too, in his white flannels, sitting in the hammock on the old Bohanan lawn. How much in love they had been!

Will the Romance Be the Same?

How romantically, deeply, terribly so! Not all the masculine movie stars were more ardent in their love-making than Sam had been. Where had they gone, those old romantic moments they had planned to keep alive? Where were they now, those old thrills which they had said could never die? They had not kept them alive any more than all the other long-married, staid old couples. Their conversation now consisted for the most part of the annoying fact that Bo's teeth needed straightening, of the big expenses incurred by Hal and Louise away at school, of paving taxes and a leaky kitchen roof. Oh, *why* did romance fly out of the window when children came?

"Dear, dear!" As one hears faint far-away wind in the poplars, Mary could hear Aunt Dell's comments: "Every one of these blocks must be saved to be pieced some day," and Hettie's "Dusted 'n dusted . . . put 'em here . . . what in time . . . this corner . . . I suz . . ."

She turned the stiff, mucilage-crusted page. Alone on the page and in a bracket of purple ink, as though set aside for special honor, was a little poem, evidently cut from a magazine. There were several verses, but they all ended with:

> After years I'll come to meet you—
> Will the romance be the same?

Above the purple-inked framework a bunch of little dried violets was crushed into the soft pulpy paper.

Will the Romance Be the Same?

Under the violets, in Sam's writing, were the words: "To be read together on our silver anniversary."

It might have been written the day before, so clearly did the picture come to her, the resurrection of a little dormant memory which had been lying away under a shroud of crumbling violets. They had read the verses together, pressed the flowers together, and then Sam had taken his fountain pen and written the words. They had laughed at the mere thought of any change, at the absurdity that romance would ever die. It had been one of those certainties of life not even debatable. As for the thought of a silver wedding, that had been too far in the future to contemplate, a huge joke, that in the then glamorous present they should have spoken of a date so far removed. It had seemed centuries away. And now their silver anniversary was one week from the next Saturday.

It did not seem possible. Where had the time gone? Out from the little purple frame stared the statement: "After years I'll come to meet you." And the statement was true, true by twenty-five long years. From under the little crumbling violets stared the question: "Will the romance be the same?" And the question must be answered one week from the next Saturday.

Mary Wakely sat on the attic floor and thought of Sam, young, ardent, lithesome, wooing her under the trees of the old Bohanan home; and Sam, now, heavy, wide-girthed, bespectacled, gray patches above his ears, talking of paving taxes and dental bills and a leaky kitchen roof. That, then, would be the answer. Romance was never the same. But this was the queer part, when she stopped to analyze it, she herself was still romantic. She still cared for sentiment. That seemed always the way—one kept the romance and one ceased to remember. Suddenly she realized that the idea was almost identical with one of the Ella Wheeler Wilcox poems she had just passed in the book, and over which she had thrilled and wept in her youth. She searched until she found it and read it avidly:

> This is the way of it the wide world over
> One is beloved and one is the lover.

Yes, that was for all the world the way it had turned out. And the humbling thing about it, the pride-eating thing, was that Sam, whose soul had once been aflame with a god-like passion, was soon the beloved, and that she who had been so ardently wooed, proved in the long run to be the lover.

She turned back to the pages of the violets. "To be read together at our silver anniversary." Neither one had remembered the verses. Only by chance had she run across them. Already preparations were under way to celebrate the occasion. Very well, they *would* read the poem together. The evening of the anniversary, after the guests had gone, she and Sam would read the verses. And perhaps, no, certainly, Sam would tell her that he had never forgotten those moments of exquisite romance. Possibly, no, assuredly, it would take only the sight of the verses and the violets to have Sam reveal the fact that he had never ceased to remember those glamorous hours of young love.

All that week they worked hard at the cleaning of the big rambling house, Mary and Hettie Hess. To be sure they had some help from the other members of the household. When school was out, Ken managed to carry a few papers to the alley and burn them, and Tod, with much elaborate preparation in the way of oiling, screwing, and petting his second-hand motor-cycle so that it would navigate, in four days' time made three successful journeys to the junk pile with a few tin cans in the side-car. Gwen took so much time to change from her school things into a work dress which she thought sufficiently *chic,* rearranging a satin band around her head, that it was dinner time before she had accomplished anything. Bo, attempting to wash screens with the garden hose, was almost immediately the center of centripetal force for all the neighborhood youngsters, whereupon the screen washing deteriorated rapidly into a series of imported Indian monsoons. Aunt Dell sat heavily in the most comfortable chair in each room as it was under process of being cleaned, and held grimly on to all the old Wakely things and some of the Bohanan ones.

"She has seen the things from my side of the house

around here so long that she thinks they belong to her," Mary told Sam. "I've always suspected she made up some of the reminiscences she tells me, and now I know. She had my mother's box of sea-shells in her lap this morning and was telling Bo how she picked them up, and, Sam, she *has never been anywhere near the sea.*"

Mary and Hettie Hess worked under extreme pressure in order to get through before the anniversary. "Like horses . . ." Hettie mumbled. "I suz . . . this closet . . . looky here, Mis' Wakely . . . never stays put . . . same things . . . pick up 'n pick up . . ." A raven of a woman croaking her "nevermore."

On Wednesday of the following week, the cleaning was practically finished. By Thursday there was a tumbled slant again on all of the first rooms cleaned. "What is the *matter* with this family?" Mary would say in exasperation. "The Downings and the McIntyres can clean and it will *stay* clean. Tod, take that bird's nest out of this room immediately, and, Bo, there *are* better places for a bicycle tire than on the davenport."

On Friday, Louise arrived home from the University, gay and lovely and full of sorority gossip. Something always seemed to happen to the household when Louise blew in. It took on a foolish gaiety which it had not previously possessed. Louise had on a fetching new green and white sport suit. "I hope you don't mind, Mother. I got it at Garwin's and charged it. We hadn't planned it but when I found they were wearing sports to the Beta party instead of the printed chiffons we first thought, there wasn't time to write. I got new white pumps . . . and I picked up this green costume jewelry for a *sparrow's* song . . ."

More bills! How they crowded always in a sort of unending nightmare. But how fresh and glowing and deliciously pretty Louise looked in the gay outfit. Only one more year and she would be through.

Louise did not appear to be what one could call vitally interested in the house-cleaning. She seemed to have something vaguely important on her mind. At the first moment in which she could catch her mother alone it came out with geyser-like burst. "Mother, I've been dying to tell you . . . but with every one around . . . the kids all under foot . . . Hettie all ears . . . and Aunt Dell calling from the far end of the house: 'What's that you're sayin', Louise-y?' I haven't had a chance. Mother, next week I'm having company . . . here at home. Listen—Rod Robinson, *himself*. Can you feature it?" Hands on her mother's plump shoulders, she gazed into her mother's blue eyes with rapt expectancy.

"And who," said Mary Wakely, "is Rod Robinson—himself?"

"Oh, Mother," Louise's voice held deepest reproach, "please don't show such ignorance—such *abysmal* ignorance. Rod Robinson," she lowered her voice to a reverent whisper, "made the winning touchdown in the game with the Aggies."

Will the Romance Be the Same?

Mary dropped her eyes that they might not show their tell-tale twinkle. When she looked up her heart missed a beat, for she saw something in her daughter's own brown eyes that she could not ignore.

"Why, Louise," there was a little catch in her throat. "You—you like him?"

Louise's head dropped to her mother's shoulder. "I'm just *nuts* about him. I think of him in the daytime—" Louise's muffled voice went on, "and dream of him at night. The very glimpse of him gives me high blood pressure."

"And he—?" Mary asked. "Is he—" she dropped into Louise's vernacular, "nuts about you?"

"I don't know," Louise said forlornly. "Sometimes I think he is—but more times I think he isn't. It just keeps me palpitating between subnormal and high fever."

Dear, dear! How different girls were than they used to be. How frank! Why she herself had not even acknowledged to her mother that she loved Sam until after his proposal.

Louise was speaking again huskily. "That's why I'm so crazy about his stopping here. A week from to-morrow he's going through Oakville and he asked me if he could stop off. I just went *deeleerious*. I want everything just ideal, Mother. His family is a regular up-to-the-minute one. Things just *have* to be nice here. You and Dad will be all right—but the kids—I wish they'd be *half* civilized for once. And I want Hettie to keep her place, and her mouth shut—and it wouldn't make me sore if Aunt Dell would have that stroke she's always talking about."

"Louise!" There were limits to which Mary would allow her modern children's talk to go.

"I didn't mean that, but you'll see that she fades gently somewhere into the scenery, won't you?"

Mary was reassuring. "Don't worry. We'll have everything nice, dear. The house will be all clean, and the children, models. When did you say he was coming?"

"A week from Saturday night."

"Why, Louise, the anniversary night!"

"Oh, no, Mother," Louise was the embodiment of despair. "It's the only night he can stop. We wouldn't want the whole town coming."

"But the invitations are all out."

"Imagine—that gang being here! If he has to meet all the natives! You know yourself, Mother, that a big bunch of Oakville people look like the villagers in *Carmen.*"

"They are our friends, Louise," Mary was a little stiff. "And though they may not be as sophisticated, they are assuredly as fine people as the young man's friends."

"And there's no way out?"

"Absolutely, there's no way out. You'll just have to

entertain him some way at the party." Mary's voice held the last expression in finality.

On Monday morning Louise went back to school. All that day and the following days, Mary and Hettie Hess worked under extreme pressure in order to get through before Saturday.

But to Mary Wakely, all through the heavy work, all through the rug-beating and varnishing and turning of curtains, shone a little gleam ahead like a light in the forest. She had kept the incense burning before the shrine of romance, and perhaps Sam had kept it also. Steeped in business, hustling day after day to make a living for the big family, no doubt Sam, too, still cherished the memory of those glamorous days, would recall them with fervor on their anniversary night.

Saturday, itself, dawned bright and lovely with the scent of peonies and syringa on the sweet May air. The household was early astir, Mary and Hettie Hess beginning the baking of cakes and nut wafers immediately after a sketchy breakfast.

Louise blew in just before noon when preparations for the event were well under way. But all the activity for the party was to Louise but an accompanying chorus to herald the approach of the star performer, Mr. Robinson himself. "You're positive everybody will be up on his toes for a good impression, Mother?" she repeatedly asked.

Will the Romance Be the Same?

By six, the House of Wakely was as near perfection as it could ever hope to attain. Only once in a blue moon did it ever have that highly polished, finished appearance, Sundays, perhaps, for a few fleeting moments, the late afternoon before a holiday, an hour or so before an expected guest would arrive, was everything in place and every one well-groomed.

When Mary Wakely was dressing in the soft new silk, a little rose-colored thread of fancy wove its gay way through her heart as definitely as the rose-colored thread shimmered in the white of the new gown. When the guests would have gone, she was to meet Sam, and they would read the verses together, not as Mary Wakely, the mother of six, and Sam Wakely, the middle-aged, bespectacled bank cashier, but as young Mary Bohanan with stars for eyes, and young Sam Wakely, lithe and handsome. Sam could not have forgotten that moment of high rapture when they had read the verses in the old Bohanan hammock, could not have forgotten that pledge to romance any more than she.

To be sure there were some moments before the guests arrived which one could scarcely call of a romantic nature. Sam's waist-line having added a cubit to his latitudinal stature since last it had been encased in the suit he was to wear, necessitated setting over the buttons. He stood and waited impatiently while Mary made the change. There was one mad search by half

the family for little Bo's best necktie, in which drawers
were whisked out and the contents madly turned over,
until some one happily remembered that Bo had taken
it off Sunday afternoon and stretched it around a young
plum tree. Gwen and Louise, possessing a velvet jacket
in common, each chose this particular occasion upon
which to claim individual ownership. They argued pleasantly, but definitely and continuously, with a certain
stiff politeness.

"Pardon me, Louise, but you certainly heard me
say that I was wearing it with the blue silk crepe."

"Pardon *me*, Gwen, but with Rod Robinson coming,
most assuredly I ought to have first choice."

When Tod had dressed—oh, much too hastily—he
took occasion to work a little more on his decrepit
motor-cycle, which called forth from the more polished
Ken, weighted down with his seventeen years, "Tod,
get up from there. And don't start that darned greasy
old egg-beater to-night." To which advice, Tod made
swift, brief and decisive answer: "Go kiss a dill pickle."
Immediately thereafter, confused but pronounced
sounds issued from the side porch, as of subjective disturbances caused by two bodies of equal solidity coming in close contact.

Aunt Dell, dressed in an ancient magenta-colored
watered silk, which made her anticipated stroke seem
imminent, and with her entire cameo set—brooch, earrings, bracelet and watch chain—ornamenting her per-

son, sat heavily in the biggest chair and waited for the guests.

Hettie mumbled her way around the rooms, her mind going off on tangents: "Them ice-cream dishes . . . I suz . . . somebody's left 'em . . . tea-towels . . . I declare . . . pick up 'n pick up. . . ."

When Mary was dressed, she took a fleeting survey of herself in the glass. She saw there a blue-eyed woman in her late forties with too much weight, her blond hair sprinkled with gray, small lines about her eyes, deeper ones in her forehead and a duplex chin.

Turning away from the glass, she took the old scrap-book under her arm and started downstairs. As she passed the bathroom she saw Hettie in her too-long brown silk, holding dripping towels at arm's length, heard her muttered: "Soppin' wet . . . I suz . . . seems to me . . . them boys. . . ." Coming to Tod's and Ken's bedroom, she gave one fleeting glance therein, and as a too-ardent optimist attempts to shut out the unpleasant things of life, closed the door gently upon the special type of interior decorating visible to any passer-by.

Down the stairs she went, the old book under her arm. To an onlooker it was only a dog-eared scrap-book. To Mary Wakely it was the altar to Romance—the odor of dead violets the incense—the rhythm of the verses a prayer.

They all made comments about her: "Gee, Mom, you

look ritzy," and "A Follies girl has nothing on you."

When for a moment there was no one around, she slipped the scrap-book back of a reading lamp on a table in the big hall. It was open at the verses, and the words in their purple framing and the violets pressing their little blue faces against the poem gazed back at her with assurance. Across the border of Time they called to her:

> After years I'll come to meet you—
> Will the romance be the same?

And then the first of the guests arrived. Incongruously, they were Dick Edwards and his wife, and Sue McIntyre and her husband. Dick had been Sam's best man, and Sue had been Mary's bridesmaid twenty-five years before. Also they had been engaged. They both mentioned it, even laughed about it. To Mary Wakely, obsessed with her idea of resurrecting Romance, it seemed almost sacrilegious. How could they mention it? How could they laugh? After years they had come to meet, and the romance was not the same.

The rooms were soon filled with the gay, friendly folk of the small-town crowd who knew each other so well. Their voices floated high with talk and laughter. Sometime during the early evening, the hero of many a football war arrived and was introduced, after which Mary Wakely was vaguely conscious of the fact that he and

Will the Romance Be the Same?

Louise had slipped out to the swing on the side porch.

And then there was a little program. Grace Ivorson sang just as she had sung at the wedding. Perhaps not "just as she had sung," for Grace's voice at fifty was not what it had been at twenty-five. The minister made a talk, and Dick Edwards of the Oakville Bon Ton Grocers, on behalf of the guests, presented Sam and Mary with some very nice silver. Sam made a neat little speech in which he confided the fact that they had had the six children for the express purpose of being able to use the eight-piece set.

And all through the happy, informal, small-town party there sang a little silver song in the heart of Mary Wakely.

And then the affair was over. The last of the guests were going down the steps into the moon-filled, sweet-scented night. The last gay words floated back: "Good-night, Sam—good-night, Mary. Lovely time—coming again to the golden wedding."

Sam and Mary turned into the big hall. *The time had come.*

Sam was standing there only a few feet away from the table where the book stood open at the verses, where Romance waited to be recognized and welcomed. In their little purple bracketing the verses waited for Mary's lover.

"Nice party, Mother." Sam was not noticing the scrap-book. But one could not expect him to do so with it standing against the wall, surrounded by a half dozen other things, a vase of flowers, a reading lamp, two or three magazines, a framed photo of Louise, a dish of nut wafers.

"Sam," Mary's voice quivered in its earnestness. "There's something over there on the table I've been saving for you."

Sam sauntered over to the table. The years turned back for Mary Wakely. What was a quarter of a century to a gay, gallant knight who had picked violets and promised that after years the romance would be the same? Starry-eyed, she watched her lover approach the little altar which together they had once erected to Romance.

The moment in its deep importance, fraught with the sincerity of its meaning, should have been very quiet. It was scarcely that. The radio, tuned to a high-powered station, was emitting "Face the Music and Dance." Ken was adding to the gaiety of the nations by accompanying the ensemble with his banjo and shouting the words. That both his voice and his banjo were off-key seemed not to worry him to any extent.

From outside the dining-room window where the syringas flung their fragrant breath, came the deafening roar of the motor-cycle engine. "Whatever is that boy doing," Aunt Dell wanted to know, "after *midnight?*"

Gwen came hurriedly to the dining-room door with

Bo making excited but futile attempts to hold her back. "Mother," she called, "whatever do you *imagine?* Bo's been eating ice-cream out of a dish that some one left ... I *saw* him ... one on the sideboard. I even think it was old Mr. Jarvis's. *Ugh!* For crying out loud ... think of old Mr. Jarvis and his *whiskers* ..."

With one part of her brain Mary Wakely heard all the turbulent family noises. The other was turned toward the Great Moment, as Joan of Arc may have paid no attention to annoying trivialities, but kept her eyes turned to the Light. Sam was looking in the direction of the verses, now, the verses with their fragrance of by-gone Junes. His hand was on the book. He picked it up—looked at it in a puzzled way. And then he spoke. "I'm glad you saved me some. They're cracking good." *And he set the book aside and reached for the wafers.*

The light in Mary Wakely's eyes slowly flickered out. It gave place to a baffled expression, half chagrin, half incredulity. She looked at Sam Wakely, heavy, wide-girthed, bespectacled, with gray patches above his ears. Under his very nose the faint old fragrance of the violets pled with him, and he thought she had meant the wafers. Before his very eyes the rapture of the little poem called to him, and he thought she had saved him something to eat.

He took a handful of the brittle cakes and began

166

munching them. He swung his jaw vigorously, the crisp wafers crackling a little.

Hettie Hess came through the hall, her best brown silk crackling with the wafers. Over on the table the sweet fragrance of the dead little violets and the sweet rhythm of the forgotten little verses looked out from the old scrap-book. Hettie's ferret eyes landed on them. "Looky there, Mis' Wakely . . . good suz . . . one of them old scrap-books . . . my land . . . got down from the attic . . . such a mess . . . beats all . . . shall I take it back up?"

"No, leave it there," said Mary Wakely. She used the same tone that one might use in saying "No, leave the flowers on the grave."

Hettie trudged out of the room, mumbling mild execrations.

Sam Wakely, big, substantial, wide-girthed, stood and munched the nut cookies with keen enjoyment. "Well, Mother?" He was slipping his arm through Mary's and starting with her toward the dining-room. "They tell me the first twenty-five years are the hardest," he said blithely, "but think of the next twenty-five—with our slippers and the radio and books and magazines and a lot of grandchildren—won't they be comfortable though?"

Psychologists say that two emotions can not occupy the mind at the same time. The king, Romance, has no humor. And the king's fool, Humor, knows no romance.

Will the Romance Be the Same?

Quite suddenly, in the throne-room of Mary Wakely's mind, Humor, the fool, slipped up behind Romance, the king, sent him sprawling and threw him out. At the sight she let forth a laugh, a chuckling, rippling, body-shaking laugh.

Hal was still tap-tapping on the bare varnished floor. Ken was adding to the general confusion with the six-teenth interpretation of "Face the music and dance . . ." The backfiring of Tod's motor-cycle came from the rear of the house. Gwen and Bo, giving no intimation of an armistice were deep in "I did *not*," and "You might *catch* something. . . . *Imagine!* Old Mr. Jarvis and his *whiskers!*"

Mary Wakely laughed as she looked up at Sam Wakely, heavy, wide-girthed, unlithesome, munching nut wafers in the midst of all this familiar hilarity. "Comfortable?" she repeated, her too, too solid flesh shaking with vigorous laughter. "I'll say they will."

And then, suddenly, simultaneously, they stopped by the double windows. Outside in the cool, dark porch stood slim young figures in such close proximity that, while it was only surmise that their two minds held but a single thought, there was direct evidence that their two hearts beat as one. For the arms that had so effectively enfolded the slippery pigskin on the field of honor, now appeared to be repeating the process with a daintier, lovelier burden.

Overwhelmed at the import of the words they heard,

the parents seemed too near a state of partial paralysis to move on out of range of the low, earnest voices:

"And you'll love me all your life, Louise?"

"Oh, Rod—all my life—and forever."

Sam and Mary Wakely turned to each other, gropingly, clingingly, in the surprise of those bewildered emotions which parents inevitably experience at the first startling realization of such news. Sam's arms went around Mary and he drew her close. "Golly, Mother," he whispered, cheek to hers, "romance is always the same, isn't it?"

"Always!" Mary whispered back.

And they tiptoed away, stealthily, guiltily.

ANOTHER BROUGHT GIFTS

THE story of old Jed Miller is a story straight out of the horse and bugg—no, *cutter* days. It is as old-fashioned as the dripping tallow candles on Christmas trees in the eighties and as sentimental as a candy heart. The telling of it brings forth the memory of a combination of old odors: the delectable ones of molasses taffy and fresh popcorn balls; the pungent ones of Norway pine branches and burning wax; the stuffy one of the atmosphere in a small-town church on Christmas Eve. For Jed Miller and Christmas Eve were synonymous terms in those years.

Old Jed Miller was one of the humblest of the early inhabitants of that small inland town hewn there out of the forest on a midwestern river's bank. "Old Jed" every one had called him from his earliest days in the village, although he must have been rather young when he arrived with neither funds nor friends. Because of his weather-beaten countenance he looked old while he was still young; and because no deep worries or family responsibilities possessed him, he appeared not very much different when he had grown old. Old Jed Miller, the ageless!

He lived alone in a little unpainted house at the edge

of the town back there in the days of its building. Maple Street ran up to the boundary line of his yard and then stopped suddenly, as though realizing there was little use to continue on past so unpretentious a place. Indeed, there had been little need for the street to come even that far, for Old Jed's callers were few— a fellow townsman to get him to cut cordwood; schoolboys wanting hickory sticks for some potential hockey game; an occasional book peddler, from whom Old Jed bought no book but whom he more than likely asked to stay and eat.

As the town grew and the cordwood was largely gone, with all the stumps in Main Street out of the way so that lumber wagons and high-topped buggies might safely roll along its dusty thoroughfare, Old Jed's occupation gradually changed. It grew to be that in the springtime women all over town waited for Jed to come and spade the lettuce beds or beat the carpets thrown across the clotheslines in the prairie wind.

In the midsummer, when the arguing with various husbands over the weeds' growth in the alleys brought no immediate results, the housewives sent determinedly for Jed to bring his scythe and mow. In the fall, scarce a storm window went into place that was not guided by Jed's calloused hands.

"I'm going to have Jed the first of the week," any woman might say.

"I've already spoken for him," another might respond.

So Old Jed became as definitely town property as the new waterworks' standpipe or the little meadow which had been stylishly termed "the park" since the building of the bandstand.

Although busy from the time the sun came up behind the trees at the river's bend until it slipped over the prairie's rim, Jed's weekly earnings were small. A dime for this job, a quarter for that one—whatever the women chose to pay him—that was Jed's income. Because he could have done nothing else well, they seemed to think such modest jobs as the filling of a straw bed-tick or the planting of onion-sets should be done almost gratuitously. But he managed to get along in his own way and save a little toward that possible rainy day when the housewives might suddenly discontinue his services.

All this was on weekdays. Sunday was, as Jed himself might have expressed it, a horse of another stripe. On the Sabbath, Old Jed Miller dressed up and became a prominent citizen.

In the first of that early period, with the town but a new settlement and the church a modest frame, Jed's part in the Sunday services consisted in sitting behind the organ and pumping wind into the lungs of its cloth anatomy. His work was wholly voluntary. No one thought of paying him anything for it. In truth, in those days no one thought of paying anything for church work except the infinitesimal salary to the minister augmented by donations of coffee, sugar and molasses from the pound socials. If one had anything faintly approaching a singing voice, one donated one's musical output to the choir. If one could keep books in which exceedingly small sums of money were debited and credited, one occasionally and gratuitously became the treasurer. If one had a good flexible muscle in his right arm, as did Jed, one voluntarily turned cranks.

In time, because of the sticking of the old organ's keys and the threatened collapse of a lung, when even Jed's muscular right arm could no longer coax wind into its asthmatic interior, it was put aside and a modest pipe organ installed.

With no questioning of church authorities and without benefit of appointment, at the first practice for dedication, Jed Miller with greased hair and in a new too-blue suit, arrived to disappear importantly behind a wing of the new organ and begin another decade of pumping.

When the organist took her seat and the Gloria rolled forth, a member of the choir who could see Jed from where she sat said that his face shone with the apparent joy of being an accessory to these melodious notes. Perhaps it did something to Jed. It may be that in his simplicity of thought he gave the woman at the keys very little credit for the music, felt that it was he alone

who caused the notes to pour forth on wings of song—
for from that time he voluntarily added much of the
care of the organ and the entire church to his services.

All this constituted the whole life of the quiet little
man—a mere uninteresting existence of one who knew
neither deep sorrow nor tumultuous joy, who would
never experience either the ice or the fire of living.

If once a week, for a time, he felt real happiness, it
was a mere ripple of pleasure by the side of a great
tidal wave of excitement that overwhelmed him once a
year. This was the high point of Jed's existence. Toward
this hour was all else pointed. For this one exultant moment did he live. Christmas Eve at the church!

In those years of the eighties and nineties Santa Claus
was a single entity—an individual upon whom one
could count specifically in regard to time and place.
You heard his bells and he arrived through the side
door of the church onto the pulpit, frostladen and
breathless. He bade you farewell and disappeared
through the same door. You heard his bells die away in
the distance and knew he was gone for an interminable
year. He did not walk the streets advertising toothpaste
or barbecued sandwiches or basket-ball-games-in-the-
Coliseum-several-good-seats-left-at-thirty-five-cents.

There was one and only one Santa. In that town he
was Old Jed Miller, but of course you did not know
that for many years. You went to the church on that
night of nights clothed in several layers of flannels, a

dress, coat, muffler, knitted hood, mittens and over-shoes. Wedged between equally well-equipped adults, you rode with them in the cutter, your short feet not quite reaching the warm soapstone, your mouth and nose filled with snow-laden air and buffalo hairs.

Even as you turned the corner near the church you saw the lights shining through the colored-glass windows out over the snow and in a sickening sensation of fear wondered if you had missed one moment of the rapture. Although practically nothing could have tempted the fat old mare to budge from the spot, you had to wait while she was tethered to the rail between the hitching posts.

When, at last, over crunching snow you went up the steps, your muscles twitching, your mouth dry—almost were you ill in the pit of the stomach. At the doorway you gazed upon Paradise, with a swooning of senses at the sight. Resuscitated after that first shock, they became as acute as a bird dog's.

For the eyes there was a great Norway pine sparkling against the white of the wall, packages on and under it, the shining pipes of the new organ beside it reaching up into heaven. . . . For the ears, the rustling of papers or angels' wings, it was hard to tell which, and the voices of the congregation singing "Joy to the World" . . . For the nose, odors of cinnamon and peppermint, fresh popcorn and cooked molasses, crushed balsam and burning wax.

Another Brought Gifts

In due time there followed a program to which you did or did not personally contribute, depending largely on the timely question of whether you were in a state of health or had just passed (or were in due process of acquiring) mumps, measles, chicken-pox, whooping-cough, or the shingles. But whether or not you donated your services, the pieces spoken were practically all known to you, being largely a repetition of those that had been perpetrated the year before and many years before that. There was the perennial Notta-creatcher-wa-stir-ring-not-teven-a-mouse, and one which had been handed down from year to year but which you had never satisfactorily translated, sounding as it did like "Lattuce in they clabbered, lattuce in they say."

The program happily over, you saw Old Jed Miller go behind the pipe organ again, heard the music of an old hymn which all would sing, sensed on the verge of a nervous breakdown that after its seven verses it was finally dying away into silence. And then . . .

A stillness vast and limitless save for a hysterical giggle or two! This was the moment supreme—this the one toward which all the other moments of all the hours of the year were directed—so vital that the illness came again in the pit of your stomach, and your arms and legs twitched in an ecstasy of emotion.

There were bells tinkling faintly and far away, then closer, bringing every tingling hair root to life. Fascinated, you could not take your eyes from the side door, so that when it shook a little, you shook too. He never missed. How could he time himself so definitely to the program's end?

The bells jangled now with mad, breath-taking closeness. The door opened. He bounced in merrily, short and rotund, with a round little—*you know,* the word you ought not say out loud—that shook like a bowlful of jelly. The children roared their welcome—all but you. You hid your face for a moment because of the world-shaking event that was taking place.

He called "Merry Christmas, children!" many times and said that Pikeville was one of the places he liked best of all to come. He told what a hard time he had getting here and how the reindeer were stamping outside, impatient for him to hurry. Then he sauntered over to the tree and said well, well, he guessed he'd better begin to call the names on the packages. Thereupon he handed them out with such intimate comments that it was unbelievable how he could know so much town gossip.

When you went up for yours he said something so personal that you realized anew how uncanny was his knowledge of your everyday life. Sometimes he called the boys by family nicknames which you would scarely have expected him to know: "Tweet," or "Tubby" or "Babe," so that every one in the audience laughed.

Yes, he knew every one. "Here's somethin' fer Tom-

mie Graham. Hi, Tommie, what's this I hear tell ag'in'
ye—hitchin' on to the back of Schmidt's grocery cart?
Hev you been?"

"Y-yes, sir."

"Ye won't no more?"

"No, sir."

The audience roared, and, red-eared, Tommie received his gift.

He knew all, heard all, saw all—this Santa who
stopped here en route to other towns.

Sometimes, when the exercises were nearly over, a
swaggering older youth whispered across to you: "Ho,
ho! You think that's a real Santa Claus, don't you?
Well, it ain't. It's Old Jed Miller dressed up thataway."

But questioned, your parents had the retort supreme
for you. "Didn't you see Old Jed Miller go behind the
organ to pump and never come out?"

It was true. You admitted the fact of seeing old man
Miller disappear into the cavernous depths behind the
organ, and because you were unaware that a panel
in the sturdy oak wall slipped out of place if one knew
where to locate its sensitive spot, you admitted readily
enough that Santa Claus came in while old man Miller
was still behind there. Sometimes they added still another proof: "Wasn't Santa Claus fat? And isn't old
man Miller thin as a willow whistle?"

It silenced you, so that you were convinced for another year, and no hulking boy with bragging tongue could shake your faith.

The thing that gave you the most confidence in the fabulous wealth and generosity of the little man in red was the fact that when the gifts had all been handed out, he called the boys and girls to the platform—that is, all those who had not reached their tenth birthday. Unbelievably he gave each one money. Thirty, forty, fifty, even sixty boys and girls—he gave them all a shining quarter. He had done so for years.

He had one ruling. Every child must walk up to the tree by himself. No babies in arms and no holding parents' hands.

There were those who thought that Pikeville babies learned to walk earlier on account of the Santa Claus quarter.

It was traditional. All the presents given out, Santa walked to the edge of the platform and held up his hand for silence. . . . The older people in the audience laughed and nudged one another. "It's his big moment," and, "Just lives for it," you might hear, but not understand.

"Now I want all the boys 'n' girls who kin walk up here by theirselves—'n' is under ten—every one to come up ag'in." He patted the big pockets of his scarlet coat and called out in his commanding voice: "I've got a little somethin' else fer each one of you."

The rush to the Klondike then began.

Santa Claus held up his hand for silence. "I've watched all the children of this here town 'n' I sez to myself, sez I, they're pretty good young-uns; I guess I'll give every one some money."

There was lusty shouting, so that he held up his hand again. If you were very close you saw how worn and calloused it was, like a hand that worked in gardens, and you wondered why.

"Before I go back to my home——"

("Where you live?" a bold boy perennially asked. "Oh, up ayont Iceland er Greenland—som'ers in *the Artics*.")

"——there's three things I want ye should always remember. Live upright lives. Do some good in the world with this here money I give ye. And always keep the Christmas spirit in yer hearts, and when ye git older, bring all the happiness ye kin to other little children at Christmas time. Do ye promise?"

"Oh, yes, sir."

"All right, then—here goes!"

Shining quarters—one for each child. Again he knew about all the children. "Johnnie Quinn, you got yer last one a year agone. You was ten in July." Oh, my goodness, think of him knowing that!

You clutched your quarter tightly and went back to the pew where your parents sat grinning. "Look, he gave me money."

"Well! Well!"

Another Brought Gifts

You clutched it all the way home—this different money that came from Iceland or Greenland or *the Artics,* but was strangely the same kind of silver money your parents possessed on rare occasions. If you dropped it in the snow you bawled to the moon and held up the whole congregation on the steps until it was retrieved.

Santa had told you to do good with your money. Sometimes you gave it the very next Sunday to the Sunday school, so that you might rid yourself of all further responsibility in the ethics of its disposal. Sometimes, after due meditation in which you were torn between moral rectitude and the fleshpots, you sent it to the missionaries via the Ladies' Society with the righteous satisfaction of having converted countless heathen. Sometimes, human nature having been quite the same in the not-always-so-gay nineties, you bought huge white gum hearts and licorice with it, waiting conscience-smitten for bad luck to follow, immeasurably relieved when it failed to appear.

Always the little man ended with that same pronouncement which he gave like the benediction. "Remember! Live upright lives. Do something good with yer money. Always keep the Christmas spirit in yer hearts and try to make other children happy."

Ah, well, you were not always upright. You did not always do good with your money. But, perhaps mellowed a little by that benediction of long ago, you did resurrect the Christmas spirit each year.

Then suddenly you were ten and had passed the traditional quarter-gift age—too soon knew the disillusioning truth. Santa Claus *was* old man Miller. It was disappointing, but after the shock of the discovery was over, you joined the conspirators. Because you had so loved the great moment, you, too, kept silent and saw the other little children of the town walk up excitedly for their money.

Then after a time, when you were much older, you saw something else: the drama and the pathos that were old man Miller. You saw how all year old Jed Miller lived for this one hour of giving. It seemed foolish, saving from his small wages to give it away in one reckless hour of abandon. Don Quixote mowing lawns! Pikeville called it plain dumb.

And then the old man grew feeble and rather forgetful but still he gave much of his time to the church, although it must have been harder for him. He annoyed some of the people, particularly the Reverend Julius Parkinson who had come from a larger place, for before the services old Jed would squeak-squeak about the church, fussily passing out extra hymn-books, getting down on his knees to hunt for a child's lost penny.

The membership was changing. There were more important people in it now—Mrs. Adelbert Tobin, for instance, who was both a pillar and a power. She and

the Reverend Parkinson agreed between them that the
services would possess more dignity without the pre-
liminary squeakings of Old Jed.

"He's an institution," a few old-timers protested.

"He's a nuisance," Mrs. Tobin retorted.

So a new and younger man was asked to care for the
church and surprisingly given a small wage for doing
so.

You may tell an old family dog that he is no longer
a member of the family but it means practically nothing
to him. With this same pleasant scope of vision, Old
Jed chose to look upon the newcomer as a mere assistant
and went about his faithful, if squeaking, way.

And then, Christmas was coming. Mrs. Tobin was to
have charge of the exercises and she explained to Jed
that they were dispensing with his services behind the
organ and simultaneously with his Santa Claus impersonation.

"I won't have him spoiling my program with his
crude ways and illiterate speech," she announced. "The
time has come to tell him so in plain words."

There could be no mistaking the plainness of Mrs.
Tobin's words. She told Jed they were to have a pageant
this year—a beautiful, moving artistic pageant. There
would be Joseph and Mary and the Christ Child, shepherds and wise men and angels. Children would rep-
resent Hope and Courage, Fear and Selfishness, Truth
and Service, Love and Faith. In fact, every perfection

and every frailty attendant upon humans was to be represented in Mrs. Tobin's artistic pageant; everything in short, except a fat Santa Claus in a disreputable old red suit and dirty white whiskers. She told the other ladies that she thought for once Old Jed had got it through his head.

And she was quite right. Old Jed got it through his head. All the life went out of him. He disappeared from church and from his old haunts. When it occurred to some one that he had not been seen around much, Doctor Waters went down to the unpainted house at the end of Maple Street. He found Old Jed in bed, told questioners uptown that he guessed the old man was about done for. He left him medicine, told him to keep quiet and promised to drop in again.

Christmas Eve came with the lights from the church streaming out on the snow and the Norway pine green and sparkling against the white wall.

Every one had to give Mrs. Tobin credit for her pageant. It *was* more artistic than the old "pieces" spoken in hodge-podge order. There was a nice dignity about the whole program with its aura of spiritual significance, as Mrs. Tobin had so aptly predicted. The wise men and the shepherds, Truth and Service, Hope and Love were letter-perfect. The angels sang their final song and the pageant was over, when bells sounded loudly at the side door. Mrs. Tobin looked startled, and every child drew in an excited breath.

Another Brought Gifts

The door opened and into the midst of the artistry and the spiritual significance bounced a little old Santa Claus in a disreputable red suit and dirty white whiskers. Every child let out its breath in one wild shout. Every parent said, "Of all things!" or, "Thought he was sick."

Doctor Waters half rose from his seat and sat down again. Mrs. Tobin gave a very good imitation of a lady smiling when taking castor-oil.

"Bet ye thought I might not git here, but here I be." He might have swayed a little.

The dignified pageant turned to a riot, noisy and hilarious. Santa gave out the presents, calling names with gusto and adding personal comments to every excited child who came for them.

" 'N' now I got somepin fer everybody here under ten." He slapped his heavy pockets. "I be'n watchin' the children o' this here town 'n' I sez they's pretty good. So I looks all around my house. . . ."

"Where is it?" called the perennially bold one.

"Oh, I ain't tellin'. Som'ers up ayont Iceland er Greenland—er *the Artics*."

There was a quarter for each one, as there had been for over thirty years. It was just as the silver shower ended that it happened.

A little flame suddenly darted up from a dipping candle on the tree, curled its yellow-red tongue around the branch, leaped to the next one.

Women screamed. Men jumped to their feet. Children stood fascinated with horror, watching the little red tongues crackle toward the upper branches.

And then the little old Santa sprang to it, grasped the flaming thing in both arms, wrenched it from its sand-filled keg, and kicking open the side door, went out with his torchlike burden.

Doctor Waters hurried after the old man; a dozen adults followed.

They brought him in from the snow to the side room of the church. Doctor Waters said it was not the burns: that the old man should never have left his bed. "Must have been mighty hard for him to get dressed and come up here."

There was scarcely a dry eye there in the little room filled with grown people. It was not just that Old Jed was dying. It was the memory of those Christmas Eves when they had been little, so that it seemed Youth and Childish Happiness were going out with him now.

"The's three things." He roused himself, thinking they were children there around him. "Live upright lives. Do good with this here money. Always keep the Christmas spirit . . . 'n' make . . . other children happy. Do ye promise?"

"We promise."

Outside, people were grouped around the door. Children, clutching quarters, pestered their parents with questions. "What's happened to Santa? Did he get hurt?"

"No, nothing can happen to Santa."

"Well, who's that in there, then?"

"That's Old Jed Miller."

"Well, what's happened to *him?*"

"He's going away."

"Where?"

"Oh, up—maybe up beyond *the Artics.*"

Afterward, recalling how little work he had been able to do that year, every one realized how he must have skimped himself to save for that last Christmas.

Telling it after many years, the whole thing sounds too sentimental for this practical age. Such an out-moded tale about Old Jed Miller giving away his hard-earned money to the children—as old-fashioned as that one about the men who long ago brought Another Child gifts of gold and frankincense and myrrh.

JUNO'S SWANS

EMMA-JO THOMAS bent her fat little body over her desk and looked across at Angie Bryson sitting two rows away. Her round pink face plainly asked of Angie: "How do you like *that?*" And Angie without so much as moving her lips telegraphed back: "Grand." Some friendships are like that: wordless, significant, all-embracing.

Miss Clarkson, the music instructor, standing in front of the pupils, had just announced that the grades were to give an operetta some evening in the last week of June. It was a perfectly lovely operetta, Miss Clarkson was telling them in the vivacious voice that Emma-Jo sometimes thought too sugary. Miss Ray, the real teacher, now sitting over at her big desk, always talked to them in an ordinary way as though they were her own age, but Miss Clarkson, who came twice a week, made her voice gay and excited and a little babyish unless she grew provoked at something, and then it sounded mad and natural. This afternoon she was making it as sweet as a flute and very enthusiastic.

"There are several parts that will take a great deal of practice," she was saying—"starring parts."

Emma-Jo, gazing across at her chum again, distinctly saw Angie look self-conscious It was a foregone conclusion that Angie would have one of those starring parts. She always did. There was not the slightest trace of envy in Emma-Jo's loyal heart, for Angie could sing in a clear true voice, and—to Emma-Jo's uncritical mind—could act better than any of the four girls in "Little Women." Miss Clarkson was saying that the operetta was called "The Forest Child's Dream," which even more definitely settled matters in Emma-Jo's mind, for it followed that Angie would be either the Forest Child or the Dream.

There were to be squirrels and birds and flowers and butterflies, and it all sounded tremendously exciting to Emma-Jo and the other feminine listeners. But as usual, there was noticeable a most exasperating lethargy among the less deadly of the species. Not one of the boys seemed to be getting up any temperature over the potential impersonation of squirrels, birds and butterflies.

Miss Clarkson was working the girls into a perfect lather of anticipation, but the boys remained bored, as with a weary surfeiting of much participation in grand opera. Jimmie Landers even formed his lips and tongue into a realistic, if merely pantomimic, representation of the noisy offering known as the raspberry. And when Miss Clarkson said in a sprightly tone that some one was to be a funny, funny grasshopper and illustrated the jumping, Herman Stutz laughed out loud, but not mirthfully.

It exasperated Miss Clarkson to such an extent she was moved to say that unless they exhibited a little more interest she would not have *one* of the boys in it. Afterward she told Miss Ray *that* statement would bring them around to a show of interest if she knew her Applied Psychology. But Miss Ray, who thought that Applied Psychology was nothing more or less than applied common sense, merely laughed and said that she never paid any attention to that unenthusiastic attitude, that it was a familiar masculine trait and employed merely as a mask.

School having been dismissed with no more definite information on the future musical soirée, conversation by the Misses Bryson and Thomas, en route home, consisted largely of speculation over the coming event. A block down the street their close communion was interrupted by the approach of old Mr. Moseby, the father of their own Mr. Moseby, the superintendent. Old Mr. Moseby had once been a college professor, but this last year he had lived in Huntsville with his son's family. He stopped now, leaning on his cane and looking down his long red nose.

"Well, well," he said cheerfully, "here are the two little inseparables again—Rosalind and her Celia. Do you know who they were?"

Emma-Jo volunteered the guess that they might

be some of his relatives. But Mr. Moseby said no, they were friends in a play called *As You Like It,* written by Shakespeare. And did they know him?

"My father does, I think," said Angie brightly, adding modestly that railroad conductors knew most every one.

"I do declare!" chuckled Mr. Moseby.

Emma-Jo was ashamed that Angie had said that, for somehow she had a feeling that the man was dead. People who had written books were usually dead, and at home there was a long row of books with this one's name on them. When Cousin Mel's little boy Georgie came to dinner he had to sit on *King Lear,* but when the littler Johnnie came, it also required the services of *Hamlet* to connect Johnnie with his food.

"Yes, you're like Rosalind and Celia." The old man was enjoying himself.

The names sounded rather nice. Not long before, Angie and Emma-Jo had been Greta Garbo and Mae West, but their impersonations had ended so disastrously that they never mentioned the two now.

The little girls were getting anxious to move on but Mr. Moseby, with time hanging heavily on his hands, had more to say about Rosalind and Celia. In a voice like a radio announcer he quoted:

> "... we still have slept together,
> Rose at an instant, learn'd, play'd, eat together,
> And wheresoe'er we went, like Juno's swans,
> Still we went coupled and inseparable."

Juno's Swans

At that the two edged politely away, Angie muttering under her breath, "The old bore." But Emma-Jo rather liked it, especially the part about Juno's swans. She said it out loud several times, enjoying the way the syllables slipped over her tongue like cream pudding. To be sure, her personal interpretation was slightly original, inasmuch as she thought Juno was merely a poetical way of referring to the month of June.

She even remembered it the next day when she looked across at Angie two rows away. The nice, gay month of June was here with its roses and operetta. She and Angie were like that Rosalind and Celia.

Her heart swelled with friendship for Angie. Angie was a swan. *She* was a swan. *Juno's swans.*

But even as Emma-Jo was having her pleasant and rather poetical thoughts of friendship—even then, the serpent was creeping into her Eden. For the door opened to admit Mr. Moseby, the superintendent, and a strange girl.

All eyes—raised surreptitiously above books—were upon the two. Mr. Moseby was explaining something to Miss Ray, and Emma-Jo could hear part of the conversation. The new girl was the niece of Mrs. William Rider. She was from Capitol City and she was to be in school for the rest of the term. Her parents had been called away East, and because she was obliged to come and stay with her aunt, she must finish her grade here.

To say that the newcomer was pretty is a fractional

truth. She was a vision. She was dashing. She had on a tan-colored pleated skirt and a vivid green silk sweater, turned-down tan hose, tan-and-green sports shoes, and two green bracelets. Her hair was the fluffiest canary-yellow bob, her lips were bright red, her eyes large and blue. She stood at ease in front of the room and looked the pupils all over, tapping one sports shoe impatiently and biting her full red lips. Emma-Jo in her excitement telegraphed repeatedly to Angie. But Angie, gazing in fascination at the stranger, was not at the keyboard.

When Mr. Moseby left, Miss Ray told the pupils that their new classmate's name was Faustina Farr. It kept running through Emma-Jo's mind like a song. Faustina Farr! It sounded frosty and sparkling and as pretty as "Juno's swans."

Faustina Farr, in spite of hailing from Capitol City, did not recite noticeably better than the others, but she succeeded somehow in giving the impression that this whole thing called education was beneath her, and a little silly.

At recess time, play on the feminine side of the grounds lagged noticeably; there seemed nothing to do but surround Faustina Farr in a constantly widening circle, from the equidistant center of which the newcomer told the perimeter of girls a great many interesting things of a statistical nature, largely about herself. She said there were as many pupils in her building in Capitol City as in this whole two-by-four town. She said that she was asked to be in practically every entertainment there, that she had crooned in the Elks Club and that she had been prevailed upon to broadcast torch songs from three different stations. She casually remarked that she had colored bracelets to go with every dress she owned and admitted to owning many dresses.

She offered gratuitously the following items: that her photograph had won a prize at an exhibit of pictures, that sometimes she was called a "child prottigy" and that almost every one thought she should be in the movies. Her last observation, as the bell rang, was concise, terse and critical—namely, that she didn't know whatever she could do in this little stick town for several weeks.

It depressed Emma-Jo. She looked up and down the street where the pleasant old elms and maples met overhead and wondered what they could offer so rare a guest by way of entertainment. And then she remembered. *The operetta!* But some presentiment of coming trouble must have possessed her, for as the girls turned reluctantly away from the Charmer, she flung a plump little arm around Angie in vague motherly concern.

When school was dismissed, Miss Faustina Farr cast her large blue orbs over the feminine contingent. In search of a companion en route home, she discarded all comers but Angie, and Angie, as fascinated as elated, went with her. But when Faustina asked Angie who the funny fat little person was trailing behind them, and Angie, with the same nonchalance a rooster might have used toward a worm, said: "Oh, that's just a neighbor of ours, Emma-Jo Thomas," the world and the solar system crashed about the funny fat little person.

The second evening, after Faustina had laughed at everything Angie and Emma-Jo had once thought lovely; had burst into mirth at the thought of cutting out movie actresses and pasting them in a book; had gone into a mild form of hysteria over the idea of making jewelry out of flowers; nay, more, had been joined in this ribald outburst by Angie herself—Emma-Jo took her troubles to that source of all wisdom, her mother.

Mrs. Thomas told a tearful little daughter she was sorry for her, but not to care—that if *that* was all Angie's friendship had meant, it wasn't worth anything. She told her a great many other things—that friendship was like a sheltering tree; that real friends stick to one at all times; that she who cannot stay by a friend through all experiences is no friend at all. But Emma-Jo's stanch little heart did not move one iota against Angie—only against the serpent which had beguiled her.

Faustina proved to be everything that stolid little Emma-Jo was not. She knew the latest slang. She knew the latest songs. She attracted masculinity. She could play the piano with dash; rather sketchily, to be sure, and with much blurring of chords, but for getting over the ground there was not her equal in Huntsville. It all captivated the heart of Angie, so that where'er went Faustina Farr, there went Angie Bryson. And Emma-Jo trod the lonely path of exile.

Old Mr. Moseby, meeting Emma-Jo one day on the street, asked what had become of the other little girl, and when Emma-Jo made an evasive answer, even he sensed something wrong.

But after all, there was the operetta. Life, even in its darkest aspects, does not withdraw all its allurements.

Operetta practice was on in full swing. And it was all and more than Miss Clarkson had so sportively predicted for it. Its authors had been most lavish in their presentation of characters. There were to be robins, butterflies, sparrows, a mocking-bird, squirrels, a brown thrush, an old witch, goldenrod, a gardener, a cuckoo. . . . Practically everything that ever grew, climbed, crept, ran or flew in the forest was to be impersonated, excepting poison-ivy and wood-ticks.

Five of the leading parts fell to pupils in Miss Ray's room. Brown Thrush proved to be Angie Bryson. Mocking-bird was Faustina Farr. It might have been a matter for open debate as to why the talented ladies who wrote the operetta had placed a mock-

ing-bird in a pine and birch forest, but no doubt
they were more musical than arboreal and avifaunal.
The gardener was Jimmie Landers; he who had once
raised only raspberries was now to have a garden in
the clearing. Cuckoo was Herman Stutz who had once
laughed without merriment, proving again that he who
laughs first, laughs last.

And wonder of wonders—the old witch was none
other than Emma-Jo Thomas in person! This dazzled
Emma-Jo limitlessly, for she was the kind of child who
seldom stars. All her young life she had been relegated
to the back row of the chorus of daisies or made a
member of the peasantry; and now she was to be the
old witch with a tall pointed hat, a yellow cape and a
long crooked stick with which—like a ringmaster—she
was to command all the inhabitants of the forest. She
was almost ill with nervous excitement at the glory of it.
Not once did she stop to think that her part was all
talking—no solo work! For alas! Emma-Jo was no
more musical than she was mathematical.

That was a queer thing she could never tell any
one. She wished people knew how musical she felt
inside her. She could hear lovely tunes in her head,
but when she sang them they were not quite recognizable. And lovely words were always repeating themselves over and over in her mind. To say "Minnehaha,
laughing water" made her flesh feel quivery; and "By
the shining Big-Sea-Water stood the wigwam of Noko-

mis" made tears come to her eyes. She may have been dumb in arithmetic but she leaped to meet her reading lessons as the tides leap to meet the moon. Poetry rippled over her like the curling waves of Lake Crystal at the picnic grounds. When Herman Stutz or Jimmie Landers read poems in their slow halting way it was as painful to her as piano discords to a musician.

But now she had a great deal of talking to do and it was all in poetry—at least Emma-Jo called it that although Miss Ray was well aware that it would never have been chosen for an anthology.

From that time on Emma-Jo Thomas was a disciple of poesy. No longer did she talk as she had been wont to do. She became a sister to the Goddess Thalia, her habitat Parnassus. Day after day she drank of the water that flows from Helicon's harmonious stream to the fountain of the Muses. Because Angie no longer played with her, she made of her poetics a solitary game in her own back yard. With her long stick, an elm understudy to the hickory one at school, she would point and say in impromptu fashion:

> "O lilac bush, I'll change you now
> Into a lovely *lady*
> And when you la la-la la-la
> You'll find it nice and *shady*."

At her mother's simple request to hand her the broom, the poetess would say:

"Here *is* the broom that sweeps the dirt
And I will bring it *to* you
So *sweep* the porch and *sweep* the steps
And la la-la la *do* you."

"The operetta is making Emma-Jo poetical" her
mother said. "The operetta is making Emma-Jo screwy"
her father contributed.

But if Emma-Jo had not known this new diversion
she would have been far more wretched than she was.
Even so, she had periods of deepest little-girl misery,
for it is not pleasant to see one's twin swan sailing off
with another.

Every day at school was rehearsal day now. More
and more was arithmetic shunted to the background.
More and more did poetry come to the front. The
sciences seemed to have decamped almost entirely in
favor of the arts.

The operetta became one's whole object in life. But
all the time the forces that were later to be so disrupting were forming like cyclonic clouds on the horizon.

To Emma-Jo the music was lovely, especially one
waltz song called "The Summer Song." It made her
feel like dancing whenever she heard the lilting tune.
She could feel herself float about in exact time to it, but
when she surreptitiously tried it, her fat little limbs refused to float. The spirit was willing but that too, too
solid flesh was weak. This delicious melody was the
highlight of the operetta. And Miss Clarkson said it

was to be sung either by Brown Thrush or Mocking-bird.

It is easy to be seen that what happened, then, was distinctly the fault of the two composers who had collaborated on the operetta. For after all, it could not have occurred if they had just made up their minds which character was to sing "The Summer Song." But they had left the decision poised in the air. "To be sung either by Brown Thrush or Mocking-bird" was plainly printed at the top of the page.

Because Faustina Farr was Mocking-bird and Angie Bryson was Brown Thrush, it followed that the prettiest song of all was to be sung either by Angie Bryson or Faustina Farr. Faustina asked Miss Clarkson right before every one if she could sing it. Such brazenness appalled even Angie who was no modest violet. Miss Clarkson parried by saying in her twittery voice that she would have to confer with Miss Ray.

Emma-Jo could plainly see that "confer" meant to argue. She tried not to listen; it was almost like reading a letter which did not belong to you. But from her front seat she could hear snatches of the conversation. She knew that Miss Clarkson was wanting Faustina—something about "the Riders liking it." And just as distinctly she could hear Miss Ray say something about "unfairness to regular pupils." Twice she heard her say very low, "*so* affected."

Emma-Jo made a mental reservation to hunt up the

word in the dictionary the moment she got home. She said it off and on out loud all the way there so she would not forget it, but inasmuch as there was a slight discrepancy between the word Miss Ray had used and the word "effected" which Emma-Jo looked up, she found that it merely meant "to be performed, accomplished, achieved," which, of course, was nothing against Faustina.

But even so, each night Emma-Jo prayed consistently that Angie might be chosen. She and Angie might not be chums any more, but friendship was a sheltering tree. So when Miss Clarkson said Brown Thrush— Angie—was to sing the song, Emma-Jo, realizing the efficacy of prayer, turned her eyes guiltily from Faustina's angry countenance as one who has prayerfully maneuvered the whole thing.

The operetta was to be on Thursday night. Miss Ray said they were to come back to school on Friday morning merely to get their books and promotion cards. Sometimes Emma-Jo caught her breath in the gripping fear that she would not be promoted—that the ogre, Arithmetic, would hold her back with his clutching hands. But a glint of hope would invariably shine in the distance. After all, she always *had* been promoted, some unseen force had seemed always to push her from class to class. It was as though those friends, Reading, Writing and Spelling, with whom she was on speaking terms came to her aid each time and would not permit the ugly stranger, Arithmetic, to harm her. But it was going to be terrible not to know the worst until Friday morning.

Rehearsals went on. The last one was held on the big stage of the Community Building, where the voices sounded hollow and unnatural.

The Community Building was new and smelled of plaster. The curtain was a huge velvet thing that ascended somewhere to the heights of heaven and hung suspended from the stars. It was interesting even to Emma-Jo, but the little awe-stricken kindergartners, who were sparrows, could not take their fascinated eyes from the faraway spaces among the rafters so that Miss Clarkson kept rapping for their attention.

This last practice was called a dress rehearsal, and practically everything went wrong. The squirrels kept singing off key. Angie failed to take the first notes of the waltz song with the orchestra. The gardener went on at first without his rake and, hurrying breathlessly back with it over his shoulder, raked off the blue jay's top-knot and a goodly portion of scalp.

The cuckoo, proving himself to be inordinately fond of cuckooing, had to be squelched vigorously and limited to a minimum output. A little sparrow, while gazing open-mouthed up to the vast space among the rafters, tripped over a fellow sparrow, which had the marvelous and mechanical effect of sending the whole row of little brown birds down like dominoes.

Juno's Swans

It was all disheartening. Miss Clarkson was upset, nervous and cross—and there was not the slightest warm twitter to her voice. Miss Ray was nervous, but not cross—merely caught in the spell of a great grim silence. It was as though she were saying: "Let fate do its worst. Nothing could be more terrible."

Faustina snickered audibly and said in an undertone that the Capitol City teachers would have just *died* to see all this. Altogether, it made Emma-Jo feel a vast and awful responsibility, though she herself was letter-perfect.

At supper time she sat down with substantial food before her, at which she pretended to nibble because her mother was insisting, but it was sawdust on her protesting palate. She had a bath; she was dressed. And she was one of the first to arrive at the Community Building.

In almost no time it was all noise and confusion behind the scenes. Miss Ray, pretty and smelling of apple orchards, "made up" the witch. When Emma-Jo turned her plump pink face up to her teacher so seriously, Miss Ray suddenly said: "Emma-Jo, it's a shame to make your sweet little face into an old witch." And then she did a very peculiar thing. She bent and placed a quick warm kiss on Emma-Jo's forehead, for quite suddenly it had occurred to Miss Ray that, after all, dumbness in arithmetic is a very slight evil in this world.

She said, "Emma-Jo, you've been so nice in school all year, I'll hate to have you leave me."

Emma-Jo's heart was bursting with happiness. That was the answer to the question about promotion. She was to go on. It didn't seem possible after all those wrong answers about "If a train..." and "If a farm..."

People were coming in; there was a constant noise of chairs and voices and shuffling feet. The denizens of the forest took turns in peeking around the edge of the curtain; Herman Stutz stuck out his head and cuckooed so often that by the time they were ready to begin, his own part of the program was virtually over. Emma-Jo caught a hurried glimpse of her mother and father, her brother Bob and his girl, Mr. and Mrs. Rider, and old Mr. Moseby. It was going to be wonderful to show all these people how she could turn children into birds at the wave of her stick.

Faustina laughed at the excitement of the others. She said you ought to be in a broadcasting station once if you thought this little hick-town program was anything so hot.

But she could not hurt Emma-Jo to-night. Something very queer hung over Emma-Jo—a sense of the unrealities of the everyday world, the realities of the play. It was not possible that they were from the families of Thomas, Bryson, Stutz, Landers, *et al.* It was the forest folk who were real. The spirit of the play was gripping Emma-Jo. If raindrops had fallen from the rafters high overhead or lightning flashed across the stage, it would not have surprised her.

It was going to be a wonderful occasion, and the grandest part of all was to be that lovely waltz song of Angie's. Even if she and Angie were not chums any more, she retained her old pride in Angie.

The high-school orchestra was playing "Over the Waves." It may have been a little top-heavy as to brass, but to Emma-Jo it was the perfect symphony. Then Miss Clarkson was tapping her baton, which was the signal for the great heavy velvet curtain to lift— and there was Marian Reynolds sitting on the log in the forest, saying:

> "Oh, dear, oh, dear, I'm lonely here
> In the forest by the hill."

That was Emma-Jo's cue. Emma-Jo's heart was beating painfully. Her throat was so dry she wondered if she could swallow. She walked into the forest with her stick, and a voice that seemed to come from far away mechanically said the very thing it should have said:

> "Ho! ho! my dear! It seems so queer
> That you should lonely be.
> With all the woods so full of friends
> For you to hear and see."

Strangely enough, everything went off rather well. That unfortunate rehearsal was but a memory. The little girl saw all the things in the forest she should have seen, and left unseen all the things she should not have seen. The robins sang; so did the squirrels and the butterflies. And Emma-Jo commanded and changed things at the point of her stick so successfully that it gave her a sense of overwhelming superiority.

It was nearing the end of the play now—time for the lovely summer song, the waltz song, that Angie was to sing. Emma-Jo stepped back under the trees next to Faustina Mocking-bird. And then the most terrible thing happened. Emma-Jo thought she was in a dream, an awful breath-destroying nightmare. At the first orchestral notes of the swinging melody Faustina said in an undertone: "Watch *me!*" Emma-Jo could not believe her eyes; before the chords which were to be Angie's cue to take her place, Faustina had gone forward to the edge of the platform and stood ready to sing the first notes of the song. Faustina Farr, in her grown-up crooning voice, was starting to sing Angie's lovely summer waltz song!

No one in the Huntsville schools had ever done such a terrible thing, but Faustina Farr from Capitol City had the nerve to do it. She was going away early the next morning and probably didn't care what happened.

Emma-Jo could not look all ways at once—at Miss Clarkson, who looked terribly surprised but went on swaying her baton; at Miss Ray, whose face was redder than anything; at Angie, who had taken one step forward and then back—so she concentrated on Angie. Angie's face was red, too, and she looked ready to cry. Emma-Jo had seen Angie mad a hundred times, but she couldn't remember seeing her look hurt. It was as though the iron statue of Mr. Hunt who started the town would have looked that way.

All this, happening in the space of a moment or two, set Emma-Jo's mind working far faster than usual. Responsibility sat heavily upon her. She, the old witch, must do something for Angie.

To understand what followed, one must delve into the realm of heredity. Emma-Jo's mother had been the coolest member of the neighborhood the time the Landers' house caught fire. Suddenly, Emma-Jo was her mother. Emma-Jo's grandmother, left alone on the farm once, had stayed up all night in the barn because a horse thief was about. At this moment, Emma-Jo was her grandmother. Emma-Jo's great-grandmother had once torn away the mud chinking in her log cabin, thrust a rifle through the hole and dared an Indian to come on. Just now, Emma-Jo was her great-grandmother. Stolid little Emma-Jo Thomas was suddenly all her courageous pioneer forbears. She was Right! She was Law! She was Justice with her Scales! She was Truth-Forever-On-Its-Throne.

She could command all things in the forest. A great strength was upon her. She strode forward with her long crooked stick.

"Stop!" she said in a clear high voice, so dictatorial that Faustina broke off on the syllable, Miss Clarkson's baton wavered, the orchestra died away on a lingering note.

The audience, thinking it part of the operetta, sat unmoved. Had they not been seeing a small fat witch making sudden transformations all evening, just by swinging her stick? Little did they know history was being made.

Emma-Jo in her short life had never made an extemporaneous speech before an audience. The chances were she never would again. But now she made one. Out from somewhere—for who can tell whence spring all the little lilting rhymes of the poet?—came the words. Not for nothing had Emma-Jo Thomas conversed for weeks in verse.

Thinking it out simultaneously with her speaking, she said:

> "Mockingbird...your song is heard...
> But brown thrush now must *sing*...
> Good-by, farewell! ... Good-by, farewell! ..."

There was a perceptible pause. Fate juggled poor little Emma-Jo Thomas in its cruel hand. But the Muses had not forsaken their child. It came:

> "You *must* be on the *wing*."

And miraculously the thing was done. Emma-Jo Thomas' Big Moment was over.

Juno's Swans

It was too much for Faustina. She had a bewildered, beaten look as though her colossal nerve had at last deserted her. Miss Ray's face was as red as old Mr. Moseby's nose, and she might have been cast in bronze as "Amazement." Miss Clarkson also was the personification of perplexed surprise. All the birds and the flowers and the animals were wide-eyed with the peculiarity of the thing they had just witnessed. Only the little brown sparrows, gazing in open-mouthed fascination into the vastness of the rafters high overhead, remained immune to any bewilderment over a change in the program.

Faustina walked back under the trees. Angie, returning to normalcy, stepped out to her legitimate place on the stage. Miss Ray, cast in bronze, felt the blood start to flow again in her veins. Miss Clarkson's baton came up. The orchestra picked up the scattered notes of the waltz song. The little old witch slipped back to her place. Angie sang her song.

Then the grand finale with all the beasts and birds and flowers of the forest bursting into a wild revel of song, intoxicated with the thought that this was the last of the school year, the cuckoo adding a half-dozen raucous calls for good measure—and the operetta was over.

Immediately all was confusion. Emma-Jo stood alone, dazed, all her recent strength gone from her like a cast-off garment; stood there until Angie came flying through the milling crowd to throw both arms around her.

"Emma-Jo, how *could* you *do* it? Oh, Emma-Jo, you're my friend—my best friend for all my life." But such affectionate emotion was not natural to Angie. Immediately she was saying: "That *old* Faustina—that old *meanie*—that *old*——"

And then Faustina herself was coming by, her red silk coat over her arm. She tossed her yellow head, addressed Emma-Jo Thomas pointedly and without restraint. "You think you're smart, don't you? You little—little *cluck* of a *fat* hen!"

But Emma-Jo was wrapped in the warmth of Angie's arm and sustained by the glowering face of Angie turned Faustina-ward. And in that friendly shelter she knew she was not a fat hen nor yet the cluck of a fat hen. She was a swan—a graceful swan—and so was Angie. Inseparable friends! Like that Rosalind and Celia! Twin swans in the lovely month of Juno!

IT'S NEVER TOO LATE TO LIVE

OLD ELLA BURKE climbed laboriously down
from the ramshackle buggy, walked gingerly
around to the heads of the heavy horses standing
stolidly in the muddy gutter, and tied them to one of
the two hitching-posts left in town. Bird having surprisingly acquired the notion to stamp one shaggy leg,
Ella held her long dress carefully away from the flying
particles of mud.

She tied the last knot in the leather hitch-straps and
stepped up on the sidewalk. There she took off a big,
clumsy pair of men's gloves and tucked a wisp of gray
hair up under the back of her hat. The hat was symbolic—the very epitome of old Ella Burke's life. It
was drooping, forlorn, rusty, on one side a wilted little
bunch of violets which had once been jauntily purple,
even as Ella had once been jauntily colorful.

From some mysterious region of the petticoats Ella
extracted a man's wallet and opened it. The pocket-
book had belonged to Jake Burke, her husband, and
the only reason that old Ella dared carry it to-day was
the simple one that Jake had died two weeks before,
and almost unbelievably had not taken the familiar

wallet with him on this last journey. The fact was that he had not planned to take the trip at all.

He had always scouted the idea of death. People died occasionally, to be sure—but not Jake Burke. No sir, not by a jugful did Jake Burke ever die. More than once he had given his neighbors to understand that he thought it all tommyrot to succumb. He had never made a will, either—boasted that he could look after his property, he guessed, without having any shyster telling him where to get off. But death had played a mean joke by slipping up on him with no more advance notice than a cold, which proved in the end as stubborn as old Jake himself. At Ella's timid and frightened suggestion that the doctor come out to the farm, old Jake had gone into a rage. No sir, not by a damsight would any doctor have a chance to get hands on him, charging him for the visit and for mileage into the country. And so when old Jake, breathing raspingly through the night, at last gasped, "Mebbe—he'd better—come," old Ella had run across the frosty meadow to a neighbor's house to phone. When she returned, death, who charged neither for the visit nor for mileage, had been there and gone.

And now, with Jake strangely non-committal out there in the Prairie Hill cemetery, Ella cautiously opened the big brown leather pouch. Almost unconsciously she looked over the heads of Bird and Belle as though expecting to see an impatient, irritable old man step around the buggy and snatch the battered pocket-book from her hands.

Standing there in the lee of the buggy, out of the crisp fall wind, Ella carefully extracted an envelop from the wallet. It was directed to her, and up in the corner there was printing—*Prairie Hill State Bank*. She pulled out the letter inside and read it for perhaps the ninth or tenth time. "At your earliest convenience, will you call at the bank?" was the principal sentence —and it was signed with Mr. Thomas R. Howard's name—the president of the bank.

Old Ella had taken butter to town and delivered it at Mr. Thomas Howard's back door many times. A woman in a white apron and white cap always took it, but once or twice Mrs. Thomas Howard had come by and said pleasantly: "Won't you come in and get warm?" or "Won't you step inside and cool off a little?" Old Ella had never done so, for Jake had always been waiting, but she loved the glimpse of the shining kitchen through the open door.

"At your earliest convenience, will you call—?" She had received the letter last Saturday. It had not been convenient to come to town on Monday or Tuesday. Habit, the tryant, had held her captive to Monday's washing and Tuesday's ironing.

Old Ella walked down the side street now and turned into the paved Main Street, passing the Prairie Hill Drygoods Emporium with its windows filled with

gay-gowned wax ladies. She had always wanted to stop
and linger by the windows, but with Jake waiting
impatiently by his team, she had never been able to
do so. She passed the Bon Ton Shoe Shop, the Easy-
payment Hardware, and Jackson's Music Store. She
walked by the narrow yellow front of the Sunset Café
where she took eggs every Friday, and came then to
the Prairie Hill State Bank on the corner.

It was the first time she had passed between the
pillars and into the vestibule of the bank without Jake
leading the way. There was a seat near the door, and
always before, Jake had said: "Set there." And she
had sat, waiting until he was through with his business.
So now, hesitant, she paused and looked about her.

And then a strange thing happened. Mr. Thomas R.
Howard himself came hurriedly through an iron gate
and spoke: "Come right in, Mrs. Burke."

He opened a heavy door, and Ella, sensing that he
meant for her to go in first, slipped past him, like the
fleeting shadow of a woman, into a small room. Mr.
Thomas R. Howard stepped to another door and spoke
to a small, slim man with close-cropped gray mustache,
who came in immediately; Mr. Victor P. Mapes that
was, the cashier of the bank.

It was Mr. Mapes who had been appointed administrator by the court, a foolish procedure in old Ella's
mind, when there was so little to look after. And it
was Mr. Mapes who spoke now, crisply, in nervous

phrases: "We have a rather distasteful piece of news for you, Mrs. Burke. We have communicated with the townspeople in Mr. Burke's old home and find that there is another heir; and so, according to the laws of our state, your husband having left no will, you will only get one-half of the property, the other half reverting to his heirs, which in this case is a nephew."

Old Ella did not quite understand it. She turned bewildered eyes toward Mr. Thomas R. Howard. There was something about Mr. Howard that seemed more sympathetic.

"Yes," Mr. Howard said kindly, "it is just as Mr. Mapes says—one-half of the property must go to your husband's heir. We are sorry—you deserve it all."

"Well," said Ella, her gnarled fingers working nervously with the wallet, "I can get along. The chickens and the two cows will pay the taxes—and I don't take much. I'll have to have some help with the planting, but I can cultivate—and husk."

Mr. Howard looked at her, a little queerly, old Ella thought. "I guess that will hardly be necessary. You know, of course, that your husband held two mortgages —on the Rasmussen and Talbot farms, which brought him good interest."

Ella was frightened. *Mortgage*—the word had an evil sound. All his life Jake had held it over her head. "A carpet for the floor? What do you mean? You want we should have a mortgage over our heads?" There came to her a swift, horrible picture of being turned out of the little weather-beaten house.

"They hold some mortgages over me?" she queried.

"No, oh, *no.*" Mr. Howard was smiling, his fat face looking boyish. "*You* hold mortgages on them. Eight thousand on the Rasmussen farm, eleven thousand on the Talbot farm. You own now—or will when the estate is settled—one-half of all Jake's property; and these two mortgages total nineteen thousand dollars. Then you know, of course, there are about twenty-seven thousand dollars' worth of bonds, and a little over four thousand dollars on a time certificate here in the bank —in addition to the home place."

No, old Ella did not know it.

She was dazed. It seemed that she could not think clearly. "Will you explain it all to me again?" she said.

"In addition to the farm in which you hold your homestead rights, half of your husband's estate of approximately fifty thousand dollars will be yours."

Surprise, incredulity, took possession of old Ella's mind—and then, as the knowledge fastened itself in her mentality—bitter resentment. She had slaved all her life *and it had not been necessary.*

More swiftly than her timid sluggish brain had worked for years, pictures slipped through it—a picture of herself dressing chickens in the cold lean-to kitchen, her hands tortured between the iciness of the temperature and the heat of the water—a picture of herself emptying the sudsy wash water to get the one tub ready for the rinsing water—of herself ironing with two old flat-irons next to a cob fire—turning her rusty black dress until it was falling to pieces. *And it had not been necessary.* Money in the bank, money on interest, bonds, mortgages on other folks' farms. And Jake had made her think there was barely enough to scrape together to pay the taxes!

She was brought to the present suddenly by Mr. Mapes' quick, nervous voice: "One thing we want to find out to-day is what you want to do about this time certificate. This four thousand dollars is due now and we wondered whether you wanted it renewed or put in your checking account."

Old Ella did not know a time certificate from a centipede, and checking accounts were as foreign to her as Greek philosophy.

So Mr. Howard took a hand again. "If the time certificate is renewed—that is, if we put it back the way it has been—you can't draw the money out until the time is up—at least, not without losing your interest; but if it's in your checking account, you can use it along just as you wish. Do you have any special need for ready money now?"

Old Ella raised faded eyes to Mr. Howard—eyes that were like an old shepherd dog's.

"Yes," said Ella, "I've always wanted another wash-tub and to have some company visit me."

It's Never Too Late to Live

Mr. Thomas R. Howard dropped his own eyes, and took off his horn-rimmed glasses, intently occupied for a moment in working their bows. Then he said briskly: "All right—we'll convert that certificate into cash, before we make a new one, and part of the money can go into the checking account. How much do you want in there, Mrs. Burke?"

Old Ella did not know. Beyond the limits of a few dollars, all amounts of money seemed lost in a meaningless haze.

"About—" it was her very own, she assured herself, "about—fifty dollars." It seemed a fortune, limitless in its possibilities.

Mr. Howard made out the new time certificate and then gave her a little narrow book. He explained its use, showed her the way to write a check, patiently waited for her to write a model one for him so that she would be sure of herself, told her how he sometimes wrote the object of his purchase down in the left corner for his own benefit, assured her, as she prepared to leave, "I think you'll have good business judgment, Mrs. Burke."

The call was over. And it was well for old Ella that she did not hear Mr. Victor P. Mapes' comments when she had gone.

"Administrator!" he was saying acridly to the older president. *"Guardian*—that's what *that* woman needs, and it's what there will have to be in a few months.

She's no more competent to handle money than a child."

"Oh, I don't know." Mr. Howard was more optimistic. "I think she's all right. She'll be competent."

Up the street, old Ella untied Bird and Belle, their shaggy legs pulling up at a few flies which the first frost had not killed.

Into the west rode Ella Burke, her tanned, seamed face turned toward the sun.

She was strangely exultant. A thrilling sensation enveloped her whole body. It made her hands and feet tingle. She felt that she was floating up and away from the ancient, odorous leather of the buggy seat. She kept feeling for the little black book. It was the key to a long-locked door—a symbol of things to come.

Cars swept by her, their dust lost in the distance while Bird and Belle were covering a few scant yards. When she passed the country cemetery with its abandoned church standing back in a cluster of cottonwoods, she did not look that way. Her heart thumped strangely at its acknowledged lack of sorrow and reverence. All the little meannesses, all the larger trials of her life were accentuated now. She recalled those first few years of tears—and then when there had been no more tears—nothing but a dull acquiescence to life. All the way home she felt hard and triumphant.

Arrived there, she unhitched and turned the old team into the pasture for the night. Released from their heavy harnesses, the stolid old mares broke into clumsy and kittenish gallops, and then stopped suddenly as though realizing their age.

Ella unlocked the back door and went through the low lean-to kitchen into her bedroom. She put the little black book carefully in a bureau drawer, then took off her dark dress and substituted a calico of colorless material and ancient cut. She went outdoors, fed and watered the chickens, and gathered the eggs. The coops were scattered through the grove; makeshift affairs, laboriously botched together out of weather-stained boards. She milked the two cows with strong, knotty hands. When she had strained the milk in her dark pantry, she prepared some supper for herself.

She went early to bed. But she did not sleep. For a long time she lay staring into the night—tense—excited—planning—planning——

All the next day Ella scrubbed and cleaned the old house to soap-and-suds neatness. By four o'clock in the afternoon she was at the back door of the Reeder Memorial Home. She had taken butter there the summer before.

There was no hitching-post at the Home, and one of the little girls had always run out and stood by old Bird and Belle when Ella took in the butter. Anna May Peters, her name was. Ella smiled now to remember the time she had asked it, and the youngster had said, "*Miss* Anna May Peters."

It's Never Too Late to Live

It did not take long for the matron to come to a decision. She saw no reason why Anna May could not spend a few days with Mrs. Burke, the respectable old butter woman. In fact, she thought it would be a nice experience. "Poor child," she said to Ella, "we do get to depending on her to look after the smaller ones." And she helped Miss Anna May Peters put a forlorn little wardrobe into an equally forlorn little bag.

Anna May, a bit of the flotsam of life, was nine years old. Her canary-colored hair was stringy, and her face sloped thinly to the acute angle of her chin. But she was happy to the point of exultation over three days on a farm.

Conversation on the way back to the farm was limited, the hostess apparently as diffident as the guest. Once Ella asked with sedate politeness: "What did your ma die of?"

And Anna May, with equally sedate politeness, answered: "Tombstones."

Old Ella, wondering if she had heard aright, asked her what she had said, so that Anna May enlarged upon the topic. "She died of tombstones. She had a gall-bladder and they found it was full of tombstones."

Ella turned her head. My, my, didn't children say funny things!

"Now, play around," old Ella said, when they had alighted from the ramshackle buggy. "Make some noise if you want to. Make a *lot* of noise," she added reck-lessly.

But Anna May did not make a lot of noise. She walked quietly among the patched chicken-coops and gnarled apple trees.

There was not a great deal of conversation over the supper table, and when the dishes were washed and the kerosene lamp was lighted, Ella tried to think of some way to entertain her guest. Once she went into her bed-room and came back with a little jar.

"Smell!" she said.

Anna May pushed a diminutive, freckled nose down into the jar.

"Can you smell?" Ella waited.

"Yes," said Anna May, "just faint—somethin' sweet."

"Roses . . ." old Ella said. "Roses I picked thirty-nine years ago."

"My gracious!" Anna May clucked her astonishment. "Roses in a jar—thirty-nine years!"

" 'Tis *so*," said old Ella, "and when I think about the day I picked 'em, it seems like it's *me* that's been in that little jar thirty-nine years. I guess you couldn't understand that."

"No," said Anna May, frankly, "*you* couldn't a-been packed in a jar—I guess you're jokin'."

It was the next day that Ella put into execution the great plan that had formed itself in her mind. It was

It's Never Too Late to Live

Friday—the day she always took her eggs to the Sunset Café. To see old Ella and Anna May start to town in the afternoon, one never would have suspected that the journey was of the same import as that taken by one Ponce de Leon, some few centuries before.

Arrived in town, they drove through the alley back of the restaurant and left the eggs. And then—the moment had come. Old Ella began to pluck the fruits of desire. With Anna May—the one no more experienced than the other—old Ella went into the Drygoods Emporium. There the child who was like an old woman, and the old woman who was like a child, each picked out a dress for herself. It was so simple—just to write one's name, and the name of the merchant, and the amount of the purchase. Then, as Mr. Howard had shown her, she wrote the name of the article in the left-hand corner of the check.

They went next into the Bon Ton Shoe Shop and both bought pairs of shoes. Next door the Easy-Payment Hardware Store beckoned the adventurers, and Ella bought a large galvanized wash-tub.

She did her shopping in orderly fashion, not missing a store. The Jackson Music Store looming next on the shopping horizon, Ella went in and bought a banjo. When asked by the mystified clerk whether she wanted a teacher, old Ella said no, he needn't bother about her, that she thanked him very kindly just the same, but she merely wanted to strum on it a little.

It's Never Too Late to Live

In each place up and down Main Street, old Ella and Anna May made purchases. Even the Sunset Café did not faze her. She and Anna May went in and sat down in one of the little stalls that looked so much like church pews. And when the red-lipped, sloe-eyed waitress asked her what she would have, Ella was courtesy itself: "Oh, most anything that won't put you to too much trouble." At which the girl, suppressing a mint-flavored giggle, suggested Sunset Special sandwiches. Ella was a little disappointed when the sandwiches came, for they seemed to have only lettuce and hard-boiled eggs in them.

When the orgy of buying was over, Ella and Anna May rode home behind the fat old mares. Ella was happier than she had ever been in all the years since she was married—Anna May by her side, and all the things she had wanted so long there in the wagon.

When they passed the cemetery, old Ella looked straight ahead, her eyes in the sun slipping down behind the elms and cottonwoods along Plum Creek. But Anna May called attention to the very thing Ella did not want discussed. "Mr. Burke would-a liked to know you was havin' all these grand things, wouldn't he?" And when Ella made no reply, she continued politely: "He must a-been a nice old man."

"He was a hard worker," Ella parried. "Nobody could ever beat Jake up or into the field."

"I wished he'd lived so I could know him. I'd a-liked him, wouldn't I?"

Ella, who knew that Anna May would never have visited at the farm had Jake lived, swept a lean arm around the little girl and drew her up in a spasm of awkward devotion. "Couldn't anybody help but likin' *you*, Anna May," she countered.

At the weather-beaten back door they unloaded the purchases. They took out the banjo and a set of dishes, the bright new wash-tub and the dresses and shoes. They carried in an oak rocking-chair with a blue plush bottom, a yellow and purple hammock, and a fat lamp with a frosted globe shade. They unpacked a dozen green glass tumblers, a checked table-cloth of a vivid redness, and a half dollar's worth of peppermints.

All night long old Ella Burke dreamed of the things —a chaotic mass of color and form and odor, that tumbled and turned and twisted before her eyes, and would not let her rest.

On Saturday morning the work of the Prairie Hill State Bank was well under way, the six employees speeding up their labors in preparation for the usual busy farmer trade of the afternoon. Toward noon Mr. Victor P. Mapes came up to the president's desk, snapping a bunch of checks nervously against his hand.

"Look here, Tom. What did I tell you? That old

Mrs. Burke's checks . . ." His voice held deep disgust as he uttered the one word: *"Overdrawn.* Way overdrawn on her checking account. As far as I can see, there's a check here from practically every store in town."

Mr. Howard took the checks in his hand and ran through them, reading the cramped notations in each lower left-hand corner: *Dishes, shoes, dresses, washtub, lamp, banjo* . . .

"Well—what do you think about her now?" Mr. Mapes urged.

Thomas R. Howard grinned. "Just what I thought at first—that she's not incompetent. She'll be careful later. But I would say right now she's on a wild spree, a regular buying jag. When she sobers up, I bet she'll be as stingy as the old man himself."

At that very moment, out at the old unpainted farmhouse, Ella was saying to Anna May: "My! My! Anna May. I spent an awful lot of money yesterday, didn't I?"

"I should say!" Anna May clucked her sympathy. "Most a million dollars, I guess." And with precocious instinct she added: "You ain't worryin' about it, be you, Mis' Burke?"

"I should say I am, Anna May—worryin' a lot about it this morning. I haven't thought of nothin' else but me doin' that tomfool thing of spending all that money. I'll have to look out or I'll land in the poor-

226

house. Do I want I should have a mortgage over my head? I reckon I was plumb crazy to get all them things."

Then her eye fell on the bright new wash-tub standing jauntily in the middle of the lean-to kitchen. She threw up her head. "No, I ain't, Anna May. I ain't *one mite* sorry. I'd do it all over again. I'd get every single thing I got, unless——" her voice trailed off, a little dubious—"unless it was them sandwiches. I can't say I think them sandwiches was a good buy. Anna May, did you ever stop to think we sold our eggs at the back door of the Sunset Caf-fee for twenty-eight cents a dozen, and then went right around to the front door and bought two of 'em back in sandwiches for thirty cents? And *that*," said old Ella with amazing sagacity, *"that ain't good business judgment."*

THE MOUNTAINS LOOK ON
MARATHON

FATHER, you must take a nap this afternoon. If you're going to try to make a talk at the Knife and Fork dinner to-morrow night, you must conserve your strength."

The decisive voice of Mrs. Chester Cunningham bounced against old Judge Cunningham's ears from some point behind him. The crisp click of his daughter-in-law's thin heels on the tile of the sun-room floor seemed to put the command into italics. The definite odor of a penetrating perfume struck his nostrils as she passed him. Two of her bracelets tapped together distinctly.

There were no halfway characteristics about Rita Cunningham, no pastel shades in any of her personal traits. Where others might have made suggestions, Rita gave commands. When others lounged comfortably about, Rita sat upright, ready for action. Even her gowns were chosen from definite primary colors. Just now the old judge could see out of the tail of a belligerent eye that she was in red—the flamboyant turkey red of an Indian's blanket. Red! On this hot afternoon. It irritated him beyond measure.

The Mountains Look on Marathon

She click-clicked now over to a window shade, lowered it with quick, efficient movements, turned with a swish of the barbaric gown and a snap of silver bracelets. "I'm playing contract this afternoon, father." She would be, he thought. The hotter the day the better her game, he'd bet. "Don't forget the afternoon soda water. And above all, *don't* neglect to take the nap."

The old judge emitted something unintelligible which might have been "huh" and "well"; but running in together as they did, the result was scarcely an example of refined speech.

After her departure he continued to sit unmoving in the huge chair of English chintz, his short stocky legs reposing on a stool of French needlework and his mind vaguely registering the sound of a Mexican orchestra broadcasting a German waltz. Sitting there in apparent relaxation in the midst of these international contributors to his comfort, he looked the picture of supreme contentment—which only goes to prove that one, Phædrus, was quite right when, many centuries ago, he gave forth: "Things are not always what they seem and first appearances deceive many." For old Judge Cunningham was not comfortable, wholly unrelaxed, and most decidedly not contented.

Rita! How she irritated him with her quick, efficient ways and her brisk commands from which there was never escape. Was it because she had once been a trained nurse that she now assumed he was a buck private and she the head of the War Department? No. For a few moments he pictured her in different settings —a teacher, a stenographer, a newspaper woman—and always she was the same brisk, dictatorial creature. If he had known what freedom he was giving up when he disposed of the substantial brick home over in Silver City and came here to live in the pretentious one of his son's, nothing could have induced him to make the change.

He recalled Chet's "You'll not have to do a thing any more, dad," and Rita's "Yes, father, we're going to take care of you now." Well, they had kept their word all right; there was no discounting that. He had grown fatter and logy and definitely stupid. The first two weeks had been pleasurable, the next few passable, and the last few painful. He who had given freedom to many a tortured one was now himself a prisoner, bound by a thousand strands of repressions. He had sold his birthright for a mess of his son's and daughter-in-law's pottage. He felt intensely sorry for himself.

"Eat some spinach, dad. You need the iron." "Don't go out now, father. It's raining." Even little Margaret was beginning, "Where are you going, grandpa? *Should* you?" All day it went on. At first it had seemed merely gracious and interested. Now, by heck, it was tyrannical. It was getting on his nerves. If he left his light on half an hour longer than usual, some one came to his door and asked if he was sick. If he turned it out half an hour sooner than usual, they tiptoed in to the bed, probably to see if he had gone into a state of coma. He was tired of it, by thunder!

Liberty! Freedom! They were the two most glorious words in the language. And they were no longer in his vocabulary. He tried to put his finger on the exact time that he had lost them. It must have been during those few days of sickness. But that hadn't amounted to anything. Pshaw! Just because Chet was a doctor he didn't know everything. Made mountains of mole hills. Doctors were all like that. Acted as though you were going to die. If you did they'd crow because they'd been right in their surmise. If you didn't they'd brag about the grand job of saving you they had done.

Well, he hadn't died, but he might as well have done so, as far as calling his soul his own. And he was as sound now as he ever was. Going to make a little talk to-morrow night at the dinner. That proved he was all right again, didn't it? Why, in the name of all that was sensible, didn't the family drop this eternal bossing him around, then? If he could only shake off the sensation of their eternal supervision and feel like himself! He was no old man. Strong as an ox, quick and agile.

At that, he sat up suddenly, grabbed a plump knee and groaned aloud, looking around hastily to make sure no one was near. Then he pulled himself heavily from the depths of the big chair and went out to the hall to get his hat and cane. He opened the side door softly and started down the long grassy slope toward a gate in the clipped hedge.

"Oh, grandpa——" The fresh young voice came from an upper window. He knew it. *He knew it*. It was not possible to leave that house without interference. "Mother said to watch and if you started away from the house to tell you not to be gone long—the sun is too hot."

He walked stubbornly on, unheeding. His ears were as sharp as a chipmunk's, but if they thought he was such a decrepit old man, he could be deaf too. He went on past the pool where the goldfish nosed stupidly against the lily pads, past the hydrangeas clumped together near the side gate, and passed through the hedge out to the street. He stood for a moment looking up and down the avenue much like a little boy trying to decide what to play, and then started down toward the river, swinging his ebony cane—with "Presented by the Cedar County Bar Association" on its gold knob.

As he walked he was wishing he could take a trip by himself. But something told him it was no longer possible. They would make some excuse. He would wager his last dollar that if he should propose it, Rita would find some reason to tag along. Even if he succeeded in getting away, their influence over him would stretch out like long flexible fingers, following him wherever he went. "Tell us your exact route, father." "Where will you be on Sunday, dad? I'll send you

those tablets." No, he'd just give up. Genuine freedom
—it would never be his.

He walked heavily along in the hot sun, the cane
whacking maliciously at hedges, his thoughts as belligerent as a little boy's.

The river reflected back the sun with blinding
brilliance, but the old judge walked stubbornly out to
the end of the wharf and stood gazing across the water.
Right up there—about where that strip of pines jutted
out—was the place he and some of the old gang used
to go when they were kids. Seemed a hundred years
ago—and yesterday.

As he lingered, a dingy boat pulled up to the dock,
a wizened-looking man at the oars. He watched the
queer little fellow swing an agile leg over the boat's
edge and clamber up the piling, a string of river cat
in his hand, their bodies glistening in the strong light.
From his appearance the judge could not tell whether
he was an active old man or a weather-beaten young
one. His face was tanned and seamed, the chin and
lower cheeks covered with smoke-colored hair. His
clothes were nondescript—soiled loose trousers and a
shirt of black and white checkerboard squares pinned
with a safety pin across his dark chest.

Coming up to the judge now he gave a wide, hairy,
half-toothless grin, so that he presented the appearance
of an animated baboon.

The Mountains Look on Marathon

"Guess you don't know me?"

The judge was shaking his head slowly, and then—something in the little ice-blue eyes, the shape of the small head, an outstanding left ear, and so rapidly does the mind travel that in the flash of introspection Judge Cunningham was remembering a boy from "up the river" waiting for him in the dark dawn, lying outside in the lush grass. Together they had slipped away and together they had stayed in the woods for a day and a night. That day had stood out on his boyhood's calendar unbelievably red—a day of complete freedom. Only they two had lived in a world of their own. No one knew where they had gone. They had hunted and fished and penetrated deep into the timber. They seemed to belong to no civilization or time. It was as though they were non-existent. All night, too, they stayed in the cool depths of the forest, lost to the wonder of the dark. In the dim early morning they returned home, he to distraught parents who had been up all night seeking him, the other boy to an indifferent family who had no worries concerning their offspring's lax ways. He remembered even now the nonchalance with which Jim Shaffer had left him and gone on home, whistling, while his own family gathered around with excited comments. Almost he could hear the gay, insolent tune:

> Oh, come with me in my little canoe,
> Where the sky is calm and the sea is blue.

And so old Judge Cunningham, standing there in his tailored clothes with his presented-by-the-bar-association cane, was saying to the dirty old river rat:

"Not . . . it isn't . . . Jim Shaffer?"

The grin widened in assent.

"Well . . . well. . . ." The judge presented a fat smooth hand to a bony soiled one. "Jim . . . I haven't heard anything about you for years. How are you? Where do you live?"

"Got a shack over by Lake Tanner."

"Tanner! Why, that's where you and I ran away to —that time. Remember? Golly, how scared my folks were!"

Jim was nodding. "Ya. Same place." His little ice-blue eyes twinkled above the leather of his cheeks.

"How did you know me, Jim?"

"Took fish up to your son's home. Saw you through the window. Didn't say nothin'. Too swell."

The judge ignored that. "Whatever came of some of the rest of the boys? That little devil of a Red Prescott? Where's he?"

Old Jim grimaced. "Methodist parson," he said dryly.

"Don't tell me," Judge Cunningham chuckled. "And Goody-goody Meeker—teacher's pet—where's he?"

Old Jim pursed his lips and aimed a dusky-hued stream at a dock post. "In the pen," he said laconically. And they both laughed at the irony of it.

The Mountains Look on Marathon

"Well, well, Jim! What do you do with yourself?"

"Fish a lot. Pick blueberries 'n' chokecherries. Lay around. Hear the loons call across the lake. Watch the herons go slippin' 'cross the sky. Sleep under the pines. Come 'n' go when I please."

Old Judge Cunningham eyed the dirty little man with something which approached perilously near to envy. "Lord, Jim, that sounds pleasant."

" 'Tis. Wouldn't change places with nobody. First one to see the flash of a teal's wing in spring. Partridges feed on pin cherries right outside my cabin. Squirrels run over the roof. Mallards settle down in the rushes in front."

"How about winter, though? Do you stay there then?"

"Sure. Just as good. Stop up the cracks with putty. Big fire in the stove. Listen to the pitch sizzlin' out the pine. Melt maple sugar. Pop corn. Go huntin' rabbits. Lots o' wild things around. Little deer come nosin' around last winter. Fox tracks. Trap muskrats. Got four minks last year."

To old Judge Cunningham, bound to civilization and his son's family by a thousand strands of inhibitions, the pictures drawn by old Jim Shaffer seemed fascinating. There was something alluring in the vision. It was as if old Jim were playing upon some chord in the judge's make-up which responded with music. And the music was of poignant sweetness.

The Mountains Look on Marathon

Quite as though he were putting words to the music, the old judge said throatily:

> "The mountains look on Marathon,
>   And Marathon looks on the sea;
> And musing there an hour alone,
>   I dreamed that Greece might still be free."

"Huh?" said Jim Shaffer politely, his first-hand knowledge of Byron being somewhat limited.

"Just an old man's fancies, Jim. Say, Jim, you're two years older than I am. But, by George, you seem twenty years younger—agile, wiry, spry as a grasshopper. How does that happen?"

Old Jim shrugged a checkerboard shoulder. "No worries. Just livin' fer a day at a time. Lay in the sun. Splash in the lake. Smell the balsam."

Judge Cunningham gave a hasty glance backward down the years—studying cases . . . night work . . . speeches . . . the troubles of the community on his mind. . . .

He sighed, and then said, "So you never married." It was a statement rather than a question.

"Sure," old Jim said testily. "Sure I married. Three times."

"Three times. Why—what happened?"

"Well, one was drowned; the other two just walked off . . . vamoosed into thin air."

"That's hard luck, Jim. A death and two divorces."

"Never come up against no divorce."

"But how—you didn't remarry without one?"

"Well, she was gone, wa'n't she?" Old Jim shrugged an indifferent shoulder. "How'd I know where she'd went?"

Why, the old reprobate! He had remarried without benefit of court.

"And so you just come and go as you please."

Old Jim nodded silently. The tears came to his little ice-blue eyes. Freedom was too sacred a thing upon which to comment. He felt immeasurably sorry for the old man standing by him in the pressed suit and swell hat. "Tied down, Sam?"

Judge Cunningham's first inclination was to cover it largely. "Oh, no, no. I've a little money. I can go anywhere." But in his heart he knew well enough that it was not true.

So he leaned forward. "Terribly, Jim. I half envy you your freedom. Why, do you know, one of the happiest memories I have is the time I ran away with you. Remember catching bass in the early dawn . . . doing our own cooking over a fire . . . fish and bread and coffee . . . not seeing anybody all day and all night . . . not hearing anything but the noises of the woods?"

Old Jim nodded in wordless sympathy.

"Lord, I'd like to live that all over, Jim."

"Well"—Jim wiped a hairy brown paw across a stained mouth—"what's hurtin'?"

"What do you mean, Jim?"

"What's hurtin' you run away again?"

"Nothin'." Unconsciously Judge Cunningham dropped into Jim's and his own boyhood vernacular. "Nothin's hurtin' that I know."

"Come on, then." He motioned airily to the dingy flat-bottomed boat.

"No, thanks, I couldn't to-day, Jim."

" 'Fraid of your son and swell daughter-in-law?" the old river rat jibed.

"Afraid of—" the old judge grew almost apoplectic. It was as though he were little Sammy Cunningham again, fearful of the opinion of the independent Jim Shaffer. "Say, what's eatin' you, Jim? 'Fraid of nobody. I'll go. Sure I'll go. But not now. How's early to-morrow morning?"

"Any time with me." That was the old Jim, ready to do anything, any time—free.

All evening the old judge harbored the guilty secret. To-morrow morning at the ungodly hour of three o'clock, he was going on a fishing trip with Jim. It was true, he admitted, he did have a sort of lurking fear of the family. He could hear Chet's joking, "Father, I'm afraid you're getting into bad company in your old age." Could imagine Rita's chagrin and disgust at the sight of dirty old Jim. It was ridiculous that he had to slip out like a thief, but they watched over him every moment.

He made an excuse to go to bed early and, just as

he expected, it caused comment. "You aren't sick, are you, father?" "Sure you feel all right, dad?"

Rita came click-clicking down the hall as he was getting out an old panama hat, so that he slipped hastily into bed.

He couldn't get to sleep. For a long time he twisted and turned. Then he slept fitfully and wakened at two. Fearful then that he would oversleep, he lay waiting for three. Strange, how boyish and happy he felt!

He rose and dressed and, shoes in his hand, slipped stealthily down the back stairs. On the kitchen table he left a note for Rita: "Will be back in time to dress for the dinner." He chuckled to think how he was out-witting her. If she had known where he was going, she would have driven him to the dock and taken along a camp chair and pillows and a first-aid kit.

Down the street he went in the semi-dark, and the faint faraway smell of the river greeted his nostrils so that he quickened his pace.

There was the wharf, now, outlined against the gray water. There was Jim rowing along in the faint light, the swish of his oars soft and rhythmic.

And then old Jim had pulled up and was waiting for him to get in. He tried to drop down as easily as he knew Jim could have done, but it was a sorry attempt. With suppressed puffings and wheezing he finally crawled down backward, an entirely unsports-manlike proceeding.

The Mountains Look on Marathon

Then they were off, with a soft sound of oars. This was the life, the old judge thought. No little mill girl of Browning's Pippa Passes could have so enjoyed the freedom of her one great day, he was sure.

A light wind played along the top of the water. Old Jim sniffed and turned his face into it. "Bass morning," he said laconically. And the old judge nodded, wordless, too full of gratitude to his old playmate for speech.

Across the river old Jim docked, jumped out and pulled the flat-bottomed boat with the fat judge in it farther up on the sand. Evidently, the little wiry man had the strength of a burro.

Together they plunged into the undergrowth of the woods where light had not yet penetrated, only the white of the birches standing out from the dark shadows. The odors were fragrant—crushed ferns and little wild flowers and the pungent smell of the pines.

In time they came out to the lake set like a lovely stone in the green filigree of the woods. Old Jim led the way down the steep winding path to another shell of a boat in which there were rods and bait. There was a slight delay and then they were off, old Jim's brown sinewy arms rowing steadily, slowly, up the shore line just outside the rushes, while old Sam trolled. Far up the lake they changed to casting.

Old Jim was right. Jim had always been right about Nature's signs. Bass were biting. The fresh wind whipped the water in ruffles of waves along the fringe of rushes. Old Judge Cunningham, reeling in a big-mouth bass, was in a state of perfect contentment.

All day long that contentment grew. After a lunch of fish and bread the two sprawled on the needle-carpeted ground and drank in the pungent odor of the pines while old Jim talked about woodsy things. The years had swept back. They were boyhood pals.

In the afternoon they anchored for still fishing in a sheltered cove. Jim wound in and out of the rushes, sighting a spot opposite a fallen monster of a tree. They caught a crappie or two, their flat bodies flashing silver. Suddenly, it grew warmer and more sultry. The water took on a dark gray hue. The leaves of the birches drooped listlessly. Old Jim turned his face to the woods and sniffed. "Rain," he said laconically. "With wind."

"Rain?" Why, there hadn't been rain for quite a while. To-day, of all days! "I must get right back, then. I have to attend a meeting, Jim."

"Have to get a move on you, then."

Even as old Jim pulled up anchor, the great billowing clouds began foaming up above the birches. Greenish-yellow they were, like the cheeks of some sickly, jaundiced giant. It seemed an interminable time that it took to get to Jim's old weather-beaten dock.

Up the sloping bank to Jim's shack, and then the storm struck. The rain crashed on the roof like stones.

The judge held his watch in his hand. "Now," he snapped it shut. "Now, I've *got* to go, storm or no

storm." But when he went to the door the wind and rain
forced him back against Jim's old rusty stove. It was
exasperating, ridiculous that he was held here in this
old shack. At home a closed car would have taken him to
the dinner without wetting a hair of his head. Chet and
Rita—how worried they would be! What a monstrous
thing to cause them one moment of anxiety!

At ten o'clock, sick with remorse, he gave up going.
The rain was still pelting in great driving sheets, the
wind roaring in its fury. Jim gave him his own bed. He
shuddered as he looked at it.

All night long on the dirty bed the judge twisted and
turned and called himself choice names. He was cold.
One of the two covers over him was a dressed cowhide.
Toward morning he felt ill, as though he had eaten
great hot balls of fire. Jim's greasy cooking, that was.

At the first suggestion of dawn he shook Jim from
a snoring sleep. No, he couldn't wait for coffee. Every
bone in his body cried aloud, his head was bursting.

Together they started through the woods that still
dripped clammily. The soggy underbrush slapped the
judge in his face. Every leaf was a miniature dipper
to throw its contents on him. It was hard to walk.
There were a dozen strong, disagreeable odors—crushed
plantain leaf and decayed toadstools and rotting wood.
His feet squashed in the oozy interior of his shoes. The
boat contained so much water that they had to bail it.
The judge's back hurt with every toss of the tin can he

was using. That pain in his side—he believed it was pleurisy.

"Want I should go along up to the house with you?" Old Jim was playing the host to the bitter end.

The judge turned a mottled face to him. If that pain should turn out to be pneumonia—— "Maybe you'd better, Jim."

All the way up the side streets in the ghostly dawn Jim Shaffer stepped along blithely. Wet to the skin, he was merely a little brown gnome—one with the woods, child of the river.

The judge wished he could get rid of him before they came to the house. It wasn't quite square to feel that way after Jim's hospitality, but he would rather Chet and Rita needn't see him. At the end of the street where he was to turn he put out his hand. "Thanks, now, Jim."

They were no longer boyhood pals. One was a judge and the other a river rat.

"You don't need to go any farther, Jim. I'll be all right. Good luck to you." He must be cordial. It wasn't old Jim's fault that he had made one grand fool of himself. "Better look me up one of these days—maybe I could get you some better quarters here in town for winter." That is, *if he lived*. Someway, he was not sure he would ever recover.

"Good-by, Sam. See you later." Old Jim Shaffer turned and went jauntily down the street past the lovely

244

suburban homes. The old judge could hear him whistling blithely:

> Oh, come with me in my little canoe,
> Where the sky is calm and the sea is blue.

Off and on all day the judge slept in his soft bed, warm food within him and hot water bottles without. Whenever he woke it was with a deep sense of well-being.

When Rita had taken away the supper tray with its delicious broth, she came back with the evening paper and his glasses, fitting pillows to his back. With a feeling of utter peace, he opened the sheet. His eyes took on a rigid stare.

"Federal officers," the item said, "raided the shack of Jim Shaffer on Lake Tanner this morning and arrested the owner. . . ." The old judge's pulse was throbbing wildly and there was a queer creeping sensation in the back of his neck. ". . . officers were planning to make the raid yesterday afternoon, but the storm broke and they remained at a local hotel all night. . . ."

Rita was coming into the bedroom, her heels playing a staccato tune whenever she stepped off the soft rugs. She had on an orange blouse. Little pendants in her earrings tinkled. The pronounced odor of her strong perfume preceded her.

"You are to take this, father," she spoke authoritatively. "Open your mouth."

The old judge shut his eyes and swallowed meekly.

"You're a good girl." He looked up at her with the humble eyes of an old dog. "I hope I appreciate you."

"I hope you do," she said briskly.

"And, Rita"—his old eyes twinkled a little—"do you know that Schiller once said a very true, a very beautiful thing. He said, 'Freedom is only in the land of dreams.' " He patted her hand. "Now, run along, Rita dear. I'm a tired old man and I want to sleep."

WELCOME HOME, HAL!

THE last school bell rang throatily, and Judith Marsh, leaving her desk, stepped to the hallway of Room 3 as quickly as though she were a robot connected by some mysterious wiring with the mechanism of the unseen clapper. This quick response to duty may have been very creditable to her as a teacher, but when that immediate reaction to the sound of a noisy brass summons has been going on steadily for eight years, it might, forsooth, also be termed monotonous.

Miss Marsh, of the third grade, was pretty and dainty, and a stranger would have said very young. But when one is teaching in the town of one's nativity—and a small town at that—one's age is neither a matter of mystery nor of speculation. So there was not an old woman in Mayville who did not remember the blizzard of the specific year and month in which Judith Marsh was born, not a parent of her pupils but could say glibly: "Judith Marsh is twenty-nine years old, for she was seventeen the year she graduated, and I remember distinctly the year she graduated." Verily, to abide permanently in the land of one's fathers has its pains and its penalties.

The children came trooping into the hall now for the

afternoon session with the same characteristic entrance that all those other seven sets of pupils had affected since Judith started teaching—the first class of which was now of second-year high-school age and engaged at this particular moment in straggling up the long stairway to its study hall. If the third-grade teacher looked no different to them than she had when they were in her room, it was because of the truthfulness of the fact that her soft brown hair lay in just as attractive shining waves, her wide blue eyes looked as merry as ever, and the texture of her skin remained as delicately pink.

These present third-grade pupils, having hung up their wraps, were passing into the school-room now—the girls first, with that pious air of desiring to get right to work which is a wholly feminine one; the boys depositing their baseball bats noisily and dragging their heavy, thick-soled shoes in that quarry-slave-at-night-scourged-to-his-dungeon attitude which is wholly masculine.

Judith sent Red Murray back to the hall to brush his wildly upstanding carrot locks—this performance having become a ceremonial part of every school session, as one might always open services with a litany. Red returned almost immediately, his hair showing a faint suggestion of having made the hasty acquaintance of either a toothless comb or a garden rake and thus rendered obeisance to the god of appearances.

Welcome Home, Hal!

Near the front entrance, Emil, the janitor, who had been shoveling coal, stood ready to sound the tardy gong, like a grimy St. Peter about to close the pearly gates.

From the far end of the main hall, her face red with her exertions, a little girl came running breathlessly. She was Ruth Jean Edminston, the child of Judith's girlhood chum.

"Miss Marsh"—Ruth Jean was obliged to use the formal name at school, although her teacher was merely "Judith" to the family—"Miss Marsh . . . I was so scared I was going to be tardy. Daddy was late getting home and he had a letter he was reading to mother, and I waited a few minutes to hear it. Miss Marsh, you *never* could guess! We're going to have company Saturday and Sunday. *Important* company! *From New York!* Miss Marsh, he's a Mr. Hal Dening *from New York*. He's a cartoonist *from New York*. Daddy says *in New York*—"

Well, Ruth Jean could not have known it, of course. If she had brought one of the baseball bats from the end of the hall and struck Miss Marsh a smashing blow between the eyes, the results would have been both surprising and painful, but not more devastating.

Miss Marsh looked at the child with the same blank expression she might have used had the bat done its deadly work. Then a sibilant tidal wave of whispering behind her brought her out of the frozen stupor and she was all teacher, dismissing the child with "All right, Ruth Jean."

So Hal was coming home.

Ruth Jean could not know that Hal Dening was the romantic reason that Miss Marsh had not yet married, the reason that she could not quite bring herself to marry good, substantial Doctor McDonald, even though he was offering her one of the nicest homes in Mayville; that whenever she had almost persuaded herself to take the step, it was the memory of that wicked grin of Hal's intruding itself or the twinkle of his eyes—or any one of a dozen lovable characteristics—that kept her from it. Unfortunately, one may not happily mate with Æsculapius if she has known Pierrot.

School began.

It is no less than miraculous how the human mind can divide itself into two compartments. The teacher, Miss Marsh, living on the ground floor of her mental apartment house, so to speak, now conducted a very creditable reading class with no perceptible diminishing of her constant oversight of the lesson. "You may take the part of the peacock, Marian. The part of the duck, Jay." While the girl, Judith Marsh, inhabiting the upper apartment, simultaneously talked with Hal Dening, walked with him, rode with him, went up the river with him, saw him in his Grandmother Dening's house as a big gangling boy in Mayville, long before he had become nationally known.

"I do not see why you st-st-strut so," masculinity was floundering.

"Because I am proud of my fine feathers," the deadlier of the species read glibly.

"You may go on from there—Ruth Jean and Edgar."

And while the peacock swaggered and the duck threw the cold water of a stupid philosophy upon his gay happiness, Judith recalled many things.

She remembered little Grandmother Dening, whose one endeavor in life seemed to have been to bring up Hal so he would miss neither his mother nor the father who had been her only boy. And Grandma Dening's hands apparently had been full, for Hal was constantly dipping into all the small town's mischief-making. And incidentally, he had thoroughly decorated that town with chalk and pencil. High board fences, woodsheds and sidewalks bore his imprint. School-books introduced to snickering onlookers a rakish Columbus sailing unknown seas in a bathtub, a silly-looking Benjamin Franklin knocked into ludicrous insensibility by his lightning, foppish Indians calling out ridiculous questions to a pertly retorting bunch of Pilgrims. The bottom of Grandma Dening's dresser drawers, her cupboard doors, the whitewashed cellarway—from all of them those absurd figures of Hal's had looked at one with their foolish sayings billowing out from grotesque mouths in elliptical-shaped pencilings.

Grandma had endured them all until the day she

found the caricature of a terrible tramplike person in those bold strokes embellishing the freshness of her newly pasted kitchen wall paper. Hal must have been as large as grandma by that time; but size or no size, in her indignation she had given him a sound cuffing —but admitted she had merely cried a little and laughed a little the next day when, across from the tramp, she found a companion piece of an abnormally diminutive person who was herself, and over her knees an exaggeratedly large boy whose long legs trailed out across the picture, with a "Wah! Wah!" in that balloon-shaped flourish of pencil coming from his cavernous mouth.

In the clarity of the recollection Judith smiled, and the children, thinking she was overcome by the antics of the duck and the peacock, all laughed immoderately.

"The last page—Edgar and May."

Well, to grandma's prideful relief and perhaps her ever-wondering surprise, Hal, instead of turning out to be a nitwit, had turned out to be genius. And, at least in the eyes of Mayville, rather rich. For the great American public, liking nothing so much as to have its risibilities tickled, pays its clowns more than its statesmen. And as though in reparation for all his trouble to her, Hal had later given grandma everything her heart could wish—everything but her youth.

So all through the afternoon it went—like the sound of music through the monotonous reciting and writing and study periods. Hal was coming. Hal was to spend two days with his boyhood friends, Joe and Mabel, who in the old days had made up the foursome with Hal and herself.

He had been back only twice before in all the years. That last time; all the walks and talks—she had thought— But he had gone away with all that might have been said, unsaid.

Looking out through the window now, she could see the back yard behind Joe and Mabel's pretty brick house, the low white fence and the last of the season's garden chrysanthemums. A suit of Joe's on the line turned and whirled and flapped its sleeves in the autumn wind, as though Joe were inside and dancing about in an ecstasy of gladness that his old chum was coming home.

She wondered what Saturday and Sunday would be like; hoped that they would be lovely, so the four of them could turn back the clock and go picnicking up the river just as of old. Mabel's mother could look after Ruth Jean and the baby at her home. Everything would be just as it used to be—the scarlet oaks, the old log cabin for lunching, the river running its lazy way to the sea, Joe and Mabel and she and Hal. Nothing would be different. All afternoon her heart sang a little song of thanksgiving that was both solemn and merry.

It was dismissal time now, and the pupils were passing out with complete and ironic reversal of their entry, the boys enthusiastically, the girls half reluctant to leave.

Ruth Jean stepped out of line because of the weighty thing she wanted to tell Miss Marsh. "Miss Marsh, I have to hurry home and help mother." She had that little girl's importance of helping which becomes quite lost a few years later. "Mother's got a lot to do before our company comes *from New York*. Mother says coming from *New York* that way they will be used to everything nice."

"They?" said Judith weakly.

"Oh, yes, Miss Marsh; I forgot to tell you. He said in the letter there'd be a young lady with him. *From New York*. Her name is Grace." She came close to Judith, raised herself on her toes and whispered through her fat little hands, *"His girl,* mother says."

"I see."

"Good night, Miss Marsh."

"Good night, children. No, Mark. You don't need to stay. I'll erase the board myself this time, thank you."

Judith slipped back into her room and closed the door, tried with all her strength to close it on the sweetness of the memories in which she had reveled that afternoon—but it would not shut them out.

Oh, why was he coming? To have buried your heart and to have tried to forget where the grave was—and then at a piece of news to run right to the spot and begin frantically digging it up, only to find it all red and alive and palpitating. It wasn't fair. If he had stayed away—he and his Grace—where he belonged! Why, only recently she had begun to think that perhaps —after all—good, steady Doctor McDonald—

The wind blew around the school-house. Leaves whirled and spiraled, as foolishly active as her memories.

For a long time she sat idly at the desk until Emil, the janitor, still grimy from the coal, came in and deposited an assortment of jangling pails, mops and brooms, so that she mechanically took down her hat and coat and started home.

To-night she would not stop at Mabel's. On second thought, better to run in for a few moments, face the music, and get it over. Thanks to her own poise, and self-control, they did not know she still cared, thought her interest in Doctor McDonald growing so that they had begun to accept the fact that the affair was serious.

"Oh, hello, Judy. Did Ruth Jean tell you the news?" Mabel was trying to take off the baby's coat while he bounced up and down like an animated pump handle.

"Yes. Isn't it fine?" She was proud of her straight-forward look.

"He's driving through—going on to Hollywood. Something about screening some of his stuff. Doesn't that sound important? And"—she bent over the baby —"bringing his girl. My word, Judy, can you imagine your mother or mine letting us drive across country with our beaus, engaged or not engaged?"

"I should say not. Proof that we're outmoded, Mabel." She was as cool as she could have wished.

Ruth Jean fixed the two with her solemn round eyes. "Maybe," said the small oracle, "she's got married to him by this time."

"Maybe she has." They both laughed.

Judith rose to go, but stopped at hearing Joe come into the drive. She would wait to see Joe, too, a minute. She felt strong; now that the first ice was broken she would be all right permanently.

"Hello, Judy."

"Hello, Joe." How poised she was.

"Hear about Hal?"

"Yes—isn't it lovely?"

Mabel separated the baby's mouth and one of the chair's tassels. "Joe and I sort of sketchily planned this noon just what we'd do for them. We think, on account of their driving in that way sometime in the afternoon of Saturday, we'll have just a small dinner for six or eight of us. Then on Sunday we'll get father's bigger car and all drive to Millard to dinner at the Chief. Maybe Hal might want to make a few calls over there where his mother's people used to live. Then Sunday night we'll have an informal buffet supper here with perhaps twenty—as many of the old crowd as we can scrape together anyway—and a few of the newer people who would like to meet him. He's leaving early Monday morning, he says. About the small dinner, Judy. Shall we have Doctor McDonald for you?"

"*No*," said Judith in a frantic refusal, "*Oh, no.*" And it had happened.

With no control of her emotions, the thing was said. With words no more important than those simple ones, she had done the damage. It was as though a curtain had been pulled aside and she stood naked and ashamed before her two best friends. Pink and embarrassed and sick with distress, she knew that they had suddenly seen what she had intended no one to see—merely by saying she could not come to a dinner for Hal with Doctor McDonald. For years she had laughed with Joe and Mabel at Hal's foolery in the papers, saved comic strips for them which they might have missed, discussed freely his rise to popularity, lived the constant pretense that he was nothing more to her than a good friend of the old days—and now this.

"Oh, well," Mabel set the baby down and said quickly to fill the embarrassing gap: "I tell you—we'll just wait a day to see what our plans are, for sure, whether we'll do that way or . . ." Her voice trailed off vaguely.

And Judy went home sick with the hurt in her heart and the wound to her pride.

At home she told her father and mother with elaborately assumed cheerfulness that Hal Dening was coming home and bringing his girl—at which her father launched into a chuckling tale of reminiscences involving the youthful Hal and some contraband watermelons; but with the uncanny knowledge of mothers, Mrs. Marsh kept a discreet and suspicious silence.

During dinner the phone rang. It was Mrs. Clement Waldo Stryker, and she was summoning Judith to a called meeting of the division heads of the Mayville Community Ladies' Welfare Club. The meeting was to be at 8:30 at her home, and the dictum was absolute.

Mrs. Clement Waldo Stryker was the mayor's wife— old Clem having held office for twelve years and bidding fair to hold it another dozen, for one went right on voting for him term after term, realizing that one's ballot was not so much for old Clem as it was vicariously cast for his wife. Mrs. Stryker was the head of so many of Mayville's organizations that, in truth, if Hercules had appeared in Mayville and cut off one of them, in good old mythological fashion, two new organizations would have appeared to take its place, and both heads would have been Mrs. Clement Waldo Stryker.

It seemed now that Mrs. Stryker had just learned of the coming visit to Mayville of Hal Dening and, half incensed at the six hours' delay in being apprised of it, had forthwith decided that there should be a welcoming dinner for him at seven o'clock on Saturday night at the new community building. As she elucidated over the wires, there the new building stood, all completed, so that it seemed as if providence had taken a hand and sent them Mayville's distinguished son just in time to introduce the two to each other as the populace looked on.

In vain Judith began an explanation that Hal was to be Joe and Mabel's guest; that they were planning a small dinner party; that he was bringing a girl friend, so the time did not seem auspicious—

It fell on deaf ears. Mrs. Stryker was the official greeter of the town, and on this particular occasion held no intention of allowing her place to be usurped.

Judith went stubbornly to the committee meeting. It seemed so silly to have a dinner of that type—so small-townish. If Hal were coming alone! But the girl—what would she think? The best they could do would be one of those hospitable noisy village demonstrations. A dozen women in Mayville could have given a very creditable little dinner that would not have been glaringly defective from a social standpoint. They were not all back-woodsy. But a huge conglomerate gathering! It was a horrible thing to perpetrate on Hal and the girl. She began to see everything through the eyes of the strange girl who was coming with him, and the metamorphosis was not pleasant to contemplate.

The Mayville Community Ladies' Welfare Club was divided, through the chief's armylike leadership, into four divisions, each headed by a chairman and Mrs.

Stryker—and the greatest of these was Mrs. Stryker. The four were Mrs. Otto Schneiderman, Mrs. Hattie Durkin, Mrs. Ralph Hitchcock and Judith.

Judith was the last of these to arrive, for she had taken time to go around by Mabel's and tell her what Mrs. Stryker was putting across, willy-nilly. Mabel had capitulated, as one must before the Mesdames Strykers of the world; had said that she didn't want to be selfish, and if Mrs. Stryker really felt that Hal should be given some kind of ovation by the town—

"Yours not to wonder why—yours but to do or die." Judith had congratulated herself on her self-possession. Perhaps by adhering strictly to this renewed poise she could counteract any impression she might have given Joe and Mabel earlier in the day.

As she mounted the stairs to remove her wraps in Mrs. Stryker's guest chamber, she could hear the other ladies in conversation—specifically the voice of Mrs. Hattie Durkin remarking acridly: ". . . embarrassing to be an old girl he ditched."

"Hold on to yourself, Judith," she said under her breath; "consider the source."

For Mrs. Hattie Durkin, head of Division II, was the town's human flea, not a wasp whose sting is formidable, but a mere flea, which is "a wingless, blood sucking creature with extraordinary powers of leaping." From one person to another Mrs. Hattie Durkin darted, sticking her tiny proboscis of gossip into one, piercing the outer texture of his sensibilities, while her thin lips smiled and her small beady eyes shifted cannily toward her prey.

"Oh, hello, Judith," she said now. "You'll be glad to see Hal—you were such old friends." Then she bit Mrs. Ralph Hitchcock, whose husband's business had failed: "Hal will see changes in *your* life, Etta." And enjoyed the victim's momentary irritation at the puncture.

They all went downstairs to begin plans for an event which Judith loathed with every fiber of her being.

Mrs. Stryker, having figuratively donned her general's uniform upon first hearing of Hal's coming, was ready with her bombardment. She made her assignments immediately.

Mrs. Otto Schneiderman was to have charge of the food, a very sanguine procedure, for Mrs. Schneiderman's theory of life was that earth held no sorrow that food could not heal; her motto, "A bird on the table is worth two in the hen house"; her prayer, "Give us this day our daily bread," contained no spiritual interpretation. So she came like a warhorse to the Battle of the Menu. One would have thought, to hear her talk, that Hal had never known a square meal since he shook the dust of Mayville from his nimble feet. She was all for vegetable soup, chicken pie, noodles, oysters, roast beef, rolls, cabbage salad, fruit salad—

Judith looked at her through the eyes of the girl who was coming. She seemed to be able to visualize that girl

—dark and tall and slender, and the last word in modish attire. She could imagine her soft smile, guarded but supercilious; hear her laugh with Hal later. She could bear anything better than to think that Hal would laugh with her.

If Mrs. Otto Schneiderman was concerned with the food to be consumed, Mrs. Ralph Hitchcock was torn by social problems: where Hal should sit; where the toastmaster, the girl; the order in which the speakers and singers should be honored in the seating problem. Would the Rev. Arthur Caldwell be hurt if the Rev. Benjamin Hass were asked to give the invocation? Should the girl have a corsage at her plate?

"After all," said Mrs. Stryker pompously, "the dinner is for Hal. We really don't know the status of the girl."

Mrs. Hattie Durkin immediately lighted and bit: "Good land, he's engaged to her, or he wouldn't have brung her"—and darted her small beady eyes at Judith.

She hated it all, did Judith: the deep discussions over trifles; whether to put raisins in the dark cakes or leave them out; whether to have the salad placed fresh on the plates as Mrs. Schneiderman wanted it, or embalmed in gelatin as Mrs. Stryker insisted.

Eventually all four, however, were assigned to their respective posts: Mrs. Otto Schneiderman for food; Mrs. Ralph Hitchcock for the program; Mrs. Hattie Durkin for publicity, tickets and finances; Judith for tables, dishes and decoration; with Mrs. Clement

Welcome Home, Hal!

Waldo Stryker, in the language of Mr. Kipling, as he correctly, if unintentionally, described her, "sitting up in a conning-tower bossing three hundred men."

Out of a chaos of plans and suggestions, ludicrous, feasible and impossible, there slowly and painfully evolved a program for the occasion. She who can handle a small town community affair could be ambassador to the Court of St. James's. Tickets were to be sold to the public.

"He belongs to every man, woman and child in the community," Mrs. Hitchcock had said, with ready emotional moisture in her eyes.

Mrs. Hattie Durkin had leaped. "I'd say he belongs to his girl," she cackled, and shot Judith a furtive glance.

The dinner was to be at seven, or as nearly afterward as it was possible for Mayville's beauty and chivalry to assemble. The high-school orchestra was to play. The Rev. Benjamin Hass was to give an invocation before they were seated. Although it took physical bravery and a goodly portion of tact, Mrs. Otto Schneiderman was to be held down to three courses of food.

Mrs. Walter Merrick, who had studied music in Chicago, was to sing. "To render" sometimes meaning "to inflict," the Methodist men's quartet was to render a piece. Hannah Thompson Emmett was to read an original poem. Mayor Stryker was to make the official welcoming speech in behalf of the town. Joe Edminston was to give an expurgated summary of Hal's boyhood, after which résumé, and appropriately, as atonement follows confession of past sins, the Rev. Arthur Caldwell was to pay tribute to Hal's later and supposedly less lurid life.

This assortment of literary, musical and spiritual contributions to Hal Dening's welcome was good as far as it went, but to Mrs. Hitchcock's emotional nature it did not go far enough.

"As I said before"—her sensitive chin quivered in comradely alliance with her warm heart—"Hal Dening belongs to every man, woman and child in the community, and I repeat 'child'—but notice that up to this minute not one of the little darlings has a part in the program. I want the little folks to have a share in this welcome, too. Judith, couldn't you train a group—some little flag drill or something of that kind?"

"No, I couldn't," said Judith, and cast about wildly for an excuse that would not wabble too noticeably. "I —we're beginning a new and hard number work Monday, and I always—always make a good deal of preparation for it."

And inasmuch as not one of the other four had ever taught, the frail little excuse limped past them without reproach.

Oh, she hated it all. If it were Hal alone! But the girl—it would be a ridiculous thing for her to witness. Why should these good, kind people, salt of the earth, as the Reverend Caldwell called them, work their heads off for three days to welcome Hal home, only to be laughed at for their pains? Yesterday she had loved all these home folks—well, almost all of them—to-night she hated them for proposing and expecting to carry out this wild small-town festivity, this village orgy, this —this wineless bacchanalia.

But it was always of the girl she was thinking. Hal would fit in anywhere. But that "rag and bone and hank of hair" who was coming with him; how could she understand the love and affection for Hal that was going into this ridiculous dinner? Hal, alone, would understand, but Hal was not to be alone. Men were so susceptible to the opinions of the girls with whom they were in love—and Hal was in love.

Thursday and Friday were lived through, but for that matter, it was nothing providential—so were Marie Antoinette's last two days before the ax fell. On Friday afternoon Judith went to the woods with the school children for autumn leaves with which to decorate the freshly plastered sides of the new barn-like room called by courtesy the banquet hall.

Saturday dawned mild and warm and sunshiny. October's Indian summer was welcoming Hal, too, with the haze in the distance that he loved, and the smell of fall-turned loam and wild haws and bonfires coming over the town on the wings of the autumn breeze.

Just before noon Judith made her angel-food cake—a

huge fifteen-egg affair that in its completed white perfection soothed her pride for the space of a few moments. In the early afternoon she went down to the community building and set her tables. At home again she bathed and dressed for evening in a soft gray-blue gown the exact shade of her eyes. Hal had once liked— "Little fool," she warned herself. At five o'clock she took her cake in its basket and started back to the community building. Even so walked Antoinette out onto the balcony at Versailles.

Because there was no car at Joe and Mabel's she stopped for a brief moment, half in fear that the couple would come before she could get away. She found Mabel tired and irritable with the nervousness that comes from preparing to entertain a stranger. Ruth Jean was practicing monotonously "one . . . two . . . one . . . two." The baby was nibbling a piece of paraffin, so Judith extracted it from his mouth and cuddled him for a few moments. *"She* may not like children," she thought, and for no special reason had a fleeting hope that she would not.

All the way down to the dinner she looked at the town through the coming stranger's eyes: the small park with its simple little fountain—once she had been proud of that newly acquired fountain; the wide country-lane streets, with the trees nearly meeting overhead—once she had reveled in their soothing shade; the hodgepodge homes—square frames, bungalows, cottages, red-brick two-storied ones—once they had looked pleasant and adequate because they housed old friends; the community building itself, now a huge, gray-stucco affair, its architecture merely inverted soup tureen—once she had worked hard for that building, given school programs to earn money for it, been proud of its completion. To-day she saw nothing but through alien eyes— and a small Midwestern town through alien eyes is sometimes not a lovely thing.

She went up the walk to the south door. Box-elder bugs swarmed over the whole side, the warmth of the Indian summer day having brought them out of their fall hibernation. They clung to the gray of the stucco like an army of Reds carrying their flags under each wing. They irritated her, as though they too were merely small-town bugs, as though city bugs might have flaunted more modest colors, been better behaved.

She went directly into the kitchen with its new pine built-in tables and sinks. The room seemed too warm with the heat from a range, so she took her cake on into the far end of the cool plastered furnace room and placed it on a shelf near a partly open window, covering it securely with a snow-white tea towel.

Back in the kitchen she encountered Mrs. Clement Waldo Stryker, her portly figure incased in black satin, jet earrings against the pink smoothness of her fat cheeks, just now a huge apron swathing the satin dress. How grotesque! How the girl would laugh at the combination. Where besides a small town did one ever encounter such an association of servant-and-hostess ideas and clothes?

Mrs. Hattie Durkin came in. She darted a swift glance at Judith with her little shifting eyes. "Judith, you and Hal was such old friends—you should have et with him instead o' workin'."

Judith felt the bite, pretended it hadn't stung, said casually, "Oh, somebody always has to put over a social affair."

Mrs. Ralph Hitchcock was there, worrying whether the Congregational quartet would be hurt because the Methodist one was going to sing—whether any more of the children in the welcome drill had broken out with measles. Mrs. Otto Schneiderman was there, hoping that the vast quantities of food prepared would permit body and soul of the citizenry to hang together until breakfast time. And now Judith was there—praying that she could get decently through the ordeal.

The helpers were arriving—the two women hired to pare potatoes. Everything was so confusing in the kitchen that Judith slipped into the large dining hall, where her tables stretched their forms down the room like block-long white-sheeted panels. Only field phones would have allowed any one to converse with another than those seated on either side. The tablecloths were of a dozen varied patterns. Mrs. Schneiderman's Irish damask ones overlapped Mrs. Hattie Durkin's mercerized ones. The flowers were home-grown, the vases a heterogeneous collection borrowed from high and low. All the leaves that the children had brought could not hide the bareness of the newly plastered walls. There were not anywhere near enough new chairs for the crowd, and now the high-school boys were noisily stumbling in with a jumble of drug-store chairs, funeral-parlor chairs, Mrs. Merrick's early-American, Mrs. Stryker's modern-Jacobean and Mrs. Hattie Durkin's painted kitchen ones.

The high-school girls who were to wait on tables arrived in fifteen-year-old breathless excitement over the coming of the romantic couple. Judith fixed salads. A million little quivering pyramids of pale green gelatin arose from their pale green lettuce beds, giving specific proof that Mrs. Stryker, still wielding her scepter, had won in the salad argument.

That majestic personage was now engaged in giving every one orders. "As soon as I give the signal, start in to arrange the second course. As soon as the second course is being removed, start cutting cakes. It must all go off like clockwork."

Judith had a wild notion that the whole affair was being conducted from the trenches; that this was just before the zero hour, and soon they were all to go over the top. How she would have loved to laugh about it with Hal, imitate Mrs. Stryker's bombastic orders and Mrs. Schneiderman's perturbation over the amount of provender. She could see the way Hal's mouth would have drawn up at the corners and the wicked grin give way to contagious chuckles. Oh, would the girl have a sense of that same deep humor, understand that delicious whimsy?

It was nearly time now. People were in the "parlors," freshly plastered and decorated with the autumn leaves and the G. A. R., Spanish-American and World War flags. She could hear laughing, talking; through the constantly swinging doors catch glimpses of the town's merchants and professional men, farmers and laborers, a cosmopolitan group of men, and such wives, sisters and daughters as were not actively engaged in the food belt.

Three high-school girls stuck their heads through three swinging doors simultaneously to shrill: *"They're here!"*

The members of the Mayville Community Ladies' Welfare Club forgot their cues, ignored their field marshal, crowded to the swinging doors to peek at the guest of honor and his young lady. Mesdames Durkin, Schneiderman and Hitchcock all went out to shake hands with the returning hero and his sweetheart, headed by no less a personage than their bellwether, Mrs. Clement Waldo Stryker.

Judith knew she should have trailed along, too. But she could not—not with the eyes of the town upon her. She had been a traitor to herself at Joe and Mabel's, and now she could not trust the unreliable person she had thought to be her placid self. It seemed suffocating here in the kitchen. In a few minutes she would be all right, but just now her heart was pounding so hard that its noise was in her ears, the pulsation of her throat was so apparent that she put her hand there to still its beating. Suddenly she turned and slipped into the cool quiet of the furnace room, colliding, as she did so, with Joe, who had just deposited an ice-cream freezer therein.

"Oh, Joe—sorry!" she said. And finished lamely, "I have to see about my cake."

And then to fool herself, pretending to herself to prove her point, she walked over to the far end of the room where the cake sat, to unveil its white perfection.

And stared. Some four hundred box-elder bugs were toiling their way patiently up the treacherous iced sides like so many hearty Alpine climbers. Several dozen, having gained their objective, peered out from frosted crevices at the top. The gayest adventurers of them all, a few clumsy fellows, flew flappingly up from their highly original investigation of the dark shaft of the center hole. From the open window a long line of happy fellow soldiers of fortune were hurrying cakeward.

It seemed the last straw on a breaking camel, the paramount horror of a hideous nightmare, the final drop of a three-day deluge of small-town stuff. She clenched her fists in her nervousness. Angry tears came to her eyes, so that she pinched her tongue with her teeth to keep back the hysteria. She was ashamed of Mayville, ashamed of every one in it and everything they did. She was going to slip out of that far outside door and leave the——

Because she heard a door open behind her and saw a shaft of light she turned.

"Hal!"

"Judy!"

"How did you——"

"Joe told me you were in here, crawling into the furnace."

After a lifetime of longing for him, years of dreaming it all out, days of the anticipation of meeting him again, all she could think to say was, "Oh, Hal, my cake's ruined with a thousand box-elder bugs." Thus do we meet life's deepest crises.

"What's a bug or two between friends, Judy?" Hal was grinning in that never-to-be-forgotten way, with the corners of his mouth drawing up, and holding out his arms.

Before she could think, before reason had time to command, and only foolish sentiment directed, she was in those arms and Hal had held her close and kissed her. Like a flower to the sun, or the tides to the moon, she had gone, before she remembered how or why she had let herself go. After all, Hal was modern, probably kissed indiscriminately these days if he chose. She had always been a little old-fashioned about it. Well, she still was. More small-town stuff, maybe, but it was the way she felt.

"Oh, Hal! I'm sorry. I shouldn't have—nor let you."

"And why not, Judy-Prudy?" It was the first time she had heard that old nickname for years.

"Well—the girl—"

She was laughing in embarrassment. After all, she shouldn't attach any importance to the very natural thing of that friendly greeting—except for the fact that it had seemed so much more than friendly!

"The girl? What girl? Whose girl? Why a girl?"

"Why—the girl you brought." She looked up at Hal, startled. "You did bring her, didn't you?"

Hal threw back his head and laughed long and merrily behind the furnace in the plaster-smelling room. "My girl's eighty-one—grandma. I told Joe I was bringing her, but it seems that my penmanship isn't all that it might be, and in my hastily scribbled note the word 'Gran' looked like 'Grace,' and Joe and Mabel were all set to welcome a real fiancée. You should have seen their faces when I helped little old Gran out of the car." Then he pulled Judith close again. "Lord, Judy, you're sweet and dear. I don't know why we've wasted any—" He broke off to say hurriedly, "I'm dropping grandma off here to visit and I'm taking you on to the Coast with me. Will you, Judy? Marry me before Monday morning and drive on to the Coast with me?"

Welcome Home, Hal!

And without waiting for an answer: "How do you get married around here now, anyway? Do you have to tack up a notice in the post-office, or does old preacher Hass announce it from the pulpit along with prayer meeting and choir practice?...I get married so seldom these days."

Judy was laughing. Was she always to laugh now? "Oh, Hal—I couldn't."

For the first time he was serious. "There's no one else? None of these new men? If there is—"

"No, there never was any one but you." Doctor McDonald might have been in Tasmania. "But—I mean—not Monday. Why, I couldn't. I'm a teacher. We're—we're taking up new number work Monday morning."

"So am I. I'm subtracting grandma and adding you and dividing my income and"—Hal would—"we'll talk about multiplying later."

Joe opened a door, stuck his head around the furnace and emitted an ancient small-town joke: "Hey, folks—sorry to interrupt, but we can't start things out here without the prodigal calf."

And Hal had to go. He kept Judy's hand a moment, kissed the soft pink palm. "Aren't you coming in to sit with me?"

"Heavens, no, Hal; go on—hurry! I'm chairman of Division IV of the Mayville Ladies' Community Welfare Club."

"My word—and to think I once also glimpsed the Sultan of Turkey." And Hal was gone.

And Judith, her heart shouting to the four winds that she was going away with Hal, had to go back into the kitchen to hand out quivering green-gelatin pyramids through an aperture in the wall.

The kitchen was now a mass of moving, hurrying, perspiring members of the Ladies' Community Welfare Club obeying the orders of their chief. When the last of the second course had gone the way of the opening in the wall, the order was on to start the cakes. Judith cut a layer cake of mulatto hue, chocolate filled and chocolate covered; Mrs. Hattie Durkin, next to her, cut an albino-complexioned one of lemon origin.

"My! Hal's swell, ain't he?" was her opening wedge. "And did you hear it was only Grandma Dening he brought?"

"Yes—oh, yes," said Judith, so very, very happy that it was only Grandma Dening he had brought.

Mrs. Hattie Durkin prepared to light. "But he's goin' to get married, though. Pa asked him, and he laughed and told pa 'soon,' and pa just had time to tell me when I was comin' back in."

"Yes, so I heard, too."

Having lit, Mrs. Hattie Durkin prepared to bite. "You're hardly good enough friends with Hal now, I suppose"—she darted her little eyes sidewise toward Judith—"to know who she is? I been wonderin' who he's going to marry." She did not care especially who the girl was. She merely wanted to puncture human skin as she hopped lightly from one person to another. "You wouldn't know, I suppose?"

"Yes," said Judy, sweetly confidential; "they say an old girl of his that he once ditched." And she sawed away serenely on a tough, if bugless, cake.

The swinging doors to the banquet hall opened and shut constantly like the doors to heaven. And Judith knew herself to be a peri, one of those elfs of Persian myth excluded from paradise until they had paid penance—and the penance was abject humility before the god of friendships because of disloyalty to her own.

Through those swinging portals she could hear the Rev. Benjamin Hass praying for Hal's immortal soul— Hal, who had given clean and wholesome joy to a nation. She could hear Mayor Stryker welcome Hal home and give him the key to the city—Hal, whose inquisitive nose had poked itself into every culvert and cranny of the village before he was ten. She could hear them laugh uproariously at Joe's homely exposé of Hal's checkered boyhood career, and hear the Rev. Arthur Caldwell smooth it over so the Lord would not take Joe's report seriously and think too ill of Hal.

She could see a long unfurled manuscript in the hands of Hannah Thompson Emmett, and guess at the literary value of the home-grown poem. She could catch glimpses of little old Grandma Dening beaming with pride as though to say, "Just look at the man I paddled him up to be."

She could hear the high-school orchestra, rather top-heavy as to brass; could hear Mrs. Walter Merrick sing in her best Chicago voice "Home ag-a-a-in...home ag-a-a-in...from a faaaw-rin shore," and the slightly discordant but lusty Methodist quartet render, "There zno pla sli kome."

Her work done, she stepped through the swinging door in time to see Mrs. Ralph Hitchcock's little darlings welcome home Mayville's distinguished son in their own blithe way. Mrs. Hitchcock, with emotional moisture in her eyes, and much after-school practice, had trained a group of kindergartners to go through a little drill, at the close of which they were, with startling surprise, to form suddenly with lettered cards held high above their heads the touching tribute:

WELCOME HOME, HAL!

In her most enthusiastically hopeful moment Mrs. Hitchcock had underestimated both the startling nature of the procedure and the efficacy of the surprise. Measles having somewhat disrupted the *entente cordiale* during the practice, and substitutes at a late hour having taken the places of a few of the original cast, there was now, as the drill was ending, a bit of confusion in the assembling of the component parts of the surprise greeting. A few of the late recruits, including the exclamation point and the comma, who had not rehearsed at all, becoming confused concerning their respective positions, and fearful of being left out altogether, were elbowing, not to say fighting, their way into the display with more zeal than discrimination. For suddenly, to Mrs. Hitchcock's red-faced mortification and the company's raucous hilarity, the greeting stood forth in all the simplicity of its hospitable invitation:

AW, HELL! COME HOME

Judith laughed with the others until she cried. Hal was shouting like a schoolboy. The effect was disrupting to whatever shreds of formality might have clung to the event. Happily it was the last thing on the program, for no other participant could have been taken seriously.

Chairs were pushed back—modern-Jacobean, early-American, the funeral-parlor ones, the soda-fountain ones and the yellow-painted ones. People were crowding around Hal, shaking hands with him, laughing, adding their own extemporaneous speeches to Joe's summary of anecdotes concerning the town's prize mischief-maker. A sort of jovial pandemonium reigned supreme. The kindergartners, released from their devastating responsibility of welcoming the home boy who made good, were trying their hands—and mouths—at the various deserted orchestra instruments, with ear-splitting results—all but the exclamation point and the comma, who were surreptitiously finishing the left-over ice-cream. In their patrician way the Irish damask table-cloths were as guilty of being awry as the plebeian mercerized ones. Crumbs of homemade cake lay soggily in green puddles that had once jauntily looked the world in the eye as salad pryamids. A thousand dirty dishes awaited washing by a tired membership of the Ladies' Community Welfare Club. A box-elder bug in jolly exploring mood sailed back and forth across the scene, piloting his red-painted aëroplane impartially from table to table.

It was all small-town stuff put on by small-town people in a small-town way. But Judith, whose heart was singing, felt only a warmth of affection toward them all. Hal would understand the sincerity and kindness that had prompted the whole event. Only a strange girl with critical alien eyes would not be able to understand. And there was no strange girl with critical alien eyes. Just Judith Marsh with tender love-filled ones.

THE SILENT STARS GO BY

THE woman turned her head monotonously back and forth on the pillow in the restless way of the very ill. Her arms swung out from under the silken quilts with the regularity of a swimmer and with equal regularity were covered by the white-gowned nurse at her side. Little inarticulate murmurs like the moaning of a peevish child slipped from her lips.

They were the only sounds in the stillness of the big house save the muffled steps of the woman's husband pacing up and down the thick-carpeted hall like a sentinel on duty. If children's voices from below sometimes penetrated the quiet room they were broken off suddenly, hushed by an unseen authority.

Beyond the silken daintiness of the noiseless room, great moist snowflakes fluttered lazily onto the window sills and the wide expanse of dead lawn. Only beyond the driveway with its retaining rope stretched between stone posts at the entrance was there activity —the sound of cars moving up and down the avenue, the laughter of young people running up the steps of the church near by, Christmas greens in their arms.

The woman vaguely sensed it all—the unusual quiet, the tense atmosphere, the strange experience of being ill at the Christmas season. At times her mind was hazy, unmindful of its surroundings, off on some far-away journey of unreality. At other times it snapped into lucidity, became so keen that it saw pictures in detailed clarity, as though magnified by a huge glass.

It was then that she remembered how cruel Life had been to her. It had betrayed her. She who had so loved Life had watched it turn upon her, crushing her. Now she was ill. And she did not particularly care.

Restlessly her eyes roved to the picture of the Christus in its silver frame across the room. She had bought it in Rome—had liked the tender look of compassion in the eyes and the pleading attitude of the outstretched arms. That was the summer she and Neal. . . . Her mind grew hazy and she could not recall the incident of the buying. For several moments she slipped away weakly on some dim, wandering journey, while the snowflakes fell clammily on the sills and the young people laughed on the near-by church steps.

Then suddenly she was snatched back to that clarity of vision in which the events of the past year were mercilessly detailed.

The year had been one long nightmare domineered by a colossal giant that people called Depression, as though they spoke the name of a human being. At first she had tried to joke away this phantom of the times—to ignore it. But the Thing had developed a Machiavellian strength; had thrust its cruel, leering face upon them at every turn. There was the time when Neal had come home and said soberly, hesitatingly, "Janet, if the business should go..."

She had laughed at that. Assuredly the business couldn't go—not the old House of Broderick founded in the early days of the state; not the wholesale firm established by the first old pioneer Broderick and carried on by his son and his son's son. Why, that business was as substantial as the good old soil and rocks upon which the great buildings stood.

But the business *had* gone. Nothing, apparently, could stop it—not the advance on Neal's life insurance, the mortgage on the home, the loans on real estate holdings, the Broderick farm, the sale of the summer cottage, her own money, invested since the days of her voice teaching—not all these, combined, could stay the oncoming of the hideous Thing.

Far into countless nights Neal had wrestled with the problem, but it had been time wasted. There was the dark day when he had come home and said it was all over. In that moment Life for her had been over, too. But if Life in its larger sense had ceased, mere existence had not. That went on—an animal-like state of being, in which one merely made an attempt to eat and sleep.

She had been obliged to drag on, even though the very house in which she now lay ill was no longer their own. The house she had planned with prideful forethought, had furnished with such taste that all their

friends admired the beauty of it! She had no right to
be here now in her own room. But she had been taken
ill, and some one—whoever it was—must have been
kind and told them to stay until she was well. *Kind!*
Was there kindness in the world any more?

Involuntarily her eyes went to the Christ. Even He
did not feel the compassion toward people He once
felt. She was sure of that.

The nurse brought medicine and rearranged a pillow.
In a few moments the woman floated off again on dark
waters and did not know where she was drifting.

After a time a bell, tapping at the church, roused her
so that her mind snapped back again to its former
acuteness and took up its ceaseless burden of thought.

Broderick's had failed. And failure was something
she could not tolerate in a human. She ought not to
blame Neal. He had been caught like a wild thing in a
trap. He had twisted and turned and writhed, but the
trap had been made of the impregnable steel of unforeseen conditions. Other men had hung on though, somehow, and now that things were righting themselves,
they were saved. Neal should have done something
more to prevent the crash.

But there was no use going over all that again.
Everything was gone, everything worth while, the entire setting of their lives, all that gave them their position in the community. Slowly and painfully she called
the roll of their former activities: Chamber of Com-

merce—Neal was a past president. The Musical Arts Club—she had long been a director. Country Club, Tuesday Dinner Club . . .

A young boy's voice called out suddenly from below stairs and was as suddenly hushed.

The children! That was the most bitter draft of all. To fail Michael and Dorothy! Michael, who would have been the fourth in line for the business! Dorothy, who would have been a débutante some day in the city's most exclusive circle! To have brought children into the world, and then to fail them!

Everything of importance had been taken from the children: Miss Proudet, the French governess; Spence, the dancing teacher; all the people who had been training them for the future. If the children could not have modern advantages, what was there left for them in life? Parents who could not give their children the benefits of cultural things in this day and age were complete failures.

Some dual part of her mentality reasoned for a moment that she herself had known but the common comforts of a plain home and had been both happy and successful. But that had been years ago and times had changed. Her children ought to know nothing of those old economies. But all her plans for them were ended now—travel, social background. She could not give them anything without money. Life was too cruel.

Out on that misty, unknown sea she drifted for a

moment, and then came back to sharply defined realities. She remembered that day in which Neal had come home with news. He had seemed quite like himself, energetic, alert, a little gay for the first time. Courage and faith and hope had shone from his eyes. But she had seen them fade at her lack of elation. Carter and Price were opening a new department and they had come to him about taking charge. It was the first step toward rehabilitating himself, he had said.

Perhaps she should have been more pleased. But she had felt too bitter. Neal Broderick in another man's store, taking orders from other men! Of the various people in town who had experienced business reverses, none had fallen from such a height. There would be sneers and pity for the Brodericks. And she could stand the pity no better than the sneers.

Up to this time the rope stretched across the stone gates had been sufficient for keeping out disturbances. But it was failing now in its service. It could not successfully keep out the music. For, suddenly, from the old stone church on the corner a wave of melody came past the rope into the quiet of the sick room. The deep, resonant tones of the pipe-organ sent out the old song:

> O little town of Bethlehem!
> How still we see thee lie ...

In through the open window, where the snowflakes fluttered, it came with lovely cadence:

The Silent Stars Go By

> Above thy deep and dreamless sleep
> The silent stars go by.

The nurse moved as if to close the window, remembered the doctor's orders for fresh air, and left it open.

The woman's music-loving soul groped toward the liquid notes of the melody as toward a light. The verses of the hymn were as distinct to her as though the organ were singing them. In reality she was merely sensing the words, having sung them so many times, but every syllable came clearly on the winter wind:

> Above thy deep and dreamless sleep
> The silent stars go by.

As her burdened heart felt the soothing message, her burning eyes sought the compassionate ones of the Christ and clung to them. In the haziness of her ill mind the thought of stars took possession of her, so that she felt no surprise when they began going past her, misty, brilliant, pale, large, with one of surpassing beauty in the distance. It hung quiveringly just above the Man holding out his arms with yearning compassion.

The stars seemed drowning her now, so that she gave a convulsive gasp and tried desperately to get her breath in the deep waves of light. She was vaguely conscious that the nurse was calling to some one beyond the doorway. The Christ became more faint. The music, too, grew fainter and far away.

The Silent Stars Go By

Above thy deep and dreamless sleep
The silent stars go by.

She saw nothing now but the arms of the Christ held
out to her. And suddenly the outstretched arms were
no longer those of the Christ, but of her mother. She
was vaguely surprised and happy.

"Do you remember—?" It was the old familiar voice,
silenced now for a dozen years. "I promised to help
you if you needed me. And I have come."

The woman felt a delicious sense of restfulness, a
child-like faith that Mother would make everything all
right. The sensation of lightness was as though a
stone had been lifted from her heart. In her happiness
she slipped out of bed and placed her hand in that of
her mother. She had to look far up to the gentle face, as
in her childhood days. It gave her such a feeling of
childishness that when she glanced down again she
was not greatly surprised to see that she had on a queer
little plaid cloak with huge tin-looking buttons, and
that her shoes were heavy and square-toed.

Hand in hand, the two went down the thickly car-
peted hall and the wide stairway. No one paid any
attention to their passing.

Only the silent stars went by.

At the outer door she hesitated, at a loss to know
what was vaguely worrying her. Something hung over
her, some forgotten duty held her back. It was queer
that she felt both childish and maternal.

"The children," she explained to her waiting mother. "Michael and Dorothy. I must get them." She seemed to have a dual personality, to be both the child of her mother and the mother of her children.

"Of course; you must always look after the children."

So there was nothing incongruous in the children's coming from the library and completing the group, Michael in his jaunty suit and Dorothy in her tailored dress. And she in the funny plaid cloak with the tin-looking buttons.

Together the three went down the steps with the tall, gentle mother, and it was as if she were the mother of them all.

Nor was there anything so surprising about the fact that her father was waiting for them in a double-seated cutter, her brother and sister on the front seat with him. Her sturdy father helped them all in, clucked to the fat old horse, who moved off with a jangle of bells.

Down dark streets they rode on the crusted snow, sleigh bells ringing and children laughing.

> Yet in thy dark streets shineth
> The everlasting light.

It was Christmas Eve and the family was on its way to the church, the old breath-taking glamour over it all.

> The hopes and fears of all the years
> Are met in thee to-night.

She was filled with an almost delirious ecstasy. "Isn't it nice? Isn't it fun? Don't you love it?" She peered around into the faces of Michael and Dorothy.

She had a peculiar feeling of being a mediator to stand between the two groups—the old and the new—interpreting each to the other. She felt a sense of complete harmony with each, desiring tremendously that Michael and Dorothy should like her plain, substantial father and mother, wanting her father and mother, brother and sister to be pleased with Michael and Dorothy.

At the church there was that old childish delight in wax candles on the tall fir trees, the expectation of receiving a gift, the wonder of the music.

> For Christ is born of Mary,
> And gathered all above,
> While mortals sleep, the angels keep
> Their watch of wondering love.

There was a present for each, including a funny little doll with homemade dresses for Dorothy and a huge jack-knife for Michael. She felt apologetic toward them for the simplicity of the gifts, yet they seemed not to mind. And evidently they were liking her parents. For, before the exercises were over, Dorothy was sitting close to the tall mother, and Michael, next to her father, was looking up proudly into the strong, bearded face of the man, apparently for his approval.

They all rode home in the two-seated cutter behind the fat old horse, their hilarity intensified by the anticipation of hanging up their stockings. And home, not at all strangely, was that familiar old wing-and-ell house in which her own childhood had been spent. Again she held that wistful hope of wanting Michael and Dorothy not to dislike it, not to make fun of the plain old place.

But evidently they had no intention of so doing. They entered it with interest, looked inquisitively through all the comfortable rooms, explored the low-ceilinged upper floor and the garret with its accumulations of queer old things and even went down into the cellar, sniffing with pleasure at the agreeable odors of apples and potatoes in their bins.

Mother set out a lunch on the kitchen table and, with much laughter and chatter, the family perched around the homely old room while they ate the plain but delicious food, Michael and Dorothy entering happily into the fun.

And the silent stars went by.

In the days that followed, with incongruously rapid changes of time and season, they were all making garden, were out with their sleds, were having bonfires, were at picnics on the creek bank, roasting potatoes in ashes, fishing, hunting meadow larks' nests.

With growing surprise she saw how thoroughly Michael and Dorothy entered into the life, what a comrade her father was making of Michael, what devotion existed between her mother and Dorothy.

The family did everything together, as always. Their contacts embodied much of the heart, something of the soul. Life in its simplicity was rich and full.

And now she began to be troubled. Some vague sense of responsibility for Michael and Dorothy asserted itself; some obligation that, as she had brought them here, so must she return them. She felt a haunting realization of the fact that unless she acted quickly she might lose her way back. It shook her complacency, lessened her enjoyment of the irresponsible days. In this dawning of the sense of her duty to them she became more maternal than childish; was, suddenly, all mother.

She began urging them to return.

Dorothy was deep in the mysteries of her first baking of cookies under Mother's instruction, Michael in the intricacies of putting together a piece of machinery under Father's supervision.

"But I don't want to go back."

"Neither do I."

She became worried; did not know how to break the illusion. "But you must. This isn't your life."

They seemed stubborn, standing their ground with consistent refusals.

"I don't want to."

"I don't either."

"But *why* don't you want to?"

"I like it here. I like everything. Don't you, Mikey?"

"Sure, I do. I like it lots better than back there."

She was confused, not knowing what to do. She looked about for aid in deciding the troublous question. And looking so, she saw her mother smiling down at her.

"Dear!" Her mother spoke compassionately. "Don't you understand? It was the spirit of our old home—more than the things in it." Even as she spoke she was slipping away.

The woman tried to call out to her mother, but the gentle face grew faint and far away. Only her arms were still outstretched in loving benediction. And suddenly her face became the face in the picture at the foot of the bed, and her arms were the arms of the Christus.

The woman was vaguely conscious that people were bending over her, that the doctor had his fingers on her wrist. She was aware that he was saying very low, relief in his voice, "All right now."

Neal was there at the side of the bed. "Janet, you're better?" All the concern of a worried man was in his eyes, the love of a devoted one, the protection of a strong one.

Her heart went out to him in sympathy for all his troubled days. She wanted to touch his hair, to run her fingers over the graying spots on his temples, but she had no strength. She wanted to tell him something, too, but she could not think what it was. She wanted deeply that he should understand a very lovely thing. But she could not put into language that which was merely ethereal and gossamer-winged.

"The children—where are they?" she asked weakly.

"The children," Neal said hurriedly. "She wants the children."

It was relayed down the hall—from nurse to some one else—to another below. "She wants the children."

Michael and Dorothy came into the sick room with exaggerated tiptoeing, a little frightened. To the woman they looked so little yet, she felt a deep desire to care for them, to give them more of herself, to carry on the comradeship they had but recently known.

"What is it you want, Mother?"

"Are you better, Mother?"

She gave them a brief, wan smile and whispered: "We had a nice time—back there—didn't we?"

They looked up at their father in startled inquiry.

He slipped his arms around their shoulders. "Don't worry," he explained. "Her mind wandered a bit, I guess. She's better now."

The woman looked up at the three standing there in close contact. She must tell them all a wonderful thing—something about the big things of life; something about a little home they four were going to have—

293

somewhere. She searched her mind weakly for the heart-warming experience she wanted to describe. But she could not shape it into definite form. All she could remember was that, always, *above one's deep and dreamless sleep the silent stars go by.*

(1)